WHAT THE HEART SEES

"Matt?" Sara asked. "Are you ready?"

He inclined his head in her direction, a shadow of a smile playing about his full lips. "Ready for what, Sara?" The silky texture of his voice rolled over her like a caress.

Her gaze focused on his lips. They were firm and full, the lower one jutting out just a little.

"Sara?"

There it was again. That voice, but several octaves lower. How did he make it sound so soft and sexy, like a warm summer night's breeze blowing over naked skin? He hadn't spoken to her that way this afternoon. No, then he'd cursed at her, ranted, accused and tormented. And she'd handled that so much better.

"Are you going to answer me, Sara, or ignore me?" Matt asked, smiling at her. It was a slow, lazy smile, revealing a set of even, white teeth.

Her chest tightened. "I'm not ignoring you," she snapped. "I just wanted to know if you're going with us or not."

"No, Sara, I'm not," he said. "I've seen everything before and I can't see anything now, so what's the point?" His voice was still low and quiet, but the gentleness of a moment ago had vanished, replaced by strains of bitterness.

"I just thought—"

"No." One word, spoken with such finality that she knew better than to ask again. This was the Matthew Brandon she recognized. Angry, rude, domineering. Him, she could handle. It was the seductive, gentle, one that scared her to death. . . .

PARADISE FOUND

Mary Campisi

ZEBRA BOOKS
Kensington Publishing Corp.
http://www.kensingtonbooks.com

ZEBRA BOOKS are published by

Kensington Publishing Corp.
850 Third Avenue
New York, NY 10022

All Kensington titles, imprints, and distributed lines are
available at special quantity discounts for bulk purchases for
sales promotion, premiums, fund-raising, educational or in-
stitutional use.

Special book excerpts or customized printings can also be
created to fit specific needs. For details, write or phone the
office of the Kensington Special Sales Manager: Kensington
Publishing Corp., 850 Third Avenue, New York, NY 10022.
Attn. Special Sales Department. Phone: 1-800-221-2647.

Zebra and the Z logo Reg. U.S. Pat. & TM Off.

First Printing: March 2002
10 9 8 7 6 5 4 3 2 1

Printed in the United States of America

This book is dedicated to my brothers, Bill and Mark Wooditch—the miles that separate us will never diminish the love I carry for both of you in my heart.

And to J. Wellman, driver and friend extraordinaire!

Acknowledgments

Paradise Found will always be special to me because it taught me what spirit and strength and will can do. Much of this book was written in pain—hours of it, days, months—doubled over, with a hot-water bottle pressed against my lower abdomen. The diagnosis was severe endometriosis and I underwent three surgeries in two months, the last of which was a complete hysterectomy. I had just turned forty.

A few years have passed and now I have a difficult time recalling those days and that pain, but I have not forgotten the people who were with me, caring for and about me.

And so it is with heartfelt gratitude that I say thank you to each of them:

Dr. Anthony E Bacevice, Jr., for giving me back my life

Dr. James Cantoni, for understanding my quirky reaction to drugs and guiding me through three surgeries

Marie Ingmand, for convincing me to seek help and for honest friendship

Caprice Mercer, for pharmaceutical advice, Internet expertise, and friendship

My mother, Verna Wooditch, for moving in and taking care of me, the kids, my husband, the dog, the house . . . and for all the candles and prayers

My husband, Jim, for patience and most of all unconditional love

My children, Danielle, Nicole, and Alexis and my stepchildren, T.J. and Laura, for making the best of a difficult time

And thank you also, to my editor, Amy Garvey, for believing in this book as much as I did.

One

"I don't like him."

"You don't know him."

"I know his type." *Very well.*

"Every man isn't your ex-husband."

"Thank God." Sara Hamilton stared at the man seated on the other side of the oak desk, large hands steepled under his chin. The groan of the leather chair's springs attested to his massive size, which was more suited to linebacker than his true profession. His colleagues joked that Jeff Sanders was the best damned psychologist on the East Coast because nobody dared refuse his requests, including his patients. And his partner.

"You'd only be in California until I can get things squared up here. Then I'll be right out. A few weeks at the most." He smiled. "Nina's having another ultrasound today. The bleeding's stopped."

"I'm so glad," Sara whispered, pushing the words past the lump in her throat. "I know how much you both want this baby." *As much as I wanted mine.*

Jeff nodded. "The doctor seems to think everything will be okay, but I can't leave her until we know for sure. Unfortunately, Matt needs help now. Seems he's turned into some kind of madman. His brother, Adam, said he's getting worse every day. Yesterday, he wouldn't let anybody near him."

"Not even one of those little starlets who always seem to be hovering around?" If the tabloids were accurate, company, especially the female variety, was plentiful.

Jeff's head shot up. "You shouldn't believe everything you read."

Sara felt her face grow warm. The remark was petty and childish. But in her estimation so was the person they were discussing. Matthew Brandon. Writer. Millionaire. Womanizer. Blind man.

"I'm sorry," she murmured. "That was unkind. I don't even know the man." *Nor do I want to.*

"He's a decent guy," Jeff said. "Once you get past the trappings and uncover the real man."

No, thank you. One real man in my life was too many. She nodded. "I see."

The grin on Jeff's face told her he also saw through her polite response. "Adam says since the accident, he's been a real bear. Does nothing but sit on his patio and curse the world for his misfortune."

"At least he's verbalizing," Sara said, drawn against her will to Matthew Brandon's plight. Seven months ago, he'd held the key to fame, fortune, and opportunity in the palm of his hand. One sharp maneuver down a steep ski slope had ended all that. The key was gone. Now he couldn't even find the door. Literally.

"If you call four-letter words verbalizing," Jeff countered, heaving a sigh. "He's been through four psychologists. West Coast brands, though," he said, flashing her a grin, "so they don't count."

"And you think one East Coast variety, who happens to be female," she said, pointing to herself, "is going to make him behave?"

He shrugged. "Maybe. You might be just what he needs. If all else fails, you can run interference for me until I get out there and knock some sense into him."

"We are talking about a man's life, not a football game," she said, pushing a stray lock of hair from her cheek. "And the man in question is more than a little *noncompliant.*"

Jeff laughed. "That's Matt all right. He's always been that way. Since our Penn State days. I sacked him three times during a drill one time. Told him not to try the damned quarterback sneak again or I'd bury him deeper than tomorrow. He tried it anyway." He crossed his big arms over his chest. "Zipped right past me for the touchdown."

"Well, in case you haven't noticed, he's not zipping past much of anything these days," Sara reminded him.

"But the point is, he doesn't give up. Never has. Matt's the kind of guy who thinks if he tries hard enough, persists long enough, he can make anything happen. No matter the odds. That's why he's so successful. He never takes no for an answer. Until now. He believes he'll never see again."

"What are the odds that he will?"

"Not good and getting worse with every month that passes. The point is, he should be starting to accept his fate. He's probably going to be blind for the rest of his life."

"He doesn't sound like the kind of man who

would accept anything he can't control." She'd read about the multimillion-dollar book deal he and his agent had negotiated for *Dead Moon Rising*. Four million? Or was it five? There was even talk of another movie. And a lot more money. Matthew Brandon had been a regular in *People* magazine since his first book, *Hard Truths*, hit the big screen four years ago. Hollywood had opened her arms and sucked him into her Armani-clad bosom of beauty, wealth, and power. There'd been a string—no, strings—of starlets and supermodels since then. The beautiful people. The ones to watch. He'd become as intriguing as Jack Steele, the character in his books. Men admired him, wanted to be like him. Women just wanted him. Most women, that was.

Jeff raked a big hand through his crisp, dark hair. "Matt's never been very good at settling for anything. That's why somebody like you might be able to help him. You've got a quiet strength, determined but not forceful, that would rival any man's."

"He's not likely to listen to a woman. I think he needs a firm hand like yours," she said, running her fingers down the creases in her camel-colored linen pants, concentrating on the way they popped back into place when she lifted her fingers. Some people were like that. You could flatten them and they'd bounce right back. Others stayed down for the count. Matthew Brandon was a survivor. She'd bet on it. Blind or not, he'd pull through.

"If you think about it, Sara, Matt's going through the same thing you did a few years back," Jeff said. "His whole identity's been stripped, his frame of reference distorted with the accident. You went through that when Brian left." He hesitated. "And you lost the baby. In a few months' time your whole world flipped and crashed. You lost your husband, your baby, your dream of the white picket fence."

I lost my heart. Ripped in two. "Matthew Brandon and I have nothing in common." *From what I've read, he doesn't have a heart.*

Jeff pushed his chair back and walked to the other side of the desk, dwarfing the rest of the room. "I'd say you have a lot in common," he said, his voice low. "And you might be just the one to help him, show him how to survive, adapt, overcome adversity."

"I think I'd have a hard time maintaining my objectivity," she admitted. It was hard to be objective about a man who reminded her so much of her ex-husband.

"Matt's nothing like Brian," Jeff said, reading her thoughts. "Once you get to know him, you'll see for yourself."

Sara wanted to tell him she had no desire to "get to know" Matthew Brandon. But she knew it would serve no purpose. Jeff needed her help, and as his partner and friend, she couldn't let him down.

"Two weeks? Right?"

He nodded. "Give or take a day or two."

"Okay then." She drew in a deep breath. "I'd like to get everything wrapped up here and leave as soon as possible." No sense in prolonging the inevitable.

"Great." He leaned over and clasped her hands in his. "I owe you, Sara. Thank you."

She shrugged, trying to pretend it was no big deal. "What about my clients?"

"Jessie can handle them if she needs to. Just get the paperwork in order and let them know you'll be gone for a few weeks."

"She's so young," Sara said, thinking of the perky redhead who followed her everywhere with notebook and pencil in hand, green glasses perched on her curly head, blue eyes wide and questioning.

"Twenty-five is not that young," Jeff said. "Of course, she's not ancient, like you. What are you anyway?" he asked, rubbing his chin. "Thirty-six? Thirty-seven?"

"Four," Sara said, frowning at him. "Thirty-four. The same age as your wife, as if you didn't know."

Jeff threw his hands in the air. "So I was off a few years. What does it matter? Thirty, thirty-five, forty? You'll still be beautiful at fifty."

She laughed. "Right. You must be desperate to get me to California if you've resorted to out-and-out lying."

"What are you talking about?" he asked, confusion etched in his blue eyes.

"Beauty has never been one of my greatest attributes, Jeff. I've always opted for the brains." *Though once in a great while, I have wondered what it would be like . . .*

"What are you talking about? Now you can choose your beauty, like a comfortable pair of old shoes?" The look on his face told her he thought she was joking. She wasn't. For much of her pre-adolescent and teenage life, she had felt the sting of being just plain old ordinary. Nothing spectacular, except perhaps her eyes. People had always seemed drawn to their amber-green depths, intrigued with the almond shape and slight tilt. A seductress's eyes, someone once said. Sara almost choked. What a joke. She'd never been able to seduce anything. Even her husband.

Brian was the only person who had ever made her feel beautiful with his honeyed words and slow smiles. Until he got tired of her. Until she balked at cosigning a hefty business loan for him. She'd wanted him to wait, wait until after the baby. . . .

Can't you ever, just once in your pitiful life say, "Fuck it? Fuck it, I don't care if it doesn't make sense right now, I'm going to do it anyway?" His perfect lips had pulled into a thin line. *Hell no, you can't. You're so goddamned responsible, it's suffocating. Well then, fuck you, Sara. Fuck you.* He'd grabbed his jacket and slammed out of the house, leaving her sitting there by the fireplace with her swollen belly and her shredded self-esteem.

No man would ever do that to her again, even if she had to reside in the world of the ordinary for the rest of her life. She was used to looking the other way when an interested male tried to catch her eye or ignoring the subtle suggestions of a fellow colleague trying to move their "friendship" to the next level. Ordinary was safe. Ordinary was what she wanted.

Jeff shook his head. "You know, Sara, one of these days, you and I need to have a long talk."

She raised a brow. "Oh?"

"Yeah. Oh. One of these days, we're going to talk about the incredible job you do with your clients. How you dig them out of a garbage pile of despair, brush them off, build their self-esteem and send them into healthy new relationships and worthwhile jobs."

"I care about those women. All of them. And I

believe in them." She had to, for God knew, they didn't believe in themselves, not when the pain and shock of being cast aside reverberated like a drum through every inch of their being.

"You make it personal." It was a statement, not an accusation. Jeff was right. She did make it personal. Because she'd experienced firsthand every gut-wrenching emotion they would ever encounter. And she'd survived.

"I can't help it."

He held up his hand. "I'm not finished yet. I want to know how you can have such patience and foresight where your clients are concerned and make such lousy choices in your personal life."

Sara stiffened. "We've been through this all before," she said in a tight voice.

"Of course, we have. And we're still hitting dead ends. The day you lost the baby, you gave up on hope. When Brian walked out, you gave up on love. You can help everybody else, but you can't help yourself. Why, Sara? Why?"

The clanging of the phone saved her from answering. Jeff leaned over and levered the receiver from its base. "Yes?" he answered in a crisp, professional voice, all traces of his earlier impassioned tone gone.

Sara closed her eyes, taking the momentary distraction to pull herself together. Jeff was right, of course. She knew his words made perfect sense. After all, she spoke similar ones to her clients every day. Why then, couldn't she listen to her own professional recommendations and open herself up to love again?

The answer was simple. She wasn't *willing* to risk the pain. Not again. It had almost destroyed her before; she couldn't chance it a second time. That's why she worked so hard with her clients. They were her success. They went on to live again, love again, hope again. And she was a part of that.

It was as close to the fire as she was willing to get.

Opening her eyes, Sara's breath stuck in her throat as she stared at the man before her. Jeff was leaning against the desk, clutching the receiver in his hand, his face ashen. She thought his eyes were wet.

"Jeff, what is it?" A sinking feeling settled in her chest, weighing her down, gluing her to the chair. Only one thing could reduce a man like Jeff Sanders to tears.

"It's Nina," he said, his voice raw with pain. "She's bleeding again."

The hot afternoon sun beat down on Matt, relaxing him, making him drowsy. There was nothing like California weather. Not too hot, never too cold and always just a day away from decent weather, even when it rained. It sure beat the hell out of Pittsburgh with its subzero winters, freezing rain, and ice storms, not to mention blizzards. Even summer days with their overcast skies and cool nights left a person wanting. He ought to know; he'd spent enough years there.

But California was different. It was the land of opportunity. A place for high rollers, where risk-takers rode with Lady Luck on their shoulder, smiling their beautiful smiles, making their multimillion-dollar deals and raking in the cash by the armored truckload. He used to be one of the elite, one of the high rollers.

But that was before he'd rammed into the tree that changed his life forever. He shoved his ball cap down, shielding part of his face from the heat. Blind. That's what he was. What he would be for the rest of his life. A knot twisted deep in his gut.

How many times had he replayed those last seconds on the slope? Two hundred? More like two thousand. If only that kid hadn't been downed right in his landing path. If only he had veered to the right. If only he had listened to Adam and not made the final run. If only that damned tree hadn't been there. If only.

He cursed. *If only* didn't matter. Not when he opened his eyes every morning to darkness. That was the hardest part. That, and accepting blindness as a way of life. Forever. He knew he'd have to do it. Someday. On his own terms. But he sure as hell wasn't going to put up with any more damned psychologists and their "How did that make you feel?" probing.

And then there was that last one. The woman. Claire something or other. She'd only been interested in studying the effects of blindness on his sexuality. Even offered herself up as part of the case study. Said she wanted to conduct an experiment with him. He'd yanked her by the arm and hauled her out of the house so fast she hadn't had time to button her shirt.

Matt sighed. He was through talking with everybody. Except, maybe, Jeff. He'd be here soon, not to pick and probe and dissect like all the others. But to listen. Like a friend.

* * *

LAX was like a maze with only one exit. Men with starched white shirts and purposeful strides balanced cell phones and overnight bags while women in short, silk suits with golden tans and sun-kissed hair, pulled compact travel cases behind them. Crying babies clutched their mother's shirts with pudgy fingers, balling the fabric into wrinkled messes, while toddlers wailed a separate tune from the ground as they grabbed at moving pant legs.

So many people. All in motion. All going somewhere.

Sara raked a hand through her thick brown hair and scanned the signs overhead, looking for a way out. A tall gangly youth pushed passed her, slamming her briefcase into her knee. Stifling a cry of pain, she hobbled toward the exit, hauling the briefcase in one hand and pulling her oversize suitcase with the other.

Too many people. Way too many people, she thought as she heard the last boarding call to Pittsburgh. Back East. Home. Maybe if she hurried she could catch the next flight . . .

Someone pushed her through the huge glass door, onto the hot concrete. The June heat smacked her in the face, stealing the breath from her chest. She fumbled for her sunglasses, pushed them on with two fingers and looked around. Los Angeles. Hot. Crowded. Smoggy. Sweat trickled between her shoulder blades. There seemed to be just as many people bustling about outside as there had been inside.

Dragging her bag forward, Sara concentrated on the sleek line of limousines dotting the curb. There were at least twelve. Incredible. They were as popular as minivans back home. A man emerged from the line of cars, carrying a sign with her name on it.

Sara hesitated. He didn't look like any limousine driver she'd ever seen. Not that she'd seen many, but she was certain their dress code did not consist of khaki pants and sneakers. He was a big man, at least six-feet-two, with a solid build except for a bit of a tummy protruding from his checkered vest. His eyes settled on her, and something in her expression must have told him she was the one, because he advanced on her like a grizzly bear stalking a fish.

"Dr. Hamilton?" he asked, towering over her.

Sara stared up at the mountain before her and nodded.

His face broke into a grin as he reached for her suitcase and briefcase. "A tiny thing like you shouldn't be lugging these things around," he said, taking bag and briefcase from her and shifting them into one hand as though they weighed nothing. Tiny? Her? Sara Hamilton? Wholesome. Sturdy. Healthy-looking. Nonanorexic. Those were terms she'd heard since her teens. But tiny had never been one of them. That word was reserved for cheerleaders and prom queens.

She had been neither.

"By the way, my name is Jimmy. Pleased to meet you, Dr. Hamilton." He stuck out a large paw and pumped her hand like a seesaw.

"Call me Sara, please," she said, hazarding a smile at the man whose crooked grin transformed him from grizzly to teddy bear. Her smile deepened.

"Sara," he said. "Let's get out of here before traffic heats up."

Sara took two steps to his every long, lumbering stride, trying to ignore the honking horns, squealing tires, and roaring engines and wondering what things would look like when traffic "heated up."

"We're sure happy you're here," Jimmy said, once they were settled and pulling out of the parking lot. Sara winced as he threaded his way between vehicles, pedestrians, and luggage.

"Why, thank you." She wished she could say the same, but the knots in her stomach reminded her of just how much she didn't want to be here. But she'd done it for Jeff and Nina. And their unborn child.

"Things just haven't been the same since Matt's accident," Jimmy said. "Everything's changed." His voice slipped a notch. "I couldn't tell you the last time I had this honey out for a spin." He shook his brown head. "We miss him, Doc. We want you to get him back for us."

Sara took a deep breath. She'd heard the sadness in his voice. And the pain. She knew both of those. Intimately. "I'll try to help him, Jimmy, until Dr. Sanders can get here."

Jimmy's big shoulders relaxed against the back of the seat. He looked at her from the rearview mirror and grinned. "I think you're going to be the one, Doc," he said, his brown eyes twinkling. "Yes, sir. I think you just might be the one."

"How many others have there been, Jimmy?" She kept her eyes trained on the rearview mirror.

"Others?" His brown gaze flitted to hers for a brief second. "Well, that was before . . ." His voice trailed off.

"Before what, Jimmy?"

She saw a hint of red creep up his neck and ears.

"Before . . . before you came. Oh, yes, before you came, there were four other big-name doctors. Matt didn't like any of them. Three men and one woman." He shook his head. "The men were all stuffed shirts and the woman was just," he hesitated, "pardon the expression, but she was downright crazy."

Sara stifled a smile. She liked Jimmy. He said what was on his mind. And then some. Would he be as willing to talk to her about his boss?

She felt her stomach lurch again. Very soon she'd be meeting the man himself. Would she be number five on the casualty list? Did she care?

"You look tired, Doc. We've got a ways to go yet. Why don't you just settle back and take a little nap?"

Sara smiled at Jimmy through the rearview mirror. "That's the best idea I've heard all day." She leaned into the soft black cushions and closed her eyes. "And it's Sara," she murmured. "Just plain Sara."

The rest of the trip whisked by as she curled into the luxury of the limousine, dozing off and on, mindless of the miles ticking by on the endless freeway. Not until she felt a gentle hand on her shoulder and Jimmy's soft voice floating into her consciousness, did she come fully awake. Opening her eyes, she smiled at him, stretched her arms wide, and looked out the front window.

You're not in Kansas anymore, she thought, as her gaze swept past the three-story Spanish style stucco dwelling with multitiered, terra cotta tiles adorning the roof. Bougainvillea and hibiscus lent vibrant splashes of yellow, orange, and red to the stark backdrop of stucco while flowering pink and purple cacti stood like sentinels on either side of the stone walkway. There were other flowers and shrubs, exotic ones that she'd never seen before, whose names she wouldn't even venture to guess.

Jimmy opened the door for her and she stepped into the heat, feeling its fingers on her head and back like a branding iron. The smell of sea air filled her nostrils. Her gaze sliced through the filmy haze, settling on the swatch of blue in the far distance. White peaks crested and fell, smashing into mountains of rocks with the force of a head-on collision.

Mesmerized, she watched nature's display of beauty unfold before her. The high-pitched shriek of seagulls loomed overhead as they dipped and swooped in graceful arcs.

"Nothing quite like it, is there?" Jimmy said in an almost-reverent tone.

"Everything is so," she hesitated, trying to find the right word, "beautiful." The term seemed understated. It would take a string of words, perhaps twenty strings, to pay full homage to the magnificence of the view before her.

"If you think it's beautiful from this vantage point, then you'd love it from up there," he said, nodding his head toward the sky.

"I'll bet it's incredible," Sara said, following his gaze. A cerulean cover blanketed the sky, tucking away cloud puffs beneath its warm embrace. Sara wished she could crawl up there and wrap herself in its soft cocoon.

"It's incredible, all right," he said, shielding his eyes from the blast of rays that beat down on them. "I'll show you just how incredible someday. I'll take you up there myself."

She wasn't certain she'd heard him quite right. "You're a pilot?"

Jimmy threw her his teddy bear grin. "Sure. Why not?"

"Well, it's just that I don't know many limousine drivers who fill in as pilots." She opened her mouth to speak, closed it, and then opened it again. "To be honest, I don't know many limousine drivers at all. In fact, I think you're the first one."

He laughed. "I'm not your typical driver."

Sara smiled. "So I noticed." She leaned closer, whispering, "Do you have any other professions you'd like to tell me about?"

His quick grin made her laugh. "Did I tell you I'm an aerial photographer? No? Well, how about a genuine mister fix-it, mechanic, tour guide, and gardener?"

"I don't think you mentioned any of those facts," Sara teased. They'd reached a heavy wrought-iron gate that separated the yard from the house. Its complex carvings twisted into thick black bands, strong and unyielding, warning against unwanted intruders. And it was locked.

As Jimmy fitted the long key into the opening, Sara thought that Matthew Brandon might not be much different from his gate. Complex, strong, unyielding. And most definitely closed to all unwanted intruders.

"Oh, and one more thing," Jimmy said as they headed up the stone walkway to the main entrance, "I'm a great listener." He flashed another disarming smile and opened the door for her. Sara had no time to ponder that last comment as she stepped over the threshold into a level of elegance she had only imagined in her dreams.

A three-tiered black iron chandelier caught her eye first. Its sheer size dominated the foyer, its commanding presence demanding to be noticed and appreciated. *Like the owner, no doubt,* Sara thought as her gaze trailed down the white hallway, looking for signs of Matthew Brandon. She heard voices, soft and muted, one male, one female. Was it him? Taking a deep breath, she pasted a smile on her face and followed Jimmy toward the voices, no longer aware of the magnificent wealth scattered about in the form of paintings, sculptures, and furniture. She kept her eyes trained on Jimmy's broad back, but the vision of Matthew Brandon, cool, handsome, and very unapproachable, flashed before her. The ultimate user.

This is never going to work. I haven't even met the man and I dislike him already.

Jimmy led her to a large room full of potted palm trees and white leather. A man and woman turned toward them. It had been their voices she'd heard. Not Matthew Brandon's. The man was tall and blond and looked to be somewhere in his midthirties. The woman was well into her fifties, dark complected, with a short, round body that reminded Sara of rising bread.

The man smiled, a flash of white, and walked toward Sara, holding out his right hand. "You must be Sara," he said, clasping her hands in his. She nodded, looking up into warm gray eyes.

"You must be Adam," she guessed. *The nice brother.*

His smile deepened, revealing two deep dimples on either side of his mouth. They added to his boyish charm and casual good looks. Unlike his

brother. Sara doubted there was an ounce of anything boyish or casual about Matthew Brandon.

"Ay, Díos mio," the older woman said, making the
sign of the cross. *"You* are the doctor?" She closed
in on Sara, black eyes darting from top to bottom
as she studied Sara's face, hair, clothes, shoes. Like
a bug under a microscope. Crossing her arms under her ample bosom, she repeated the scrutiny
in slow motion.

"This is Rosa, Sara," Adam said, gesturing toward the woman who watched her with such un-
disguised suspicion.

Sara nodded. She wasn't opening her mouth.
Not an inch. Next the woman would be counting
her fillings.

"This is the doctor! How can this be? *Ay, Díos
mio,"* she uttered, crossing herself again. "Señor
Adam, did you know this is the doctor?"

"I sent for her, Rosa," Adam said, shooting her
a sideways glance. "I know who she is."

Rosa made a *tsk tsk* sound, as though she hadn't
heard him. "He's no gonna like this. No. No." She
shook her salt-and-pepper head making the bun
on top bounce back and forth.

"I'll handle it, Rosa." Sara heard the sharpness
in Adam's voice.

"It's okay, Rosa," Jimmy said from the corner of
the room, his voice soft and reassuring. Sara
turned and saw him. He stood with arms crossed
over his chest, minus baggage. When had he left
and when had he returned? Silent intruder. She
added that to her list of Jimmy's professions.

Sara cleared her throat. "Excuse me, but is there
something I should know?" Her gaze traveled over
all three of them and settled on Adam.

His lips curved up in a small smile. "It's really no big deal." He shrugged his broad shoulders.

Jimmy cleared his throat. Loudly.

The woman named Rosa stood next to Sara, eyes downcast, lips moving in quiet repetition. Her fingers worked the beads of a small black rosary that hung halfway out of the deep pocket of her white apron.

"Really," Adam repeated. "Everything's okay."

Rosa lifted her head and stared at Adam, her plump fingers continuing their silent litany along the beads. " 'No more women. No more women. No more women.' That's what he say." The words flew out in quick, rapid succession like a round on a semiautomatic. *No more women? Matthew Brandon was swearing off women?* Somehow, she found that hard to believe.

"Adam?" Sara looked at the handsome man in front of her and waited.

"Matt had a bad experience with the last female psychologist I hired." He shot a quick look at Jimmy.

"He did? What happened?" *Probably blazed her ears with his fancy, four-letter vocabulary.*

A dull flush crept up Adam's tanned neck, spreading to his high cheekbones. "It seems . . . she . . ." he fumbled around, "was more interested in conducting experiments of a physical nature than in aiding his recovery."

"Oh." *She'd come on to her patient. And he'd turned her down? Perhaps Matthew Brandon had a few scruples after all. Or maybe she just hadn't been his type.*

"But you're nothing like her," Adam said, his gray eyes warming. "As soon as Matt meets you, he'll realize that. Everything will be fine," he reassured her.

She flashed a look at Rosa in time to see the braided bun on her head wobble back and forth in disbelief. Then the older woman bowed her head low, closed her eyes, and murmured rhythmic cadences in sorrowful tones.

The whole scene made Sara uncomfortable. It was as though she'd walked in on the last act of a play where everyone knew their part but her. What was going on? And where was Matthew Brandon?

"Is Matthew expecting me?" she asked with growing apprehension.

Adam avoided her gaze. And her question. He looked down, studying the tassels of his Italian loafers with great interest.

"Adam," Sara repeated with more force, "is Matthew expecting me?"

She knew the answer before he uttered the words.

"No." He shook his head. "Not exactly."

Great. "Is that not exactly as in he knows I'll be here sometime but not when?" She folded her arms across her chest. "Or is it not exactly as in he has no clue I'm coming and doesn't even know I exist?"

Sara heard a coughing sound in the far corner of the room and knew it belonged to Jimmy. Was that some kind of signal? Were he and Adam plotting something without Matthew's knowledge? A sinking feeling settled in her stomach like a ball of uncooked dough.

Adam lifted his gray eyes to meet hers. "We had no choice," he said in a soft voice. "Jeff and I felt this was the only way."

Sara blinked. Twice. "Jeff? As in Jeff Sanders? He *knew* Matthew didn't want another female doctor and he sent me here *anyway?*" Her voice rose with each word, finishing on a high squeak.

"It's my fault," Adam said, with an apologetic smile. "I was desperate. He's been getting worse every day. I begged Jeff to help me." He hesitated. "And he said you could keep things together until he got out here." His strong tanned fingers opened in a silent plea. "Please don't hold it against him, Sara. If anyone's to blame, it's me for pressuring Jeff to send us a miracle before Matt destroys himself and everyone around him."

Two

All eyes riveted on Sara, waiting for her response. Even Rosa paused the incessant clicking of her rosary beads to better hear Sara's words. And what could she say at a point like this, when Matthew Brandon's brother had all but gotten on his knees and begged her to stay? *No, thank you, I think your brother's a jerk?* Despite her personal feelings for the man, Sara felt a certain loyalty to her profession and those who cared about him. Namely, Jeff.

"I'll talk to him," she said in a quiet voice.

Adam let out a sigh of relief. "Thank you, Sara." He grasped her hand and squeezed. "Thank you so much."

"Where is he?" *Might as well meet the lion in his den.*

"Come with me," Adam said, turning around and heading back toward the hall. He passed three closed doors and stopped at the fourth. "This is his study," he said, opening the door and waiting for her to pass through. It was a warm lived-in room with a large cherry desk and matching leather chair. A computer rested on the left corner of the desk. She wondered how long it had been since its cursor blinked with activity. An elaborate entertainment center, complete with a state-of-the-art stereo system, monopolized the wall facing Matthew's desk. Rows and rows of CDs lined the shelves. Sara leaned over and scanned a few of the artists' names. Bach. Beethoven. Led Zeppelin. The Rolling Stones. She smiled at the odd mix.

"He used to spend most of his time in this room," Adam said, running his fingers along the smooth rich grain of the desk. "But it's been months since he's ventured in here."

"And his work?" Sara asked, her gaze skimming the framed awards and various recognitions mounted on the wall in front of her.

"Nothing." Adam shook his head. "Not a single word. Not even a punctuation mark." He moved to the bookcase and pulled out one of Matthew's novels, flipping through the pages.

"I'm sorry," she murmured, unable to think of anything more adequate to say.

"I know. We all are." He put the book back in its spot. "Matt's a great guy."

Sara felt a twinge in her stomach. Was it guilt? Her face felt warm. Could Adam tell? Would he know that she didn't share his opinion of his older brother?

"Where is he?" she asked.

Adam nodded his blond head toward the sliding glass door behind her. "Out there. Where he is every day."

She turned and walked to the door, peering out onto the stone patio. A man sat off to the right, partially hidden from view. She leaned closer to get a full glimpse of him. He was a big man, tall and broad, filling up the green-and-white-striped recliner with casual grace, his long legs stretched out in front, crossed at the ankles. His skin harbored the warm honeyed tones of one who's spent long hours in the sun. The white polo shirt and navy shorts he wore fit his body well, accenting muscular legs and arms. He could have been just another California male with a tanned body and bulging biceps who never failed to draw an appreciative glance from the opposite sex.

But he wasn't. He was Matthew Brandon. And no woman with a pulse was immune to his charm. At least that's what the tabloids bragged, each time they splashed a picture of him and his latest conquest across the cover of their magazine. No doubt, he was great to look at and that alone pumped up their sales. But some said his allure was more than just physical magnetism. It wasn't just the penetrating silver eyes that could strip a woman of common sense with the first hello. Or the hint of that ever-present half smile playing about his full lips as though he had secrets—bold, sensual secrets—just waiting to be shared. It wasn't even the sound of his deep gravelly voice speaking in hushed tones that made him irresistible to women.

It was the aura of the man that left most females weak-kneed and hopeful, desperate for attention, any kind of attention, and willing to do most anything to get it. Matthew Brandon knew how to smile his boyish smile, steal the essence of the moment, and slip away like a thief in the night, leaving a trail of shattered hearts behind. And so evolved the man whose very elusiveness was the greatest attraction of all. Every woman believed she would be the one to change him, to tame him, to make him stay. And each one failed miserably.

Sara squeezed her eyes shut. The images were too familiar. Too painful. She knew firsthand how a marauding bandit could pillage a woman's heart. And soul. Matthew Brandon was just like her husband. A user. Once a user, always a user.

Two weeks. Maybe less. She hoped not more. Then she'd be on her way back to Pittsburgh and her safe, comfortable life. Would she have enough time to lay the groundwork for Jeff?

Women would always want him, blind or not. And he would most likely continue to use and discard them like an empty container of Chinese takeout. Her job was to get him to care again. About something. Anything. Period.

Taking a deep, steadying breath, Sara pulled the door back and thanked God she was one of the few females left who remained immune to the likes of Matthew Brandon.

He pretended he didn't hear the door slide open. It would be Rosa. Again. Trying to pawn off another fajita, or taco, or whatever in the hell it was she'd been after him to eat for the last three hours. Since when was skipping a meal because you just weren't hungry a major offense?

"Rosa." Matt heaved a sigh. "What is it this time? Frijoles? Enchiladas? Tostadas? No, no, and no. I'm not hungry." He kept his head back, baseball cap low over his brow, sunglasses shielding his eyes.

"They all sound good to me."

His head whipped up off the cushion. That low, throaty voice did not belong to Rosa.

"Who the hell are you?"

"Sara," the woman said. "Sara Hamilton. Adam sent me."

Jesus Christ! Now Adam had really done it. He'd warned, threatened, argued, and bullied Matt for weeks, telling him he'd fix Matt but good if he didn't get his butt out of that chair and start acting like a human being instead of a waste product. Decomposing pile of compost, he'd called him. Said he needed a woman to get his mind off his miserable self. Well, from the sounds of that sexy voice pouring over his senses, Adam had got him one all right. *Jesus!*

"Whatever Adam paid you, I'll pay you double to leave."

"I gave my word I'd stay."

Since when did a prostitute's word count for anything? "I don't want you here." Matt settled his head back against the cushions, dismissing her.

"Maybe we can just talk a little while." The woman pulled a chair next to him, scraping the legs along the stone. He could smell her scent, fresh and tangy. Orange blossom sprinkled with lemon. Odd fragrance for a prostitute. Maybe she was one of those innocent-looking virgin types some men liked.

"You want to *talk* with me? That's it?" Laughter rumbled low in his throat.

"For starters," she said. Her voice rolled over him, smooth and silky with just a hint of scratchiness to it. Like she'd just downed a shot. Or spent a sleepless night with her lover. *Talking.* He laughed again.

"How long have you been in the business?" The old reporter in him wanted to ask how she'd gotten sucked into this kind of life, but he held his tongue. He wasn't a reporter anymore. Or much of anything else.

"Seven years."

"Seven years," he repeated, trying to guess at the number of times she'd bartered her body for money. The figure was staggering. Even for him.

"I'm very qualified if that's your concern." There was an edge of defiance in her voice. "Most of my work is done on an individual basis though from time to time, I have worked with couples."

Matt choked, coughed, sputtered. *Couples?*

"I'd like you to give me a chance, Matthew," she continued as though she were talking about sampling cheese spreads instead of sex.

He took off his cap, ran a hand through his unkempt hair, and plopped the cap back on his head. The woman was one cool cookie. She seemed more upset with proving she was *qualified* to have sex with him than with the actual act itself. Crazy woman.

"I'll tell you what, Sara Hamilton," Matt said. "You leave now and we keep this little secret between us. Okay? You get your money and I keep my reputation." He gave her one of his slow smiles. "Deal?" He leaned forward. "Now give me your right hand," he said, holding his own out, palm up. Matt felt her cold fingers graze his skin. Closing his fingers around hers, he took his other hand and stroked his way up her arm, feeling the satin skin beneath his rough fingertips. Smooth and soft.

"What . . . what are you doing?" she stammered.

"Just keeping you honest," he said. "In case someone asks if anything happened between us, you can say yes and it'll be the truth." Poor thing probably wasn't used to tenderness in or out of bed. His fingers splayed over her collarbone, massaging in slow rhythmic movements. He heard a sharp intake of breath. Trailing an index finger down her neck, he started to trace the plump fullness of her breast.

"How dare you!" She smacked his hand away, pulled out of his grasp. The chair clattered to the stone floor.

"What the hell are you talking about?" Matt yelled. "What did I do?"

"Do?" she shrieked. "You . . . you . . . touched me."

"So have hundreds of other men. Do you try to deck them all?"

"What . . . what are you talking about?" He heard the slight tremor in her voice. It was hard to tell if it was born of anger or fear, or maybe a little of both. She was obviously used to running her own show.

"It's a little late to start playing the virginal victim," he said, frowning.

"What are you talking about?"

"Men touch your body all the time."

"*What?*"

"You're a prostitute."

"I am not a prostitute!" He could almost feel the anger smothering her words, could almost imagine her standing before him, feet spread wide, fists clenched, hands on hips. So much for fear.

Matt slashed a hand in the air. He hadn't spoken this many words at one time, to one person, in a long time. Since the day he knew he'd never see again. So why was he wasting his breath on a whore? Because her outrage annoyed him. Because like everyone else on this screwed-up planet, she was trying to hide behind a cloak of deceit. Well, the smoke-and-mirrors routine wouldn't work with him. He would've respected her more if she'd just come clean and owned up to her profession. Straight out. No excuses. Show a little dignity. As much as one could find dignity in selling one's body.

What the hell, he thought. People sold their souls every day, chunks at a time, bartered to the highest bidder without so much as a trickle of conscience. Everything had a price. Everything. It was a damn sad fact of life.

So what in the hell was this woman's problem?

"Look, lady, I don't care right now who you are," Matt said, trying to keep the edge from his voice. "You're not a prostitute? Fine. You're Mother Teresa's niece? Great. Just take your overblown outrage and walk your little fanny out of here." He took a deep breath and pointed to the glass doors. "Now."

"Jeff sent me."

Jeff? "Jeff?" He turned toward her. *"Jeff?* What the hell does Jeff have to do with this?"

Silence.

He sat up, swinging his long legs over the side of the recliner. "Start talking."

"It was Jeff's idea that I come." She practically spit out the words. "I'm a psychologist. He and I are partners. He thought I could help you."

"Help me? With what?" Blood rushed to his head, pounding against his brain. "The last lady doctor wanted to help me by having sex. For her case study. Is that what you're after?" His hands balled into tight fists. "Sex?"

"No!"

"No? Good. Because you've got exactly three seconds to get out of here, Dr. Hamilton." Rage pulsed through his veins like molten lava, hot and deadly, seeping into every pore of his body. Another shrink. And a woman, no less.

It took her a moment to respond. He imagined her licking her lips, even though he had no idea what she looked like. Blonde, brunette, or bald, it didn't matter. He was through with shrinks. Especially the female variety.

"I think we should talk."

She was persistent, he'd give her that. "Talk, Dr. Hamilton? What should we talk about?"

"Well, we'll talk about your condition and ways to deal with it."

"My condition?" He took two steps in the direction of her voice. "My condition?" Couldn't anybody say the damn word? "Say it, Dr. Hamilton. My blindness." He was close enough to smell her citrus scent.

"Your blindness," she repeated.

"And you're going to show me how to deal with it, right?" He snapped his fingers. "Just like that."

"Of course not. Nothing is as simple as a snap of the fingers."

"But that's what you're after. Isn't it? Acceptance with minimal fanfare." He didn't wait for an answer. "Sure it is. You're all the same. Forget about the sunsets and blue skies. Don't think of the beautiful woman by your side. They no longer exist for you. Just shut up and accept your plight."

"That's your attitude, Matthew. Not mine."

Oh, she was a cold one. Frozen over like a glacier. That low, throaty voice of hers might turn a man's head, but it was all a trick. The woman had ice in her veins.

He rubbed his jaw, determined to chip away at her frosty reserve. His fingers brushed against two days of stubble. "Have you ever lost something dear to you, Dr. Hamilton? Something you took for granted, thought would be around forever, and then, poof, one day it's just gone?"

"We're here to discuss you, Matthew, not me." He heard the edge in her voice, buried beneath all the layers of cool composure.

Matt ploughed on. "And you keep hoping, and praying that maybe it's all a bad dream and you'll wake up soon? But it isn't, and deep down, you know it, even as you barter with God and the devil at the same time, promising to do anything, give everything, if only you could have this one thing back again? Even for a little while longer? But you're talking to a blank wall because no one hears you?"

Sara Hamilton made a small, muffled sound.

"You're in it all alone, your heart gouged with grief, bleeding the pain of your loss. And you want more than anything to die, but your damned heart keeps pumping away, pushing the hurt and anguish through your tormented body, until you think you'll explode." Matt rubbed the back of his neck. "But you don't. And that's the hell of it." He let out a ragged sigh. "You live."

He was so lost in his own thoughts that he never heard her move until the sound of the sliding glass door caught his attention. Had he offended the Ice Queen? He'd known she'd retreat once he let out his emotions. They were too honest, too real, too dark for her to handle. He shrugged as he found his chair and sank into it. It didn't matter. His tactics had worked. Jimmy was probably loading Dr. Sara Hamilton's luggage into the limo right this minute. Matt leaned back against the soft cushions of his recliner and heaved a sigh of relief.

Sara jerked the sliding glass door shut, grabbed her middle, and sucked in gulps of air like a lifeline. Her stomach jumped and roiled, reminding her of when she was a little girl rounding the top of the Ferris wheel. One suspended moment of fearful anticipation before her stomach flew to her throat. Matthew Brandon's cruel words pushed her over the edge, with that same dread, plummeting her from the top of her carefully constructed world to the dark depths of her painful past. He'd punctured the surface, picked at the scab, broken open an old wound.

Sara leaned against the desk, placing both palms on the smooth polished top. She closed her eyes, forcing herself to take slow even breaths.

She had to get out of here.

Matthew Brandon was too crass, too arrogant, too sarcastic. Too full of anger, the deep, visceral kind that spreads like a slow insidious cancer, eating away the last vestiges of humanity until nothing remains but an empty shell, cracked and brittle. The problem was, his kind destroyed anyone who tried to help them.

Have you ever lost something dear to you, Dr. Hamilton? The question bounced off the walls, echoing in her brain like a clanging cymbal. *Something you took for granted, thought would be around forever, and then, poof, one day it's just gone?* Oh, yes, she'd wanted to scream at him, she knew all about pain, knew what it was like to stare at the ceiling for days, too weak and hopeless to crawl out of bed, too full of despair to care. She knew all about it, could probably teach him a thing or two if the truth be known. But she'd kept her silence. That was the best course of action, especially in a direct attack like the one Matthew Brandon had launched at her.

What bothered her most was that his words blasted her defenses like SCUD missiles, ripping holes in the wall she'd constructed as though it were made of paper. No one got through without her permission. No one. And she wasn't in the habit of giving permission. Not even to Jeff, though he never stopped trying.

So why had a blind man succeeded? Because right now she was vulnerable. Jeff and Nina were in danger of losing their baby. Visions of her own child lying in a tiny white casket trimmed with gold assaulted her memory. She'd named her Rebecca. A stray tear trickled down Sara's cheek, falling unchecked onto the polished gloss of the desktop. She would've been three now. Another tear fell. Brian hadn't cared what name she put on the death certificate. He had been too busy packing so he could take up residence with his new girl-friend, which he did the day she came home from the hospital.

Brian. Deceitful, manipulative, self-centered Brian. If even half of what she'd read about Matthew Brandon were true, he made her ex-husband look like an altar boy. Jeff had told her he wasn't what he seemed, but in the fifteen minutes she'd spent with him, he appeared to live up to the rumors and more. The beast had called her a hooker! And touched her breast!

She needed answers. Now. Why hadn't Jeff told her Matthew Brandon wouldn't talk to anyone but him? He could have saved her the long tiring trip out here with a few honest words. Sara picked up the phone and, with slow, careful fingers, punched out his private number.

"Good afternoon, Doctor Sander's office. May I help you?"

"Hi, Jessie. It's me."

"Sara! Hey! How are you?" Jessie's bouncy exuberance coursed through the wires, making Sara smile.

"I'm fine. How is everything?"

"You mean since ten hours ago, when you left?" Jessie laughed. "Well, let's see." Sara could just picture the young woman looking at the ceiling and twirling a strand of curly red hair with her index finger. "April called to say the job interview went very well and she thinks she'll get an offer next week. She said to make sure I told you the next time I talked to you, which I must admit, I didn't think would be quite so soon."

"Let's hope things work out for her," Sara said. "Anybody else?"

"Heather called. Her husband's pressuring her big-time. Roses, cards, dinner. Says he'll never look at another woman again and she wants to believe this time will be different. But," Jessie sighed, "he's told her that six times already."

"I know. It's sad. Just listen to her. That's all you can do until she's ready to make a change."

They spent the next several minutes talking about clients, reviewing strategies, discussing probable outcomes. None of it was necessary. They'd been through it all countless times in the past several days. Jessie might be young and her light-hearted style different than Sara's more conservative one, but she was smart, dedicated, and clients loved her. She didn't need Sara to check behind her like a doting mother.

But Sara needed her right now. She needed the familiarity of her work, her clients, anything to bring back her focus, to center herself. And to avoid hearing the inevitable disappointment in Jeff's voice when she told him she was coming home. Far away from Matthew Brandon.

"So tell me, Sara," Jessie said, the excitement bubbling in her voice, "is he as handsome in person as he is in his photos?"

"Who?" Sara asked, marveling at the other woman's constant energy. She got exhausted just talking to her.

"Who?! How can you ask me that? You know who! Matt Brandon. Super hunk. Every woman's dream!" Her laughter filled the other end of the receiver. "Is he as handsome as his pictures?"

Oh, God, not Jessie too. The man was like a vampire, mesmerizing women, turning their brains into oatmeal. "I don't know." *Handsome?* "I haven't really noticed." She'd been too busy trying to shield herself from his verbal attacks to consider his physical attributes. What was the sense? Handsome or not, he was still ruthless, cruel, and arrogant. And that equaled worse than ugly in her book.

Of course Jessie couldn't let it go at that. "You haven't noticed?" she squealed. "How could you not notice? He's so incredibly handsome. And sexy. And beautiful."

"I think I'm going to be ill."

Jessie laughed. "Be serious, Sara. How is he?"

Now, there was a question. Matthew Brandon was a lot of things, but Sara didn't use that type of language so she settled for an obscure description. "Difficult."

"Really? Hmm? Well, I'm sure it'll take him some time to adjust to his situation, but if anybody can do it, he can."

Matthew Brandon was right. Nobody could say the damn word.

"You mean his blindness?"

"Yeah." Her tone grew serious. "What a bummer."

"It's a real bummer, all right."

"Those beautiful silver eyes," Jessie said. "Looking at you, into you, through you." She sighed. "Every picture of him makes me feel that way. Are they as breathtaking in real life?"

"I don't know. He wears dark glasses." This conversation was ridiculous. Jessie was too intelligent to get reeled in by a handsome face with a glib line. And a pair of silver eyes. "Jeff said he might stop in late in the day to get a little work done. Is he there?"

"Nope. Haven't seen him."

"Everything okay with Nina?"

"Yeah. The ultrasound looked good and no more bleeding."

"Great. Thanks, Jessie. I'll catch him at home."

"Okay, Sara. Keep me posted on the hunk. Okay? And if you can get him to take off those shades, look at his eyes. Real good. I bet they'll blow you away."

"Right. Good-bye," Sara said, placing the receiver in its cradle, more than ready to end the conversation. With responses like Jessie's, no wonder the man had such an overblown ego. Shaking her head, she dialed Jeff's number.

He answered after the third ring.

"Hello."

"Hi, Jeff." She took a deep breath, wrapping her index finger around the black phone cord. "This is Sara."

"Sara. Hi." He didn't sound at all surprised to hear her voice.

"Don't 'Sara, hi,' me. Why didn't you tell me 'Mr. Macho' wouldn't talk to anybody but you?"

He ignored the question. "Is there a problem?"

"Oh, I'd say there's a problem, all right." She twisted the phone cord tighter, squeezing the blood out of her fingertip. "The man has practically assaulted me, verbally abused me, and kicked me out of his house. All within fifteen minutes. Other than that, we're getting along just fine."

"That bad, huh?"

"Worse. Why did you send me out here, Jeff? He doesn't want me here."

"Right now Matt doesn't know what he wants. But he needs you there, irrespective of what he says or does."

"But would two weeks really have made that much of a difference? Couldn't he have just waited for you?"

"No. Not really. I'm afraid he's on the verge of shutting down and then nobody will be able to reach him. The best thing you can do right now is spend time with him, listen to him, encourage him to talk. But don't let him know it's a form of treatment. If he suspects you're playing psychologist, he'll shut you out faster than you can blink."

"You're asking an awful lot, considering we didn't exactly hit it off."

"I know, but be patient with him. I know Matt. He'll come around."

"Right. Patience." She needed a truckload right about now.

"Great. And, Sara," he said, pausing a moment as though his next words were difficult to say, "thanks for doing this. I know it isn't your first choice, especially under the circumstances. But I hope you find out that Matt isn't like all those other men who make a career out of trampling women's hearts. He's one of the good guys."

Sara bit the inside of her cheek. Now wasn't the time to enumerate Matthew Brandon's qualities or lack thereof. She settled on a simple, "You're welcome. Take care of yourself. And Nina." Leaning over, she hung up the phone.

Thirteen and a half more days. The spot between her forehead throbbed. How was she ever going to make it? Fifteen minutes with Matthew Brandon had been too much.

She spat out a four-letter word, one she hadn't used since her divorce. Until today. Until she'd met Matthew Brandon.

Three

Matt tried not to dwell on the latest casualty. He'd been pretty tough on her. It wasn't his style to be rude to women, but this one just wouldn't back down. She'd cornered him and left him no choice but to strike back. And he'd done just that.

Well, she was gone, probably several thousand feet in the air headed due east for Pittsburgh. He'd never have to see her again.

The scraping of the sliding glass door interrupted his thoughts. He really needed to have Jimmy put an extra lock on the door. And he would have the only key. He sighed. Who was it this time? Rosa again, laden with a fresh tray of fruit or a basket of salsa with chips and chiles on the side? Or would it be Adam, come to chew him out for scaring Little Red Riding Hood away?

To his shock, it was neither.

"I'm back and I'm not leaving, so save your scare tactics."

Shit. It was her. He lay very still, not moving a muscle.

"Don't pretend you're sleeping either," she said. "I've been watching you from the window and I saw you adjust your cap less than a minute ago."

Matt flipped his cap up and turned his head in the direction of her voice. "I thought you flew home on your broom."

"How could I when you so obviously need my help?" Her throaty voice was low. Sweet. And full of sarcasm. "I decided to stick around and see if I could help the lion find his courage. Or are you the tin man?" She paused. "Of course, you could definitely be the scarecrow. Yes, that would probably be you. But then again, you just might be a combination of all three. No courage. No heart. No brains."

He'd heard enough. "Get out."

"Sorry," she said, "but I'm staying until Jeff gets here."

"Like hell you are." He didn't like her attitude. She was acting as though she had a right to be here, as though she owned the place.

"Matthew, the sooner you accept the fact that I'm going to be here for the next two weeks, the better it will be for both of us."

"Stop treating me like a goddamned child," he said, pushing himself up from the recliner to a standing position, a safe distance from where he thought she might be. "I run this show. Me." He jabbed his thumb at his chest. "Not you, or Adam or anybody else. If I want you to leave, you leave. Got it?"

Metal clanged against stone as the chair clattered to the ground. That unique citrus blend filled his nostrils. She was close. Very close. And most likely very mad. Good, maybe now she'd get the hell out of here.

"Do you really think I want to be here 'Mr. High and Mighty, I'll do what I want to do'?" Her voice trembled. "Don't you think if I had a choice I'd be on my way back to Pittsburgh right now?" She took short choppy breaths and ploughed on. "Are you so arrogant that you think I would actually want to stay and help a man who hasn't an ounce of interest in helping himself?" She didn't wait for an answer, most likely didn't expect one. "Well the answer to all of the above, Matthew Brandon, with the exception of the one regarding your extreme arrogance, is an emphatic no."

He clenched both fists at his sides. It was obvious that she didn't think much of him. He ought to tell her the feeling was mutual. His curiosity won out. "So why do you want to stay?"

"I gave my word, that's why."

A woman with honor. How unique. Most of the ones he'd known felt honor-bound only as long as his wallet stayed open.

Sara cleared her throat. "I'm here to stay for the next two weeks until Jeff comes. So you might as well get used to me."

Matt rubbed the back of his neck. *Shit.* "I don't like you."

"I know. I don't like you either. At least we have that in common."

He laughed. A real laugh, not the short, fake ones he used to emphasize his irritation or the crude cynical ones he saved for the doctors, but an honest-to-God laugh. And it felt good.

"Okay, Sara Hamilton, let's negotiate," he said.

"Fine. I promised Jeff I'd stay until he can get out here. Probably two weeks, give or take a day or two."

Matt said nothing. He'd always found the key to

negotiation was waiting out the silence. He who spoke first usually lost the edge. So he waited.

"And we've got to get along."

Silence.

"Or at least try to get along," she amended, her voice lifting a notch.

He knew she was waiting for his response, but he kept his mouth clamped shut. He was actually enjoying her mounting frustration.

"Matthew?"

Nothing.

"Matthew! Aren't you going to say something?" He could tell she was about two seconds away from losing her cool.

"Yeah. I've got something to say all right."

"Well?"

He smiled. "The only people who ever called me Matthew were my mother and my fifth-grade teacher, Mrs. Peterson."

"That is *not* funny. Now are you going to coop- erate or not?"

"You can stay."

"I knew that."

"But not as my doctor."

That threw her. "What do you mean?"

Matt rubbed his chin. "Just what I said, Sara. You can stay, but not as my doctor."

"Oh, really? Exactly what would I be staying as?"

Man was she prickly. "Relax. I may be blind but I'm not desperate."

"Of all the—"

"Hold on." He held up his hands in defense. "That didn't come out right. What I meant was that when I go to bed with a woman I have to at least like her."

"My, my, such high standards."

"So you have nothing to worry about."

"Good. Good," she repeated in a stronger voice. "Because I find the very idea revolting."

Revolting?

"If you don't want me as your doctor or bed partner, what's left?"

"How about just plain old Sara Hamilton?"

You would have thought he'd asked her to turn into a Martian. "I don't think I can do that. You're . . . you're," she stumbled, "my client."

"No, Sara, I'm not. That's the other part of this deal. You can stay here until Jeff comes. But you won't be following me around with a pad of paper asking questions like, 'Tell me more,' or 'Would you care to expand on that?' And definitely not, 'How does that make you feel?' " Matt crossed his arms over his chest. He had the edge. Sara Hamilton had no choice. She was at his mercy. "No prying into my childhood, or asking questions about the accident or my blindness. Unless I bring it up."

"Okay."

"Okay?" That had been too easy. Sara Hamilton didn't seem the type to give up precious bargaining ground without a fight. Unless she was planning a sneak attack.

"Okay. I won't pressure you into telling me anything you don't want to."

Now he was certain she was up to something. She'd sounded too smug, too unconcerned with his ultimatum. Fine. Let her play her little games. He had a few of his own. There was more to Sara Hamilton than she let on and his brain needed a challenge. Who was the woman beneath the buttoned-up persona? He'd dig around, scratch the surface, maybe excavate a few old skeletons. What the hell. He had nothing else to do.

Matt smiled. "Let's shake on it," he said, extending his hand.

He felt her cool fingertips touch his palm, like a butterfly flitting about, refusing to land. Matt clamped his hand over hers, capturing her in his warm grip. The next two weeks might prove quite interesting.

Sara had just enough time to unpack her clothes and freshen up for dinner. Plums and grays dominated the room she would call her own for the next few weeks. Hints of cream scattered about complimented the primary colors. She buried her toes in the thick pile of gray carpet, enjoying the soft full texture as she moved about, hanging and arranging her clothes.

The scent of freesia filled her senses, drifting to her from a large vase in the corner. She closed her eyes and inhaled their sweet scent. Everything she'd seen so far spoke of understated elegance, from the fresh-cut flowers that adorned each room to the modern artwork that graced the walls. Even the carpeting spoke of wealth.

Sara thought of her own little bungalow in the western suburbs of Pittsburgh with its hand-braided rugs and window boxes overflowing with petunias and impatiens. Her fresh-cut flowers came from the backyard. Tulips and daffodils in the spring and bloodred roses in the summer. All nurtured with love and sunshine as opposed to a greenhouse thermostat and humidifying system.

And the artwork, well that was either her own humble dabblings or prints from the local craft store.

She loved her house. It provided respite from the cold, sometimes cruel, world around her. She already missed the ancient overstuffed rocking chair where she'd sit at night and lose herself in a book, cuddled with the blue-and-yellow afghan her grandmother had made twenty years before. It was the only time she permitted herself to dream of what-ifs.

Opening her eyes, Sara walked to the sliding glass door and looked at the patio beyond. It was similar to Matthew's. Same wrought-iron chairs and table. Same hot tub tucked in the far left corner. She'd counted four of them so far. The closest she came to something like that in her neighborhood was the rare aboveground pool. She smiled, wondering if Matthew Brandon even knew what an aboveground pool was.

Probably not. He'd lived a life of wealth and privilege, though Jeff had told her he'd come from the Pittsburgh area. High-rent district, she thought, shaking her head. The man didn't seem the type to be inconvenienced by anything and lack of money could certainly prove a major inconvenience.

Not that she'd ever cared about money, because she hadn't. She had enough to live a comfortable life. All she'd ever wanted was a family. And children. And she'd ended up with neither. Turning away from the window, Sara zipped up her empty bags and stuffed them in the closet.

A light rap at the door disturbed her thoughts.

"Sara?" Adam's soft voice drifted to her. "Supper's ready."

"Just a minute." She ran her fingers through her hair, let the wisp of bangs settle on her forehead, minus the giant cowlick sticking out on the left side. When she was a kid, she'd tried everything to keep the big comma of hair flat on her forehead. It sprang back, no matter how much Dippity-Do she'd plastered on it, until one day she finally realized that some things are just part of us and we can't change them, no matter how hard we try. She shrugged, pasted a smile on her face, and headed for the door.

When she opened it, Adam stood waiting for her, looking stylish in a blue polo shirt and tan slacks. He smiled down at her, his gray eyes warm. "How'd it go this afternoon?" he asked as they headed down the long marble-tiled hall toward the dining room.

"Fine, actually," Sara said, not meeting his gaze. "It went just fine."

"Really? That seems hard to believe." He hadn't called her a liar, hadn't even implied such a horrible thing, but Sara felt the talons of guilt gripping her, tormenting her. How could she tell him she was planning to "trick" his brother into verbalizing by becoming his friend? She couldn't and so she smiled and said nothing.

"Rosa, these enchiladas are wonderful," Sara said, munching around the edges of her second.

The older woman looked up from her plate and murmured, *"Gracías."*

Sara went back to eating her food. It was the third attempt she'd made in the past fifteen minutes to start a conversation with the woman, and

she'd gotten no more than a mumbled thank-you
or an ungracious grunt.

Adam tried to cover up Rosa's rudeness by filling
in the long gaps between Sara's questions and
Rosa's answers. Even Jimmy kept the conversation
going to avoid embarrassing Sara. Only Matthew
remained silent.

He sat at the round cherry table, eating with
such grace and precision, one would never have
guessed he was blind. Sara tried not to stare, but
she couldn't help sneaking glances in his direction, waiting for a piece of food to miss his mouth
and fall in his lap. It never happened. She was the
one losing shreds of lettuce and tomato from the
bottom of her wrap.

She stole another glance. The Pittsburgh Pirate
ball cap was gone. So was the stubble on his face.
He looked showered and fresh, his chestnut hair
still wet and combed straight back, curling toward
the nape of his tanned neck. He still wore dark
sunglasses. She thought of Jessie's comment about
his eyes. *Those beautiful silver eyes. Looking at you,
into you, through you.* Sara wondered why he opted
for sunglasses when his eyes, sightless or not,
seemed to be such a huge attraction. Perhaps
they'd been damaged during the accident. Or
maybe, Matthew Brandon didn't want everybody
looking at him, speculating, pitying him. She
guessed it might be the latter. He didn't seem like
a man who would tolerate pity. In any form.

"How about seeing the sights after dinner,
Sara?" Adam asked, taking a sip of iced tea.
"Jimmy's a great tour guide. He knows all the hot
spots and need-to-see places around here."

Sara smiled at both men. "That sounds like a lot of fun. Would you mind, Jimmy?"

Jimmy shook his brown head. "Not at all. Did I tell you I was a tour guide?"

She laughed. "Yes, you did. Among other things."

"That's right." He let out a low laugh. "I can do just about anything. And if I can't, then I know where to find somebody who can."

"Isn't that the truth. And then you talk my brother into hiring them," Adam said in a dry voice.

"Matt's a great boss. Everybody loves him," Jimmy said.

Adam shot him a quick look. "And why shouldn't they? He pays them—"

"Adam," Matt cut in, his deep voice filling the room. "I don't really think Sara wants to hear about it."

Oh, but she did want to hear about it. All of it. She wanted to know about the kind of people Jimmy brought to Matthew, wanted to know about their jobs and even what they got paid. Adam had implied Matthew was generous, too generous, in his hiring and with his wallet. But that didn't fit the picture she had of Matthew Brandon. Nor did it match the one she'd read about in all the tabloids and magazines.

She was beginning to wonder if the Matthew Brandon the media was obsessed with and the man sitting across from her were the same person. Or was one nothing more than an image? Which one? Questions swam in her head, clouding her thoughts, muddying her reasoning. The man was like one of those funky puzzles with extra pieces.

Just when you thought you had the perimeter worked out, you realized you didn't. Trial and error were the only sure methods of finding the right fit.

Sara had always prided herself on solving puzzles. Of any kind.

The rest of the meal passed in relative silence with the exchange of benign comments and small talk. Matthew Brandon might be blind and ornery, a shell of his former charming self, but he still commanded respect and obedience. And he'd sent the message that intimate conversations would not be tolerated.

Jimmy was the first to rise from the table. "If you'll excuse me, I'll get the car ready," he said. "Thanks, Rosa." He winked at her. "It was *muy bueno,* as usual."

Sara looked up from her plate to see Rosa's cheeks turn pink. Jimmy must have been taking lessons from his boss, and why shouldn't he? she wondered. He'd probably seen him in action enough times to repeat the performance without a second thought.

Adam removed the napkin from his lap and placed it on the table. "Sara," he asked, "are you ready?"

"Sure," she said, dabbing her mouth with her napkin. Her gaze flew to Matt as she rose. He made no effort to get up, his strong arms resting on either side of the ornate chair. "Matt?" she asked. "Are you ready?"

He inclined his head in her direction, a shadow of a smile playing about his full lips. "Ready for what, Sara?" The silky texture of his voice rolled over her like a caress.

Her stomach jumped. She shouldn't have eaten that second enchilada. Her gaze focused on his lips. They were firm and full, the lower one jutting out just a little.

"Sara?"

There it was again. That voice, but several octaves lower. How did he make it sound so soft and sexy, like a warm summer night's breeze blowing over naked skin? He hadn't spoken to her that way this afternoon. No, then he'd cursed at her, ranted, accused, and tormented. And she'd handled that so much better.

"Are you going to answer me, Sara, or ignore me?" Matt asked, smiling at her. It was a slow lazy smile, revealing a set of even white teeth.

Her chest tightened. Heartburn. She should've known better than to overindulge on authentic Mexican food. It must've been Rosa's chiles. "I'm not ignoring you," she snapped, angry with herself for letting her mind wander down the forbidden path of Matthew Brandon. "I just wanted to know if you're going with us or not."

"No, Sara, I'm not," he said. "I've seen everything before and I can't see anything now, so what's the point?" His voice was still low and quiet, but the gentleness of a moment ago had vanished, replaced by strains of bitterness.

"I just thought—"

"No." One word, spoken with such finality that she knew better than to ask again. His fingers clenched the end of the chair, his knuckles white. This was the Matthew Brandon she recognized. Angry, rude, domineering. Him, she could handle. It was the other side she'd seen a few moments ago, the seductive, gentle one that scared her to death.

Before she could think of anything else to say, he pushed back his chair, nodded a curt good night and strode from the room. Sara watched in amazement as he maneuvered past the furniture, through the room, and down the hall, never slowing a step.

The late afternoon sun followed them as they wound their way past the quaint little shops and boutiques of Laguna Beach. Sara peered through the tinted windows, catching glimpses of artists weaving their craft on canvas, pottery, wood, and glass.

Adam seemed to notice her keen interest and promised, "We'll come back another day and you can take it all in until you've had your fill."

She flashed him a quick grin. "Better wear a comfortable pair of shoes."

"Ridiculous," Jimmy said as they rounded a corner and saw a man painting plastic milk cartons. He had twenty or so finished ones resting on a pallet behind him.

"They're beautiful," Sara breathed, admiring the bold designs and brilliant colors that transformed an ordinary household object into a work of art.

"Junk," Jimmy muttered under his breath.

Adam laughed.

"How can you say that, Jimmy?" she asked, as they passed a young woman painting PVC pipe. "The medium doesn't matter. It's what the artist does with it that counts."

"Right. So, you're saying I could take toilet paper rolls and paint some fancy little doodads on them and call it art." His brown gaze met hers in the rearview mirror.

She smiled at him and nodded. "You probably could, Jimmy."

"And," he continued, "I could probably sell them for fifty bucks a pop."

Sara tried to keep a serious face. "Or more, depending on how original it is."

"I'll tell Greta to start saving our toilet paper rolls for you, Jimmy." Adam laughed and turned toward Sara. "That's profession number twenty-two, for our man, Jimmy."

"Who's Greta?"

"Greta," Adam said, letting out a long breath, "is Jimmy's latest find."

"And she's a darn good find, too," Jimmy added.

They were on the highway now, heading south toward a place called Dana Point. Jimmy told her they could get a taste of native life there, watching experts and amateurs with surfboards, WaveRunners and fishing boats. Sara was content to see sun, water, and endless blue skies.

"At dinner, you mentioned Jimmy's penchant for 'finding' people," she said, turning to Adam. Now was her opportunity to get some answers. "What did you mean by that?"

Adam inclined his head toward their chauffeur. "Jimmy has a habit of bringing home strays."

"Haven't they all proved very helpful?" Jimmy asked, shooting Adam a challenging look in the rearview mirror.

Adam shook his head. "Helpful and necessary are two different things. I fail to see why Matt needs a cook, a cleaning lady, a window cleaner, a laundry lady, a plant man, and a gardener."

"You forgot the car washer and light fixture man."

"Oh. How could I forget them?"

Jimmy grinned. "Matt just hired them last week."

"If he doesn't need them, why does he hire them?" Sara asked. Another interesting twist through the maze to discover the real Matthew Brandon.

"Thank you, Sara," Adam said, smiling. "It's nice to know someone else agrees with me. Matt and Jimmy, now they're a different story." He rolled his eyes. "Jimmy meets these people, from who knows where. They've all got a story. Somebody has a sick mother, or twelve kids, or is going to night school. You fill in the blank. Anyway, they come to Jimmy because word gets around that he's a sucker for a sob story."

"That is absolutely not true," Jimmy insisted, honking his horn at a car cutting in front of him. "They come to me because I'm honest." He jabbed his index finger at his chest. "Because they know I'll do right by them."

Adam rolled his eyes. "You do right by them all right. And Matt's too much of a softy to say no."

Matthew Brandon? Softy?

"I think we're pretty well staffed for the time being," Jimmy said. "Though there is that little Mexican lady who—"

"No." The firmness in Adam's voice left no room for persuasion.

"All right, all right." Jimmy shrugged. "So we'll talk to her again in the fall."

"Jimmy—"

"Winter then. Or next spring," he amended in the same breath.

Sara smiled, enjoying the playful antagonism volleying between the two men. They were much easier to relax around than Matthew Brandon. He made her too jumpy.

The easy camaraderie of the night spread to include Sara, making her laugh until tears sprung to her eyes. When they reached Dana Point, Jimmy pulled a large plaid blanket out of the trunk and went in search of the perfect spot to watch the water lovers. Adam and Sara kicked off their shoes and followed him to a sandy slope where he staked his claim. They plopped down on the blanket and spent the next hour enjoying the surfers.

When the sun rode low in the skyline, Adam leaned over and touched Sara's shoulder. She jumped.

"Sorry." His gray eyes turned apologetic. "I didn't mean to startle you."

"It's okay," she murmured, looking away. "I was so caught up with the surfers, I tuned everything else out." And that was the truth. Or at least part of it. What she didn't tell him was that after three years alone, she still cringed at the touch of a man, no matter how innocent. Strange that Matt's touch hadn't scared her earlier today. She'd been outraged, ready to claw his face off, but not frightened. *Why?* she wondered. *Why?*

"Adam?" Now was the time to ask him the question that had been plaguing her since Matt left the dinner table. "When Matt got up from dinner tonight, he walked right out of the room. Alone." Her gaze swung around to meet his. "How did he do that without falling flat on his face?"

He shot her a sideways glance. "Practice. Lots and lots of practice. When he first came home, it was a nightmare. He refused to use a cane and had more bumps and nasty bruises than you can imagine." He raked a hand through his blond hair and stared at the water in front of him, as if remembering those early days. "It went on for weeks. He refused to let anybody help him." He gave her a wry smile. "If you haven't guessed, Matt's very proud. Too proud, sometimes."

Sara smiled. "I've already figured that out." *Matthew Brandon was proud and difficult. And totally unreasonable.*

"Yeah, that's Matt. Thinks he has to have all the answers. Can't ever depend on anybody else." He frowned. "Not even me."

"Some people are just like that. They prefer to be self-sufficient." *I should know; it's been my motto for more than three years.*

"Well, it's damn hard on the rest of us," Adam said.

Sara sensed the underlying anger in his words. She knew he cared about his brother, wanted only what was best for him. "Maybe tomorrow we'll go for another ride. Jimmy can take us to that fishing place you were telling me about and we'll talk Matt into going with us. What do you think?"

If she'd sprouted three heads and an elephant nose, Adam wouldn't have looked at her any more strangely than he was now.

"Sara," he said, narrowing his gray eyes on her. "Matt would never come with us. He hasn't left the house in months."

Four

Sara padded into the kitchen dressed in shorts and a sleeveless top at a little past ten the next morning. She never slept past eight o'clock, and usually was up and showered by seven. But then again, the last time she'd seen midnight was New Year's Eve four years ago. When Jimmy and Adam dropped her off last night, the clock on the microwave display read one-fifteen. If she factored Pittsburgh time into that, it was really four-fifteen. Four-fifteen! The only time she'd ever seen four-fifteen in the morning was when she'd glanced at the clock on her nightstand after an occasional midnight bathroom trip. No wonder she'd rolled over and hit the alarm button this morning. Anything to stop that darn buzzing in her ear!

"Hi, Rosa," Sara said, picking up a black mug from the counter and heading for the coffeepot. "Where is everybody?"

"Up," the older woman mumbled from her place at the stove. She was stirring something with a long wooden spoon. "Out." The smell of peppers and onions permeated the room.

Sara poured her coffee, splashed a little cream in it, and walked over to her. Leaning against the dark green counter, she studied the cook. Her plump fingers worked the spoon, scooping and tossing a small mountain of peppers and onions in a huge frying pan. The extra flesh under her arms jiggled with each movement. Her breath came in short steady gasps, her small nostrils flared, thin lips pursed into a frown.

She was upset about something. Again.

"Rosa," Sara said, her tone gentle, encouraging. "What's the matter?"

The cook shook her head, eyes fixed on the food she was preparing.

"I know you're upset about something. Please tell me what it is." Reaching up, she laid a hand on the older woman's dark sun-weathered forearm. Rosa shot her a glance, her black eyes misted with tears.

"Why are you crying?" Sara set her coffee mug on the counter and took the wooden spoon from her.

"Onions," she said, wiping her eyes with the back of her hands. "Onions do this to Rosa."

"I don't think so," Sara said in a soft voice. She moved the frying pan to the back burner and turned toward her. "You've been upset since you met me. Please tell me why. Have I done something?"

Tears trickled down the older woman's cheeks, following the path of lines etched into her skin. They reached her jaw, hovered an instant, then fell, unchecked, onto her ample bosom.

"Tell me." What could she have done that would cause her this much distress? She hadn't even been in California twenty-four hours.

Another sniff. Rosa pulled out a white lace handkerchief from her apron pocket and blew her nose. Hard. "It is Señor Matt," she said in halting syllables. "I worry for him. He say no more women. He go crazy last time with lady doctor. Make big scene. Very, very bad." Her thick braided bun bounced back and forth as she shook her head.

"I'm sorry, Rosa," Sara said, amazed at the loyalty this man's employees showed toward him. First Jimmy and now Rosa.

"Señor Matt take care of Rosa. Give me nice job, food to eat, place to stay." She raised her eyes heavenward and blessed herself. "He say maybe hire nephew, Chico, in few months."

Sara wondered if Adam knew about Chico. Probably not.

Rosa wiped her damp eyes with the corner of her printed apron. "Rosa want Señor Matt be happy. Too much sadness for him." She sniffed again. "Too much pain."

"I want to help Señor Matt, Rosa, not hurt him. But he might not want my help at first and he may get very angry with me. *But I won't hurt him.*" She looked into the black depths of the other woman's eyes. "Okay?"

She eyed Sara a full fifteen seconds, saying nothing. *"Sí,"* she murmured. *"Sí."* Then she reached into the opening of her starched white shirt and pulled out a small gold cross. Holding it between her plump fingers she said, "You promise, Rosa, on this cross, that you no hurt Señor Matt."

Sara looked at the gleaming gold. This woman was willing to give her a chance, but only if she gained protection for her boss. The simple honest request moved her, and again, she wondered how he'd earned this kind of devotion.

Reaching for the shiny cross, Sara took it in her hand and met the old Mexican woman's steady gaze. "I promise you, Rosa, on this cross, that I will not hurt Señor Matt."

A half hour later, Sara headed down the hall toward Matt's study and the sliding door that led to his patio. From what Adam had told her, this particular patio was his refuge. He came here every day and spent several hours doing exactly what she'd seen him do yesterday.

Nothing.

Well, not today. Today was going to be different for Matthew Brandon, because in her own subtle way, she was going to get him to talk. About anything. The weather, the state of foreign affairs, the stock market. Why he wore a Pittsburgh Pirates ball cap. Nothing *too* personal. That would make him uncomfortable. Alert him to potential privacy infringements. She'd stay on the perimeter, work the safe zone for a few days. And if she didn't show her hand too early and bluffed when necessary, she might just win the pot and get him to talk about himself.

The door to his study was open. Jimmy sat in the big leather chair behind the desk, flipping through a magazine while the Rolling Stones belted out *Gimme Shelter* in the background. He looked up when she entered the room.

"Hi, Jimmy." She grinned. "I can't believe I slept so late. Next time, we better settle on a ten o'clock curfew."

He looked up from his magazine and nodded. "Maybe so."

Sara's gaze drifted to the patio and the back of Matthew Brandon's Pittsburgh Pirate ball cap. He had repositioned his chair so he couldn't be viewed from the window. Clever of him.

"I think I'll go say hello," she said, turning away from Jimmy. "I'll catch you later." She hadn't taken the first step when he called her name.

"Sara?" He sounded odd. She swung back around. He looked a little pale, too. Like he was going to be sick.

"What is it, Jimmy?"

His eyes darted around the room, from ceiling to floor, and everywhere in between. He reminded her of a fly waiting to light. "You can't go out there."

"I can't?"

He fidgeted in his chair. "Matt said no," he mumbled, looking down at his fingernails.

"Matt said no?"

A dull flush crept up his cheeks. "Said he wants some time alone."

Sara laughed. "He's had nothing *but* time alone for months." She shook her head and laughed again.

"I'm glad you're not upset."

"Upset? Why would I be upset?" She shot a glance at the Pirates cap. "That doesn't mean I'm going to honor his request and stay in here, though. It'll take more than a demand from Matthew Brandon to keep me away." She smiled at Jimmy, whose complexion had gone from red to green.

"You can't go out there."

"Yes, I can. Relax, Jimmy." She turned on her heel and flashed him a quick grin. "Watch me."

Sara strode to the sliding glass door and reached for the handle. *Get ready, Matthew Brandon, here I come.* She yanked on the door. Nothing. She pulled again, harder this time.

"Jimmy, I think this door's locked. Can you get me the key?"

Silence.

"Jimmy?" She looked over her shoulder. "Jimmy? The key?"

Guilt and dread washed over his face. "There's only one key."

"Do you know where it is?"

He nodded. "Matt's got it."

"Oh for heaven's sake," she muttered. "He *locked* me out of his patio?" Sara stared at Jimmy, hands on hips.

He shrugged.

"And I suppose all of the other sliders are locked as well. With only one key?"

"No. But Matt had me turn the security system on." Jimmy hung his head. "You can't open the sliding glass doors, unless you have the code."

"Fine." *Damn him.* "Fine." *How could he do such a thing?* "Fine." *Did he really think a silly, old lock and a security system would keep me away?*

"I'm really sorry, Sara," Jimmy said in a quiet voice. "I like you. You're not like the other docs. You're different." He lifted his broad shoulders. "Maybe he just needs a little time to see that."

"It's not your fault, Jimmy. I'm not upset with you." But his boss, now him she could strangle. Sara ran a hand through her hair, something she did when she was confused and needed to think. And she was very confused right now.

"What am I supposed to do, while I wait for him

to 'come around'?" It was a general question, born
of frustration and anger. She hadn't expected an
answer and was surprised when Jimmy provided
one.

"Well, according to Matt, you should just consider yourself 'on vacation and enjoy the sights.' "

Sara gritted her teeth. She could just hear him
saying the words in all of his exaggerated self-im-
portance.

She swung away from the door, fists clenched.
She'd play his game. For a little while. "Well,
Jimmy, if you'll excuse me, I guess I'll be retiring
to my cell . . . I mean room." Sara whizzed past
him, anxious to be by herself. When she reached
the door, she stopped and called over her shoulder, "And you can tell your boss I declare him the
victor." She waited a second before adding, "Of
round one."

"I can't eat one more thing," Sara said, shaking
her head at the pecan pie Adam offered her. "I'm
stuffed."

Adam grinned. "How can you resist pecan pie?"

"I can't, but my hips can," she said, pushing her
plate away. "Besides, didn't you just see me eat that
double fudge brownie? Where I come from, that's
considered rich enough for two desserts."

"Well, I guess you leave me no choice but to eat
it all myself. Unless of course Jimmy thinks he's
got room for more." Adam and Sara looked over
at Jimmy who was stuffing a piece of chocolate
cheesecake into his mouth. He shook his head.

"That's what I thought," Adam said, popping a
pecan in his mouth.

"We've got to stop eating like this," Sara said. "It's our second night of overindulgence. Pretty soon they'll have to roll us to our car."

Adam shrugged. "So we enjoy food. You don't have a weight problem." His eyes scanned her black-and-cream sleeveless dress. "Neither do I," he said, patting his flat stomach. "Now, Jimmy, he's the one who needs to wait in the car while we try out these restaurants." They all laughed and Jimmy saluted Adam with a huge forkful of cheese-cake.

"I think you're fine, just the way you are, Jimmy," Sara said, smiling at him.

He grinned. "Just one more reason I like you so much."

"My honesty?" she asked.

He shook his head. "Your great diplomacy. It would rival Henry Kissinger's."

Sara met Jimmy's warm brown eyes and her smile deepened. Things were good between them and she wanted to keep them that way. It had been two days since the "key" incident. Two days of shopping and playing and eating. Two days of leaving Matthew Brandon's house in the morning and not returning until evening. Two days of having that miserable miscreant avoid her.

When Adam heard about the situation, he wanted to confront his brother immediately. Sara had urged him to wait it out, play by her rules. And that's what they were doing. Playing by *her* rules. Matthew Brandon probably thought she'd succumbed to his high-handed tactics, thought she'd decided to take his advice and "see the sights" for the remainder of her stay. She was seeing them, all right. And enjoying them too. But it was all a ploy to get his guard down. Just one more day. Then she would attack.

She crept down the dark hallway, her tiny pocket flashlight providing a faint path of light. The house was still, save the faint hum of the air conditioner. Everyone appeared to be asleep.

Conditions were perfect.

Moving along the wall, her fingers trailed past uneven sections of stucco, marking each room she passed. His was the fourth one on the left. It seemed to take a lifetime to travel a few feet, but Sara couldn't afford a mistake. She reached his door and drew in a deep breath, her fingers trembling as they touched the knob.

Could she do it? Could she take such a bold step? What if someone saw her? How would she ever explain? Sara quelled the voices in her head, pushed past the fear and doubt that beat in her veins, and grabbed the knob. She turned it, pushed the door open just enough to slip through and closed it behind her.

His room was huge. Much larger than the rest. Even with the small beam from her pocket flashlight, she could make out a wet bar, large-screen TV, stereo system, and recliner. And the king-size bed that dominated the center of the left wall. Her eyes settled on the sleeping form in the middle of the bed.

He was lying on his side, his muscular back facing her. She inched closer, comforted by the slow rhythmic breathing that filled her ears. He was asleep. Thank God. Rounding the foot of the bed, she tiptoed to his side and stared down. The first thing she noticed was his long lashes. Dark, spiky, and full. She hadn't seen them before, not with the sunglasses he wore. Most women would have died for the thick fringe or at the very least, sought a high-class salon to duplicate them.

Her gaze flitted over his face shadowed in darkness, traveled along his strong jaw and neck to settle on his bare chest. It was broad and from what she could tell, covered with a thick mat of dark hair. A single sheet rode low on his hips.

She swallowed. Perhaps coming to Matthew Brandon's room at five-thirty in the morning hadn't been such a good idea. But it had seemed so brilliant last night. Of course, she'd been sitting in the safety of her own room, surrounded by light and sweet-smelling flowers, plotting the grandest of grand schemes to outwit him. She'd sneak into his room in the early morning hours, perch next to his bed and pounce on him as soon as he woke up. He'd have no choice but to acknowledge her presence. And then she'd get some answers, force some issues, set some rules.

It had all seemed perfect. Now she wasn't so sure. Perhaps she should opt for plan B. Borrowing the window cleaner's ladder to climb onto Matt's patio seemed a far more reasonable solution than standing in his bedroom at predawn hours watching him sleep with nothing but a swath of sheet wrapped around him. Sara took a small step backward. She could feel her heart pounding in her chest, the blood roaring in her ears, drowning out thought and reason. What should she do? Her gaze flew to the door then back to his bare chest. She took another step away from the bed.

A strong hand snaked out to grab her wrist, yanking her forward like a rag doll and thrusting her onto the bed. The pocket flashlight flew out of her hand and landed with a thud, blacking out the room. She tried to scream but a hand clamped over her mouth, stifling the attempt. Before she could gather her senses, Matthew Brandon had her pinned beneath him.

"What the hell do you think you're doing?"

"Get off of me," she gasped, pushing at his chest. Big mistake. Touching his bare skin only reminded her of their intimate position. She yanked her hands back.

"Not until you tell me what you're doing in my bedroom." He jerked her arms over her head and held her there with one hand.

"You've been avoiding me for days," Sara spat out, squinting in the darkness, trying to make out his expression. Nothing. Where was that darn flashlight? Not that she needed to see his face to tell he was angry. She heard it in his words, felt it in the rigid way he held his body. A body that was touching hers.

"I wanted my privacy."

"You're just afraid."

"You're crazy." Irritation seeped into his voice.

"Am I?" she challenged, trying not to think about his warm breath blowing on her cheek. Anger warred with common sense and won. Her next words spilled out in a breathless rush. "You're afraid to talk about the accident because then you'd have to deal with it. And your blindness. Straight out. No more excuses."

"Oh really?" His tone sent tiny prickles up her spine. It was half threat, half mockery, spoken in the softest of voices. "Well, Sara, I think you're the one who's afraid."

"Don't be ridiculous." She felt a twisting sensation in her belly and told herself it had nothing to do with his words or his half-naked body lying on top of her. He was just too heavy. That was the problem.

"And do you know what I think *you're* afraid of?" he asked, trailing a free hand along her cheek.

Sara turned her head away, trying to ignore the pulsing sensations coursing through her body where his fingers touched her skin. Like heat and light melted together, flowing in and over her. She didn't want to feel anything. Not with this man. Not with any man.

"I think you're afraid of me," he whispered. "Afraid of my touch."

"Just because I don't want you pawing me, doesn't mean I'm afraid of you or your lecherous hands." *Or your body,* she thought, wishing she couldn't feel the springy hair on his chest rubbing against her thin cotton T-shirt.

He laughed, a low sensual rumble that did strange things to her insides. "You're a terrible liar." His fingers ran along her jaw, brushed over her cheek, and settled on her mouth. He traced her lips with two fingers, learning the shape and curve of them, teasing the crease until they parted.

Sara knew she should stop him, knew she should at least mouth a word of protest. But she couldn't. He'd caught her up in his spell, where nothing existed but the feel of his body on hers and the touch of his fingers playing over her mouth. Her tongue darted out, flicking over his fingers like a butterfly.

He groaned, low in his throat and pulled his hand away. "God, Sara," he said, crushing his mouth to hers. It was a kiss of need and possession, burning hotter with each stroke of his tongue. He loosened his grip on her wrists, framing her face with his hands. She wound her arms around his neck, burying her fingers in his hair. Her tongue mated with his, slow and easy at first, then quick and urgent.

She moaned.

He tore his mouth from hers, cursing under his breath. His body tensed. Her arms fell away. "Jesus," he muttered again, levering himself off her to sit on the edge of the bed.

Sara scooted to the head of the bed, trying to distance herself from him and the memory of what had just happened.

"I think it's time you left," he said in a quiet voice that reminded her of the balmy breeze that fills the air just before a hurricane rips reality in half.

Dismissed. Just like that. She couldn't help but wonder if that was how he got rid of his women. A one-liner, straight up, no sugar.

"But . . . we have things to discuss." She wasn't leaving until they reached some sort of compromise.

"Not now."

"When?"

"Later. Ten o'clock." She heard the edge in his voice.

"Where?"

"My patio." He paused a second, then added, "In the hot tub."

"What?" Sara squeaked. "You've got to be kidding." What was he up to now?

"Do you hear me laughing?" No, there wasn't even a hint of amusement in his voice. He plowed on, issuing a few more conditions. "If you want to talk, be in my hot tub at ten o'clock. No pencil, no paper, no tape recorder, and no fancy technical terms. Got it?"

Sara scrambled to her feet. *Pigheaded bully.* "I've got it," she mumbled. "I'll see you at ten." She turned to leave. Now what? How was she supposed to get out of here when the only light in the room came from the digital clock on the nightstand? It would illuminate two, maybe three steps and then she'd be in total darkness again. If only she hadn't lost her flashlight.

"If you don't get out of this room right now, I'm going to think you came here to do more than talk."

She was grateful that he didn't remind her they'd been doing more than talking a few minutes ago. Much more. Inching forward, she took two small baby steps. Then two more. She'd crawl before admitting she needed his help. Sara put her hands in front of her, feeling the way for obstacles intruding on her path. Step by half step, she moved in the general direction of the door.

"Need some help?"

"No." The word was still on her lips when her big toe collided with a hard object. She let out a small yelp.

"What the hell." He grabbed her by the arm and propelled her forward. She had no choice but to put one foot in front of the other. When they

78 of Mary Campisi

reached the door, he pulled it open and waited for her to pass.

"I could've found my own way," Sara said as he led her down the dark hallway to her room. She didn't add that it might have taken the better part of an hour and several more bruised body parts to do it.

"Right." His tone told her he knew she was lying.

She should've given it up, but something in his superior attitude just wouldn't let her. "I was just a little disoriented. This is the first time I've been in your room . . . and it was dark."

They'd reached her door. Matt leaned over and opened it for her. His bare shoulder brushed hers. She jumped back. "Good night, Sara," he whispered. "Don't come to my bedroom again unless you're planning to stay. I don't like a tease."

She opened her mouth to speak, but nothing came out. By the time her brain formulated a half-intelligent response, she heard the click of his bedroom door.

Five

She wasn't coming. Not after the way he'd treated her last night. It had been uncalled-for and rude. So why had he done it? More to the point, why did he care? That was the hell of it. He didn't know. Didn't have a clue. And he'd spent the rest of the predawn morning trying to figure it out.

It was acceptable for him to act like a bastard these days. Even expected. Since the accident he could say and do most anything and women still came back for more. Not that there'd been a bevy of female companionship in the past few months. He'd ordered them all away, but initially they'd swarmed on him, unrelenting in their pursuit. Now he only had Gabrielle to contend with every once in a while, when she decided to flit in from Milan or Paris or wherever in the hell she'd been. And he could take her in small doses. Very small.

So what was his problem? Why should he care if one mouthy female from Pittsburgh felt insulted? Matt raked a hand through his curly wet hair and settled back in the hot tub. None of this would have happened if Sherlock Holmes hadn't come snooping around his room in the middle of the night. His defenses kicked in, telling him she got what she deserved. But self-justification didn't make him feel any better. Nothing would, except an apology.

Matt sighed. He hadn't apologized to a female since he was sixteen years old and found his hand up Heather McAllister's sweater. And she'd only protested so he wouldn't think she was "one of those girls." By the end of the night, she'd unbuttoned her sweater, took both hands and told him two were better than one.

And it had been that way ever since. No challenges, no maybes. They'd all been eager, willing participants. In business and in bed.

But not Sara Hamilton. Not that he wanted to bed her, because he didn't. But he did want her to be a little more compliant, not so inquisitive. Malleable, that was the word. Like a piece of clay that he could shape and design to his liking. Then they could both glide through the rest of her stay with a minimal amount of emotional expenditure.

He heard the sliding glass door open above the low hum of the hot tub jets. Had she changed her mind? Had she decided to come after all? A tangy scent filled the air. Citrus. Matt took a deep breath, inhaling the fresh fragrance.

"Señor Matt, I bring you your juice and fruit." Matt frowned. That was not the low throaty voice he had expected to hear.

"Thank you, Rosa. What do we have today?" he asked, pretending interest. Rosa felt if a person were eating, the world always looked brighter.

She rattled off the contents of the tray and their location. "Today we have your fresh-squeezed orange juice at two o'clock, grapefruit cut in half at six o'clock, two oranges, peeled and sliced at nine." She paused. "Oh, and a wedge of fresh-picked lemon at twelve."

"Two, six, nine, twelve. Got it," Matt said, laying his head back against the edge of the hot tub, arms outstretched on either side. Lemon. Oranges. Citrus. His mind wandered. Sara.

"Would you like anything else, Señor Matt?" Rosa asked.

"No. This is fine, Rosa." He smiled. "Just leave the tray in the usual spot."

"Sí, Señor Matt." She fussed around another minute, then left. He could just imagine her waddling away, black and gray bun flopping back and forth.

Reaching his left hand up and over the edge of the hot tub, Matt plucked a slice of orange from the nine o'clock position. Good old Rosa, she knew how to take care of him. Now if she could only learn to cook something that didn't have chiles or frijoles in it.

"Sorry I'm late."

Matt paused, the orange slice half way to his mouth. Sara. "I thought you weren't coming."

"I wasn't," she answered, her throaty voice deeper than usual.

"But?" He waited.

"I came to apologize. I should never have invaded your privacy." Matt heard a small splash. She must be in the water now. "I'm sorry, Matt."

He liked the way his name rolled off her tongue. Like a soft song. Or a caress. He thought of last night and the way her fingers had stroked the back of his neck and trailed over his shoulders. Jesus, why couldn't he forget her touch? He cleared his throat. It was his turn now. "I'm the one who should apologize, Sara. I was out of line." *But you felt incredible lying beneath me.*

"It's okay. Let's just forget it."

Right. That was like asking someone to forget a pink-striped elephant. "You don't want to talk about it?"

"No."

"Sure?"

"Yes."

"But I thought you doctor types wanted to talk about everything," he said, biting off a chunk of orange. "You know, why'd you do it, what were you thinking, what did it feel like—"

"No." He heard the frustration in her voice. "No. It was a simple kiss. Nothing more."

He wanted to tell her that when a man has his tongue rammed halfway down a woman's throat, it is not considered a simple kiss, but he decided against it. If she could act like it was no big deal, then fine, so could he.

"Good," he said. "Then we'll just chalk it up to misguided groping in the dark."

"That won't happen again," she added.

"I sure as hell don't want it to," he said, wondering at the truth of his words.

"Nor do I."

"Fine." He had no desire to feel her warm body pressed against his again. None at all.

"Fine," she echoed. Had he just heard a little tremor in her voice? Of course not. That would mean last night had affected her and she'd just admitted it hadn't.

Matt was more than ready to let go of the subject. He didn't even know why he'd dwelt on it so long, when she'd given him the perfect out. Not many women did that. But he was learning that Sara Hamilton wasn't like most women. In fact, he'd never met a woman quite like her.

He took a deep breath and said, "Let's start over. Hi. I'm Matt Brandon. Nice to meet you." He extended his right hand.

She let out a small laugh. "Hi. Sara Hamilton." She placed her hand in his and they shook. Contact lasted less than three seconds before she pulled her hand away.

"Care for some fruit?" he asked, gesturing to the tray.

"Yes. Thank you."

"Help yourself, just don't mess up my 'clock.' Rosa arranges all my food in relation to the hands of a clock," he explained.

"So that's how you did it! That first night, I kept wondering how you knew where everything was. I made such a mess of my food and you didn't even lose a shred of lettuce."

Matt laughed. "That comes from much practice. Rosa thinks everything should be wrapped in a tortilla with chilies and hot sauce."

"She's a sweetheart," Sara said.

"Yes, she is. But, I got the impression you two didn't hit it off very well," Matt said, popping a wedge of grapefruit in his mouth.

"Well, we didn't, at first. Actually, Rosa was the one who had reservations about me. But everything's fine now." Sara hesitated. He could feel her eyes on him. Matt wondered what color they were. Green? Blue? "I had to promise her that I wouldn't hurt you."

"And do you always keep your promises?" The

question was light, almost flippant, but he wanted to hear her answer.

"I try very hard to keep my promises."

Matt wished in that moment that he believed in promises. A light breeze blew by, filling his senses with citrus. He wondered if it was Sara or the fruit. There was one way to find out. "Did we eat all of the oranges?"

"All gone."

"Lemon?"

"Gone, too."

"Then, it's you I smell," he said, smiling.

"You think I smell?" she croaked.

"Like a special blend of oranges with a hint of lemon."

"Oh. I know it's not the latest craze but I've worn it for years." She sounded almost defensive. "The strong stuff gives me migraines."

"I like it. It's very refreshing."

"Oh. Thank you."

"The strong stuff gives me migraines, too."

She didn't respond. The quiet hum of the hot tub filled the silence, blanketing them like a cocoon. Matt slid farther down, resting his head along the edge of the tub. The warm water swirled around his body, pulling him into its soothing caress.

"I know I'm not supposed to ask you any personal questions—"

Wham! Just when he started to relax a little and let his guard down, she hit him with a fastball. In the groin.

"But you're going to anyway."

"Would you tell me about the accident?"

Shit. Here it comes. "I'm sure you read all about

it in the papers. They're much more eloquent than I am."

"I'd like to hear your version, Matt." It was a simple request, honest and sincere, without a hint of vulgar curiosity or blatant demand.

Before he knew what he was doing, Matt found himself talking. "There's not much to tell. It was a damned freak accident. I went to Vail for Thanksgiving, just like I've been doing the last five years or so. Adam was there, too. The snow was great, lots of powder. It was twilight, and I wanted one more run." He rubbed his jaw, remembering. "Adam had already gone in to get ready for dinner, so I went down alone. I flew down, faster than I ever had before, hit the ridge and went airborne. It was great, just like flying. Until I looked down and saw a body lying right in my landing path. I swerved and hit a tree head-on."

"And?" Sara's soft, low voice drifted to him.

"And I must've blanked out, because the next thing I remember was waking up in a hospital." He could still remember the pungent antiseptic and alcohol odor of his hospital room. "I could see, but it was blurry. Three days later I was blind." Blind. The word felt like a punch in the gut.

"What did the doctors say?"

That was the million-dollar question every busybody, bloodhound, and media monger wanted to know. Would Matt Brandon ever see again? They'd dogged him, stuck the microphone in his face, snapped pictures from trees, and continued their relentless pursuit to the iron gates of his home. And still he refused to answer them. That was his press agent's job.

But Sara wasn't a bloodhound searching for dirt.

"Matt?"

The words spilled out. "The formal diagnosis was Mild Traumatic Brain Injury, otherwise known as MTBI. Seems I developed a clot at the site of the injury. That's what caused the blindness."

"But it doesn't necessarily mean it's permanent, does it?" she asked.

He shrugged. "You know the odds. Every month after six reduces my chances. It's been seven."

"Do the doctors agree?"

"You know doctors," Matt said with a dry smile. "Afraid to commit to anything anymore. Too many lawsuits. They've given me some real scientific advice." He raised one finger at a time. "Time, patience, periodic medical evaluation, whatever that means," and, he paused, "concessions."

"Concessions?"

"White cane. Seeing-eye dog. Braille." He ran a hand through his hair. "And everybody's telling me what I have to do. As if I didn't know I'll never drive a car again, or ski, or do any of the thousand things I took for granted. They're all standing over me, spoon-feeding the *have to*s and *mustn't*s down my throat like I'm some kind of baby." His next words were laced with anger. "I don't have to do a goddamn thing I don't want to. Not until I'm ready."

"You're right, Matt. You don't." She was like his conscience, spurring him on.

"My family can't accept it. I've always been the strong one and they want me to deal with it, so they can stop feeling guilty. My editor calls me every other day, asking about my next book. And if he's not on the phone, it's my agent. They all want something. Every damn one of them." His voice fell five octaves. "I say screw 'em all."

His breathing came in quick uneven gulps. He sucked in air as though he'd just finished a fifty-yard dash. What the hell had come over him? He'd said volumes more than he had intended.

Why? How had she gotten him to open up like that? Anger gripped him, fierce and hot, pulsing through his veins like a brushfire gone wild. Sara Hamilton knew how to draw a person out, get him to divulge deep dark secrets without realizing it. Until it was too late. Until he'd told the tales, relived the fears, unleashed the demons. Like he'd just done.

Damn her.

He felt used. Not that it made any sense, because it didn't. But he needed anger right now, needed to hold onto it like a lifeline to keep from getting sucked into the undertow of naked truth and grim reality. One person stood in his way.

Sara Hamilton. She'd almost slipped past his defenses with her sympathetic, "I care about you" manner. Almost. But he'd recognized danger and thwarted her attempts, however innocent they were. He was beginning to have his doubts about that, too. She seemed too good, too honest, too sincere. Nobody had those qualities anymore. At least not the people he knew.

Matt took a deep breath, forcing himself to relax. It wouldn't do for her to know she'd gotten to him. And she would be studying him, watching for telltale signs of anger or frustration. Or capitulation. She could watch until she was cross-eyed for all he cared, because *capitulating* was not in his vocabulary.

Attack. Now that was a word he understood very well.

"Enough about me," Matt said. "Tell me about yourself." *Missile launched.* He'd blast that cool exterior away, even if it took twenty missiles.

Sara coughed, cleared her throat. "Me? Well, there really isn't much to tell."

He threw her a dry smile. "Of course there is." He lowered his voice to a rough velvet timbre. "You don't get to be . . . How old are you, anyway?"

"Thirty-four," she said in a tight voice.

"Okay, well, you don't get past the age of three or four and not have a history. So what's yours?" *Target sighted. Second round preparing to launch.*

"Matthew—"

"Matt," he corrected.

"Matt, I really don't discuss my personal life with my clients."

Gotcha. "As well you shouldn't," he agreed. "But, Sara, I am not your client. Remember? We're just two people having a conversation. And to my way of thinking, I just unloaded a whole heap of emotional garbage. Now it's your turn."

The hum of the hot tub filled his ears as he waited for her response. Why was she so reluctant? What was she hiding?

"What do you want to know?" Her voice was distant, muted, as though she were speaking in a tunnel.

"For starters, I'd like to know how you can just pick up and come out here for two weeks." *Missile launched.*

"It's my job."

Good answer. Perfect avoidance tactic. But not clever

enough for his former journalistic nose. "And no one stopped you. No one cared? No one said, 'I'll miss you'?"

"No." Her voice grew dimmer. If she were a battery, she'd be in desperate need of a recharge.

"No husband? No kids? No dog?"

"No." A single word, prompting hundreds of questions with thousands of possibilities. It reminded him of eighth-grade algebra.

"Why?" *Kaboom!*

"Why what?"

Sara Hamilton did not want to answer his questions. "Why is there no husband, no kids? Not even a dog?" If he had to be blunt-face bold about it, he would.

"I'm very involved with my work."

"Too involved to take a minute to have a life?" He was starting to get annoyed with her.

"Just because I don't have a family, does not mean I don't have a life, Matthew Brandon!" Sara's throaty voice rose like sandpaper rubbing against stone. That last question blew her away, like a SCUD missile hitting its target dead-center.

He decided to back down for a while. His eyes might be sightless, but he still didn't want her scratching them out, and if the conversation didn't change soon, they were headed in that direction. He raised his hands in surrender. "Okay. Okay. So you're a career woman. What kind of people do you see? Adolescents? Couples?"

"Women."

"Women? I see," he murmured, though he didn't. "What kind of women?"

"Abused women," she said. "Women who've been turned into physical and emotional wastelands by abusive husbands or boyfriends." Ah, now that was a statement. There was an odd note to her voice, almost like a subtle accusation woven into her words. "Men mistreat women all the time, stripping them of their self-esteem, stealing their self-respect. Taking and taking, until there's nothing left." Her next words were flat, emotionless. "That's when they dump them, like trash in the street, and move on to their next victim."

Talk about an attitude. "Some women set themselves up," he said, feeling a need to defend the ordinary Joe. "Some women meet a guy and re-make their whole life for him." He'd known a few of those in his time. "They eat what he eats, think like he thinks, wear only what he wants them to wear. Forget ever hearing an original idea from them again. It'll never happen. They're banking on the guy to give them everything. Love, happiness. Even self-respect." He shook his head. "And then they wonder why he leaves."

"You seem to have quite an opinion," Sara said, her tone cool and distant. "Are you speaking from personal experience?"

Matt laughed. "Not necessarily."

"From what I've read, you're quite familiar with that territory," she snapped.

What the hell was her problem? "You shouldn't believe everything you read, Sara. Besides, when you're in the public eye, you become a target for all kinds of people. Especially desperate women."

"That may be true," she said. "But I've found most men don't even entertain the word *desperate* until *after* they've had their fill of these very same women."

He opened his mouth to disagree, but the sound of Rosa's voice stopped him.

"Señor Matt, what you like for lunch?" The woman was always happy when she was around food. Cooking, cutting, cleaning, it didn't matter what it was as long as she could be near it, smell it, touch it.

"Damn, Rosa, we just finished breakfast."

"*Sí*. But now Rosa needs to think about lunch. It no hop on table."

"What are you offering today?" he asked, flashing her a grin. "Hot dogs? Pork lo mein?"

Rosa laughed. "Ah, Señor Matt, it is your favorite. Steak fajita with peppers, onions, and cheese." Otherwise known as a Philly cheese steak in a tortilla, Matt thought. Rosa would be crushed if he told her he preferred a crusty, six-inch hard roll to the soft corn wrap. She "Mexicanized" everything she cooked, from hot sauce on scrambled eggs to chilies in spaghetti sauce.

"I will set up your table in the usual place, *sí*?"

"That's fine."

"And Señorita Sara, will she be joining you?"

"No!" Sara's response left no room for doubt. So, she couldn't wait to get away from him. Not that he was in the mood for another minute of her company either, but it irked him to hear the vehemence in her voice.

"Thank you for asking, Rosa, but Señorita Sara will not be joining me today."

Six

Matt leaned over the elaborate exercise bike, sweat pouring from his body like a summer rain. He drew in a deep breath through his nostrils, held it, and exhaled through his mouth. Damn, but he'd needed this workout tonight. His neck muscles still felt tense, though he'd massaged them and even tried basic range of motion techniques. They hadn't helped. Stress tended to do that to him, bunching up his muscles and tying them into knots even a modern-day Houdini couldn't untangle.

Sara Hamilton was to blame. She was responsible for the tightness in his neck, the kink in his shoulders, and the pounding in his head. He'd been in a bad mood since lunchtime, ever since she'd whisked out of the hot tub with nothing more than a mumbled good-bye.

Now, several hours later, her actions still grated. So he'd pushed and probed a little. Well, maybe a lot more than a little. So what? She'd done the same thing to him. Those were the rules, his rules, and she couldn't handle it. And what was all that high-and-mighty "save the feminine soul" talk about? For Christ's sake, you'd think she'd been one of those women. Hardly. He'd bet his last buck no one had ever gotten close enough to take advantage of Sara Hamilton.

He grabbed the towel from around his neck and dragged it over his face. It felt good to sweat again. He needed to do it more often, not just when he felt his blood pressure reaching boiling point, which it had been doing a lot over the past few days. Ever since the arrival of Sara Hamilton.

Where in the hell was Adam with his beer?

Climbing off the bike, Matt walked the ten steps to the lifting bench and plopped down. It was twenty-five steps to the door, fifteen to the treadmill, and twelve to the rowing machine. He measured his whole world in steps these days. It had taken weeks of concentrated effort, several bumps and bruises, and a lot of cursing, but he'd mapped out his home according to his size-twelve foot. His system was perfect.

But along with his incredible ability to navigate unassisted around his home came one major drawback. The more comfortable he became in his own dwelling, the more insecure he felt about venturing outside of it. Not that he would ever admit it to anyone, because he wouldn't. Matt Brandon was a rough and tumble kind of guy who could handle anything. Fear was unacceptable, in any form.

As days passed, the world beyond the iron gates grew dimmer and dimmer. Farther from reach. He'd become a prisoner in his own home. He wouldn't use the blind man's aids, but he couldn't maneuver in the outside world without them.

Trapped in a hell of his own making, that's what he was, with no way out.

The click of the door pulled him from his dark musings.

"I'm back," Adam said. Matt listened to his brother's light sure footsteps coming toward him, stopping a few feet away. Next came the snap of a beer top and the dull thud of the can as it hit the table next to him. "There you go, bud. Let's toast."

Matt frowned, picking up the beer. "You know I don't go in for that kind of thing."

"I know you don't. But you know I do." Adam laughed. "Humor me. Okay?"

"All right, but don't get all sappy on me." Matt raised his can. "And don't take too long. I'm thirsty." Adam had a tendency to go on and on, eulogizing everything from Buster, the family mutt, to the treehouse they'd built twenty-five years ago. That was what made him such a good lawyer. He never stopped talking.

"I've got it," Adam said. "To my brother, Matt. May he live bold new dreams, conquer the unconquerable, and be strong enough to admit I can outbench him."

"Like hell you can," Matt said, taking a healthy swallow of beer. "This is the first time I've lifted weights in seven months, and you still only beat me by ten pounds."

Adam laughed. "I know, but let me bask in the limelight for a few days, okay?"

Matt smiled, lifted his can in mock salute and took another drink.

"It's good to see you in here again, Matt," Adam said, all traces of earlier humor gone.

"You mean, it's good to see me up off my ass and doing something. Right?"

"Well, that, too."

"It feels good to be in here again," he said. "It's been too long." He slapped his stomach. "And this old gut feels it, too. If I don't get moving, it'll be nothing but flab."

"I really don't think you have much to worry about, big brother," Adam said. "You're sweating it out all over the place. I'll make sure I tell the cleaning lady to wipe everything down." He paused. "What's her name? Is that one Greta or Alice? Or Consuela?"

"I think it's Alice. Jimmy would know," Matt said, shrugging and downing the last of his beer.

"If he weren't such an honest guy, I'd say he's taking a percentage of their wages as his cut," Adam said.

"Jimmy? The Good Samaritan?"

Adam chuckled. "I know. Pretty absurd, isn't it? Kind of like thinking about Mother Teresa stealing from the Church."

"Bizarre," Matt agreed. He lifted his empty beer can. "I'm all out. Want me to make the next run?"

"No need. I brought extras." Matt heard the flip top snap open. "Here you go." Adam handed the can to him.

"So . . ." he said, taking a quick swig, "that's why you took so long. Raiding the fridge. Got anything else? Cheese? Crackers?"

"No. Sorry," Adam said. "I would've been quicker, but I ran into Sara."

Matt felt his whole body tense. "Oh?" He tried to pretend a casual interest, nothing more. It proved damn difficult since he really wanted to know what the little witch was up to. She must be mighty pissed off at him because he hadn't heard from her since their little hot tub meeting this

morning. She'd even conned Jimmy into taking
her out to dinner. Presumably to try out the new
little Thai restaurant in the area. Matt knew better.
The only thing Sara Hamilton wanted to try out
was a way to avoid him.

"She was getting a little midnight snack," Adam
said.

"Somehow I can't picture her guzzling a beer,"
Matt said in a dry voice. "Kind of like thinking
about Rosa in a miniskirt." He shook his head.
"The image just doesn't work."

"That's sick," Adam said, laughing himself. "No,
Sara's not the beer type. White wine, maybe," he
mused. "But she was stealing a glass of milk and
a few of Rosa's chocolate chip cookies. Said she'd
smelled them all day and couldn't resist them any
longer."

Matt wondered if she was one of those anorexic
types who weighed and measured every ounce of
food that went in their mouth. Or she could be a
yo-yo dieter who starved herself until she couldn't
take it any longer and then started gorging. "How
many did she eat?"

"Huh? Two. Why?"

Hmm. Didn't sound like an anorexic or a gorger.
And he'd known both kinds. "What? Oh, nothing.
I was just wondering." Matt took another drink.
"Did you tell her Rosa probably spiked them with
tequila or hot sauce?"

Adam laughed. "She's not that bad."

Matt raised a dark brow.

"Okay, she is that bad. She can't help it if she
thinks everybody should be Mexican. We should
all have such strong ties to our heritage."

"It would sure make for some interesting new foods," Matt agreed.

"Yeah. It would at that."

"What does she look like?" The question came from nowhere, startling him. Why had he said that?

"Who?" Adam asked, puzzled.

Curiosity won over his annoyance with himself. What the hell. "Sara," he mumbled. "I've spent hours with her and I have no idea what she even looks like."

"She's not your type." There was a hard edge to Adam's voice.

"That's an understatement. Believe me, little brother, I have no romantic interest in Sara Hamilton." Other than a shared kiss that scorched him every time he thought about it. "She's too mouthy, too opinionated, too bullheaded for me."

"Good. Keep it that way."

Matt turned his head in Adam's direction. "Was that a threat, little brother?"

Adam ignored him. "She's a nice woman, Matt. That's all I'm saying."

"Okay, okay. Sara Hamilton's guardian angel has spoken. Now will you answer the damn question and tell me what she looks like? For all I know, Medusa could be sitting across from me every day."

"Hardly. Sara's a very unique woman. In looks and personality." Adam's gentle tone made Matt perk up. "She's not beautiful, at least not in the classic way of your models and starlets. But there's something about her, an almost ethereal quality that makes her glow. And she's so honest. And caring. With a great personality," he added.

"A real dog, huh?" Talking about personality and avoiding description was usually a bow-wow sign.

"Not at all. It's just that around Sara, you don't concentrate on her physical attributes as much as her other qualities. Her smile lights up the room. And when you speak to her, she listens. I mean, really listens, not like one of those empty-headed, big white teethers who smile and nod, but have no clue what you're talking about. She does. And she cares about *things*. You can hear the passion in her voice when she talks about something important to her." Adam paused. "But I don't need to tell you all this. You noticed it yourself, didn't you?"

Right. The woman Adam had just described was not the same one who'd stormed out of his hot tub this morning. But he couldn't tell Adam that. So, he opted for the big lie. "Of course I knew all that, Adam." He almost choked on the words. "That's why I was asking you what she looked like. So I could piece it all together and get an image of her. Visualization and all that stuff the doctors talk about." What a joke. He'd visualized Sara Hamilton plenty of times in the last several hours. With a big broom and a pointy hat. At least that was better than fixating on her supple mouth and soft skin.

"Oh. Sure. That makes sense."

Poor Adam, Matt thought. He could be so gullible sometimes.

"Well, let's see. She's about five-feet-four or five. Not very tall. Nice shape. Not too skinny. Good curves. Great legs. And there's this neat little swing to her hips when she walks. Almost like she's moving to a beat." He paused a second. "Oh, and her hair is dark brown, kind of glossy, cut a little above the shoulders with bangs. And a cowlick on the left side."

"Jesus, Adam, did you put her under a microscope?"

Adam laughed. "Hey, what can I say? It's my legal training that makes me notice details. And I can't forget her eyes. You can get lost in them when she looks at you. They're an amber green, kind of tilted at the corners. They change colors with her moods and clothes. When she's passionate about something, they turn this incredible rich amber color, flecked with gold. Like old whiskey. Really beautiful," he murmured.

Matt was still stuck on passionate. He wondered if her eyes changed shades last night when he was kissing her

"And that's about it, old boy," Adam said, interrupting his thoughts. "That's Sara Hamilton. Did you get the picture?"

Now, there was a question. Matt's lips turned up in a faint smile. "Oh, yeah, Adam, I got the picture." And he did. His little brother was falling big-time for Sara Hamilton, the Wicked Witch from Pittsburgh.

Sara stuffed her white tank top into her jean shorts and zipped them up. Her head throbbed with the beginnings of a headache. A Matthew Brandon headache. Just the thought of the man made her temples pulse in pain.

Was she going to spend the rest of her stay dodging bold interrogations like the one yesterday morning? He'd pushed and pushed, accusing and formulating his own erroneous conclusions. And she'd let him because his words had pierced her heart like an arrow, bled her soul dry, and left her numb with grief. She hadn't been able to move, let alone think. So she'd told him she was committed to her work and that's why she had no husband, no children. Nothing.

She wondered what he would have said if she'd told him the truth. *I had a husband and I almost had a baby. Almost. But he left and my little girl died. And the only life I have now is the one I live through my clients. Because I'm too damn scared to live again. It just hurts too much.*

She pressed her fingertips to her temples. Of course, she'd never say anything like that to him. Never. Turning, she headed for the sliding glass door and opened the blinds. Peering through the wide cream slats, her gaze slid to his chair. Empty. Maybe he was still sleeping. She could grab a quick bite before he got up . . .

No. She was not going to cower in the shadows like a frightened child. He would like that, had probably anticipated that reaction. Well, he was in for a surprise. A big surprise.

Taking a deep breath, Sara turned and headed toward the door. One step closer to her nemesis.

Two minutes later she entered the spacious black-and-white tiled kitchen. Jimmy sat at the table sipping a Coke and reading the newspaper. Rosa was stirring something at the stove.

"Good morning," Sara said, grabbing a mug and pouring herself a cup of coffee. A drop of cream. A hint of sugar. She took a sip. Perfect.

Jimmy looked up from his paper. "Hey, Sara, good morning."

Rosa turned and offered her a big grin that transformed her lined face into a road map. "Hola, Señorita Sara. I have good food for you today. Eggs with jalapeño cheese, *sí?*"

"No, thank you, Rosa. I was thinking of something more along the line of a piece of toast." Seeing the crestfallen look on the older woman's face, she recanted. "Well, maybe just a taste."

"Bien." Rosa grinned again. "I like you, Señorita Sara. You no like Señor Matt's other women. They no eat nothing Rosa fixes. Only coffee. Always coffee. Black coffee." She waved a plump hand in the air. "Black, black, black. And so skinny. No meat on the bones. How they gonna have the babies? But you," she nodded her gray head in approval, "you have a nice hips for babies. You and Señor Matt make lots of babies."

Sara stared at the older woman. It took her a minute to find her voice. "No, Rosa. You've got it all wrong. Matt and I . . ." she stumbled for the right word, "we aren't involved with each other."

The other woman grinned, a knowing look on her face.

"We're just friends." And that was stretching it.

"If you say so, Señorita Sara," Rosa murmured, turning back to the pot of chili she was stirring.

How had she gotten such a crazy idea? A few days ago, Rosa had wanted to drag her out on her ear. Did her change of heart have anything to do with the promise she'd made on her cross? Even so, the whole idea was too bizarre. She and Matthew Brandon? Involved with each other? As in a couple? As in dating? Sara felt her body heat as she thought of the other night. Thought of his touch, his kiss, his hard body pressing her into the bed.

It had been a mistake. A big mistake. She tried to force it from her mind.

A snicker from Jimmy's corner drew her attention. At least somebody could laugh at Rosa's blatant matchmaking attempts.

"Where is he, Jimmy?"

"Who?" he asked, covering his smile with a huge hand.

Sara gave him a warning look. "Matt," she said, through clenched teeth.

"Haven't seen him." A muffled chuckle escaped his lips. He bent his head over the paper, pretending great interest in the lower left section.

"Señor Matt was not in his room last night," Rosa said in a sing-song voice, as though she were a little bird chirping news. "Perhaps he no can sleep." She turned her head and gave Sara a pointed look with her black eyes. "Perhaps he lonely."

"Rosa, that is the most absurd—"

"Perhaps he miss his sweetheart." She chuckled.

"Who misses his sweetheart?" a low deep voice asked from the back corner of the kitchen.

Matt.

Sara swung around so fast she almost bumped her nose on the white cupboard in front of her. *How long had he been standing there? How much had he heard?* Her fingers shook as she picked up the coffeepot and poured a little more of the steaming liquid into her cup.

"Who misses his sweetheart?" Matt repeated, his voice closer.

Jimmy dove in with the grace and ease of one

well accustomed to handling sticky situations. "Nobody in particular, Matt. Rosa was just telling us about some guy and his girlfriend."

"Oh." Sara heard the scrape of wood on tile. He was at the kitchen table. Sitting down. "Hi, Rosa." He paused. "Hello, Sara."

"Hello," she breathed. How had he known she was here? He must have heard her talking.

"That lemon-orange scent tricks me every time. I'm never sure if what I'm smelling is you or the real thing," he said.

"Kind of like a fruit salad, I guess," she said, trying to sound cute. *Stupid.* That's what she'd sounded like. *A fruit salad? Good God.*

Jimmy chuckled.

Matt laughed, a rich, low timbre washing over her with its warmth. "Actually, it reminds me of your personality. Sometimes sweet. Sometimes tart. But always tangy."

Sara squeezed her eyes shut a second. Had he just complimented or insulted her? Or both? She wasn't sure. That was the problem with Matthew Brandon. She was never sure about anything with him.

Jimmy cleared his throat. "Coffee, Matt?" Thank God for Jimmy. He always seemed to know his way around an awkward situation. She guessed he'd had plenty of experience.

"Sounds great. But you sit still. I'll get it."

"I'll get it for you," Sara said, her words spilling out so fast she knew they must all be watching her. Matt more than the others. His blindness was no obstacle to his sight. Not the sight that counted, the intuitive perceptive vision that gained entry into another person's thoughts, ideas, hopes. He seemed quite adept at crawling inside, making himself comfortable, dissecting words and emotions, one feeling at a time. Especially hers. And that made him very dangerous.

"Thank you, Sara." There was an odd note to his voice. What was it? Hesitation?

She pulled another mug from the cupboard and lifted the pot. Why had he sounded so strange? Did he think she was going to try to put a little something extra in his cup? Like arsenic? She smiled. Couldn't do that. Too many witnesses.

"Black, right?" She remembered from the other day.

"Yes." Pause. "Thank you."

Jimmy cleared his throat. Again. Rosa started humming a squeaky rendition of "I Will Always Love You." Sara would have a long talk with both of these instigators later. Ignoring the rush of heat in her cheeks, she picked up Matt's mug and turned around. She'd taken no more than three steps when she forced herself to look at him.

The mug crashed to the floor, sending hot coffee and splintering shards of white ceramic everywhere. She gasped. Her eyes stayed glued to his face. And the most arresting pair of silver eyes she'd ever seen.

"Good God, Sara, are you all right?" Matt jumped up from his chair, inching forward, his arm outstretched to her.

She recovered from her initial shock. "Clumsy," she murmured. It was all she could manage.

He ignored her. "Are you all right? Did you get burned?" There was real concern in his voice.

"No." She shook her head, staring at him.

"I've got it," Jimmy said, his big bulk pushing

through the laundry room with a mop and bucket. When had he left? Sara remembered nothing but the startling shock of seeing Matt without his sunglasses.

Rosa *tsk tsked* behind her. "You no get burned, for sure, Señorita Sara?"

"I'm fine, Rosa. Just clumsy, I guess."

"Give me your hand," Matt commanded, holding a strong, tanned one out to her.

She clasped his warm fingers, felt them close over hers and urge her toward him. He led her through the living room, pushed open the sliding glass door and stepped outside. Neither spoke as they made their way toward the patio. His footsteps were measured and even. Sara guessed he was counting his way. Adam had said he'd spent weeks calculating paces so he could move about with ease. Like someone who wasn't blind.

Seven

Sara followed Matt onto the stone patio. He released her hand and said, "I'll get you a chair." He moved several paces ahead of her and located a recliner with a green-and-white striped cushion. Pulling it toward his own, he said, "Go ahead and sit down." He waited for her to settle in before taking his own seat, his long tanned legs straddling either side.

"Thank you," Sara managed, not sure if she was thanking him for showing her an unexpected gentleness or not commenting on her obvious clumsiness. She suspected a little of both.

He shrugged but said nothing.

"Matt," she said, drawn to the silver depths of his gaze. "Your eyes . . ." she trailed off.

"What?" he asked, lifting his hand to his face. "Damn it, I forgot my glasses." He started to rise, his mouth flattening into a straight line.

"Stay." Sara's soft command halted him. "Don't hide behind them anymore."

His eyes narrowed. "I'm not *hiding* behind them. It's just that I'm more comfortable when I have them on," he muttered, sitting straight up, as if he were preparing to bolt from the chair. As if he were running for shelter.

"Please, Matt. Don't."

Don't. One simple word. That's all it was. But the implications were more complicated than California driving during rush hour. If he conceded and honored her request, then she'd take that as a sign of trust. If he chose to ignore her, then she'd know where she stood with him. A big, fat nowhere.

Sara kept her eyes on him, holding her breath. He seemed to be teetering on the brink of indecision, torn between staying and leaving. His brow was furrowed, his mouth grim, his jaw clenched. She watched him draw in a long breath.

And sink back down into his chair.

The breath rushed out of her like a deflating balloon.

"I like you without your glasses," she admitted, anxious to make him feel more comfortable with his decision.

"Thanks." The word came out as little more than a low grumble. It was obvious that he wasn't one hundred percent okay with it.

She pushed on. "I've never quite seen that shade of . . . silver." She studied his eyes, her heart tugging at the blank stare in them. What would they look like filled with emotions like passion, anger, joy?

"They might be intriguing, but they're useless." Matt lay back in the recliner, heaving a big sigh that sounded a lot like disgust and crossed his arms over his broad chest. "I'd settle for plain old brown ones any day if they came with sight."

What could she say to that? He was right. No

one in their right mind would choose beautiful over functional. Well, maybe that wasn't really a good analogy. People did that every day. Women crammed their feet into three-inch high heels to slenderize their legs. Then they stuffed their bodies into super control-top panty hose to hide that extra tummy bulge. Why? To attain *The Look*. Perhaps beautiful, but certainly not functional. Men were no better. They tooled around in sports cars with no legroom and even fewer passenger accommodations. And some made a hobby of collecting gorgeous females on their arm whose only useful skill was looking beautiful.

It was a crazy world. But Matt's situation was different. He just wanted to see, no matter if the eyes were brown, green, or violet.

The swoosh of the sliding glass door interrupted her thoughts. She turned to see Rosa walking toward them, carrying a tray full of coffee, mugs, toast, eggs, and fruit. And a big bottle of hot sauce.

"I bring you your breakfast," Rosa said, smiling. She laid the tray on the glass table and started to arrange a plate. "Is your favorite, Señor Matt. Scrambled eggs with jalapeño cheese. And I bring your hot sauce, too."

"Ah, Rosa," Matt teased, "you know they say 'the way to a man's heart is through his stomach.' " He patted his own. "Well, between the salsa, the chiles, and the jalapeños, I think you're about two-thirds of the way through my stomach lining." He laughed. "I'd say you're almost there."

Sara couldn't help laughing. Rosa just clucked her tongue and ignored him. "I look for you this morning, Señor Matt. The bed is nice and neat," she said, handing him a plate heaped with eggs, toast, and melon. "Eggs is two o'clock, toast is six, and melon is ten." She wiped her hands on her cotton apron. "So, where you sleep last night?"

Matt took a bite of egg and said, "Weight room."

She scooped a healthy serving of eggs onto Sara's plate. "Weight room? *Por qué?* Why?"

Matt shrugged. "I'm getting fat, Rosa. With a gut." He sunk his teeth into a piece of toast.

"Hah!" the older woman huffed. "You no fat, Señor Matt. You perfect." She cast a sly smile in Sara's direction. "Is he no perfect, Señorita Sara?"

Sara felt a blast of heat on her cheeks. "Ah . . ." she stammered, dragging her gaze to Matt. He had a look on his face that said, "See if you can get out of this one." She was trapped. Rosa would accept no less than full agreement. Matt's smile broadened as he waited for her to answer. "Ah . . . yes. Yes, he is . . ." She couldn't bring herself to utter the word *perfect*. Not when he sat there, grinning like a Cheshire cat. Her gaze swept the length of him. Broad chest, muscular arms and legs, firm belly. Perfect. But she'd die before she admitted it to him.

Rosa smiled, satisfied with her answer. "So why you no sleep in your own bed?" she asked, handing Sara a plate. "Maybe something, say somebody on your mind and you no can sleep?" She winked at Sara.

Sara threw the troublesome matchmaker a warning look. She almost wished Rosa were still trying to oust her from the house. It would be less embarrassing. Rosa playing matchmaker was about as subtle as an elephant in tights.

Matt laughed, as if the very idea that a female would render him sleepless was outrageous. "No, nothing like that. Adam and I finished working out, had a few beers, and then I closed my eyes. The next thing I know, I'm waking up with a stiff neck and a bad case of tennis ball breath." He popped a melon into his mouth. "And no glasses." He turned his head toward Sara and smiled.

She smiled back. Her pulse kicked in an extra beat. Oh, but he had a smile. And with those silver eyes, it was a killer combination.

"You hair no look so great either, Señor Matt," Rosa said, patting her plump fingers on his head. "Is curly this way," she said, pulling on a dark brown tuft, "and stick out that way." Her fingers tried to smooth a few errant locks.

"So much for perfect. Just get me my ball cap, Rosa. Works every time."

"*Ay, Díos mio.*" Rosa shook her head. "You and your ball cap. Who knows where you leave it."

"Just go in my closet. Top shelf. Ten of 'em. All Pittsburgh Pirates. Take your pick."

"Okay, okay," she said, waving her arms in the air.

"Why Pittsburgh Pirates?" Sara asked, munching on a piece of wheat toast. "I would've thought you'd be a Dodgers fan, seeing as they're practically in your backyard."

"*Are you serious?* You're from Pittsburgh. How can you even ask that question?" She heard the enthusiasm in his voice, saw it in his expression.

Sara laughed. "I am from Pittsburgh. And I have *twelve* Pirates caps in my closet because they're the greatest baseball team in the world." She paused, then added, "With the most loyal fans."

He agreed. "Once a Pirates' fan, always a Pirates' fan."

"Even all the way out here, with all the glitter and glamour of West Coast living?" She heard the doubt in her own voice.

"It never leaves you," he said, his tone dead serious. "I can still hear the crowd in Three Rivers Stadium, still feel the excitement roaring in the stands, still see the expression on my father's face when they clinched the title back in seventy-seven." He shook his head, a hint of a smile playing about his full lips. "It's stuck in my brain all these years."

Rosa returned and plopped a cap on Matt's head. "Is Pittsburgh Pirates. Black and yellow," she said.

"Thanks, Rosa. Feel free to borrow one anytime you like." He threw her a wide grin.

She pretended outrage. "If I no like you so much, I leave this place."

"You can't do that, Rosa," he said, adjusting the bill on his cap. "I'd be heartbroken."

"Would be nice change to see you with the broken heart," she quipped. "One never knows, Señor Matt. One never knows," she said in the little singsong voice that Sara had come to recognize as her way of prophesying. "Now, I leave you two to *talk.*" She turned and winked at Sara as she bustled away.

Matt rubbed his stubbled jaw. "What's with her?"

Just a little matchmaking! And guess who the lucky couple is? "Oh, nothing," Sara said, trying to sound matter-of-fact. "I think she just likes to tease you."

He shrugged his broad shoulders. "So, when was the last time you went to a game?"

"A week before I came here. They were playing the Reds."

"They lost two to one."

"That's right," she said, impressed with his memory.

"Where do you sit?"

Sara laughed. "Wherever ten bucks will get me, which is usually upper deck, nosebleed section." She studied him a minute. "I'll bet you're box seats, behind home plate."

He shook his head. "Nope. Upper deck, left field."

"Why?" The seats he mentioned were just average, nothing special. She pictured him in a loge or at least a box seat.

"It's tradition with me. My father started taking me to see the Pirates when I was eight years old. Three Rivers Stadium was brand new. Those were our seats. Upper deck, left field, anywhere in the first five rows. Every Sunday they played, we would go see them. In an old beat-up Ford. Just the two of us. Adam never liked the game. And my kid sister was too small." He leaned back against the striped cushions and closed his eyes. "I can still see my old man shouting and cheering them on. It was the only time I think he was ever really alive. He worked in the steel mills forty-some years. Went to work every day, got paid, came home. Never said more than three words at a time." He rubbed his jaw. "Unless he was at a ball game. Then you couldn't get him to shut up."

"Is he still alive?" Some part of her needed to know.

Matt shook his head. "Died ten years ago. Two weeks after he retired."

"And your mother?" Was she still back in Pittsburgh?

"Cancer," he said, "two years ago."

"I'm sorry," Sara said, and meant it. She knew the pain of losing parents.

He shrugged. "Adam came out here after she died and joined a law outfit in Irvine. Amy is the only one left back home. She's got two little rugrats who keep her going crazy most of the time."

"Do you ever get back?" The thought of him in the same city, perhaps walking down the same street, sent an odd chill through her body.

"Once a year. I schedule my visit around opening day. Then I take Amy and the boys to the game and play the doting uncle." He flashed her a smile. "You know. Cotton candy, hot dogs, pop, peanuts. Real bellyache stuff. Amy says she doesn't know if she loves it or hates it when I come."

"You like her children?" She felt her heart flutter like a hummingbird's wings. Children. This was dangerous ground.

"I *love* her children. And I love being the uncle who spoils them rotten."

"Have you . . . seen them since the accident?"

She watched his jaw tense, saw the tiny muscle on the right twitch. Indeed, this was dangerous ground. For both of them. But for very different reasons.

"No." One word. No elaboration.

Sara tiptoed. "Well, maybe you just need a little time."

"They're used to me running and playing ball with them. Time isn't going to show me where to pitch the ball or how far out to throw the long bomb. I can't do any of those things with them anymore."

"So," she braced herself for his anger, "you're never going to visit them in person again? Or let them come here?" The idea seemed preposterous. "You're going to let those kids imagine all sorts of horrible things about their uncle?" Her voice fell to a whisper. "You can't do that, Matt."

"You don't understand, Sara. It not that simple." His words were cold, harsh. She could feel him building his wall, shutting her out, one brick at a time.

"Nothing is ever simple, Matt." She reached out and touched his hand. He jerked but didn't move it away. "Sometimes life throws us these incredibly horrible curve balls that hit us smack in the face, slamming us to the ground. And we're lying there, bloody and swollen, and it seems like no one can help us. Not even ourselves." She drew in a deep breath, memories flooding her brain. How many weeks had she spent wallowing in dirt, too weak and hopeless to open her eyes or lift her head? Too heartbroken to see past her faithless husband and dead baby?

She didn't want that for Matt. He was scared and alone in his own private hell. She knew how to dig him out.

"Let me help you," she said, her voice thick with emotion. He placed his big hand over hers. There was just a hint of pressure, not quite a squeeze of acknowledgement, but Sara took it as a good sign.

They sat in silence, content to let the warm morning breeze blow about, wrapping them in their own intimate moment. It felt right to be here. In this time. With this man. Sara closed her eyes and lifted her face to the sun. She was beginning to think Matthew Brandon was much more than the handsome face and wads of cash he flashed around in public. Much, much more.

He was the first to break the silence. His deep voice was low, almost tender. "I'll bet you're a great doctor."

She smiled, her eyes still closed, her face tipped toward the morning rays. "I am," she teased. "But you won't let me show you how good."

He let out a long sigh. "No, I won't. But somehow, I get the feeling you're analyzing and assessing everything I say anyway."

She laughed. "Against your will? Without your permission? Would I do that?"

"Damn right you would."

"You're right," she said. "I would."

"You're not like the other doctors," he said, rubbing his thumb in a distracted manner along her wrist. Sara's eyes popped open and shot to his hand. *What was he doing? Why was he doing that?* She thought about pulling away but didn't. He probably wasn't even aware of what he was doing. No sense making a big deal about it.

She just wished she didn't feel every stroke. Wished even more that she could stop thinking about the other night in his bedroom. The feel of his hands caressing her face, the smell of his skin filling her senses, the touch of his tongue mating with hers . . .

"Sara? Sara?" She heard the rich timbre of his voice calling her. "Were you daydreaming?"

"What?" She shook her head, trying to clear her brain. "Oh. Yes. Daydreaming." *About you.* "You caught me all right. I was daydreaming." *Suffering from temporary insanity was more like it.*

"You know, I've been wondering," he began. There he was with that darned thumb again. Circling, circling. "Why is it that every other doctor who came here was asking about my books before he crossed the threshold?" He paused. "Oh, except the last one who was more interested in touching than talking." He threw her a wry smile. "But not you. You haven't asked me anything about them. Why?"

Sara felt the heat rush to her face and was thankful he couldn't see her. What should she say? The truth? *I don't like your Jack Steele character with his smart mouth and overabundant supply of buxom bimbos.* How could she tell him that? It was too brutal. So she opted for a half-truth instead. "Well," she drew in a deep breath, "I assumed you would talk about your writing when you were ready." *Not bad. Sounded plausible.*

"Bullshit."

"I beg your pardon?" Had he just said what she'd thought he'd said?

"I said bullshit, Sara Hamilton. From the second I met you, you've been pushing and pulling, prying into every part of my life. Except one of the most important ones. My writing." He flipped his cap up, scratched his head and flipped it back down. "Why?"

What to say? "We have so many other issues to address."

"That's not the reason."

He was too darned perceptive. "I'd been forewarned that your writing was not open for discussion." *That part was true.*

"Since when did that stop you from meddling?" he asked, tilting his head to one side.

Sara bit her lower lip. She'd read somewhere that before he made it big with his Jack Steele Private Investigator series, Matt had been an investigative reporter. That would account for his rapid-fire questions. And his persistence.

"Sara?" The tone in his voice said he was tired of her tales.

How had he known she was stretching and reworking the truth?

"Sara?" Judging by the pitch of his voice, he was moving from slight irritation to full-blown annoyance.

Time to come clean. "Okay, okay. I was going to get around to discussing your writing in a general way because it's what you do and is very important to you." She hesitated, trying to think of a way to gentle her words. It was like sugar coating a lemon. No matter how much of the white stuff you dumped on it, it was still a lemon. With a very sour taste.

"Stop dancing, Sara. What the hell's the problem?" As soon as the question was out of his mouth, he slapped his chair with his right arm and said, "You don't like my writing!"

She wished she could slither away and hide until her embarrassment died down. Like in two thousand years. He'd guessed the awful truth. Little literary nobody, Sara Hamilton, didn't like best-selling author, Matt Brandon's work.

"I'm . . . I'm sorry, Matt."

He threw back his head and laughed. A full deep-bellied laugh that ended on a sigh. "Nobody's ever had the guts to tell me they didn't like my work. *Nobody*. I was just worth too damn much money, selling too damn many books and movie rights for anybody to tell me they thought my work stunk." He laughed again. "Until you."

Sara was horrified. "I didn't say your work stunk, Matt."

"You didn't have to. That's one thing about being blind. You learn to compensate with all of your other senses, including intuition. When I accused you of not liking my work, I felt your body tense, heard your breathing change to quick uneven puffs of air. I *knew*, Sara. I knew."

"Oh God, Matt," she said, hanging her head, "I am so embarrassed. And so sorry."

He waved a hand in the air. "Save the apologies. People apologize to me every day and they don't even know why they're doing it. Tell me what you don't like."

Sara sneaked a look at his strong, handsome face. What did she have to lose? She let out a long, slow breath. "Okay. I don't like Jack Steele. It's his attitude. He can do anything he likes, with little or no repercussions and he *always* gets the girl."

"So? What's wrong with that?" Matt asked, a wide grin on his face.

"Do you want to hear what I have to say or not?" Now that he'd given her the go ahead, she was eager to forge on, open all cannons, and blast Jack Steele right off the page.

Matt laughed, holding up a hand in mock surrender. "Just kidding. Please. Go on."

She dove right back in as though there'd been no interruption. "Actually, he always gets several girls. They fall all over him, or maybe they're just so top heavy they can't hold themselves up." He howled at that. She smiled. "Anyway, he's a horrible example for both men and women. His persona says, 'I'll ignore you until I want sex, demean you with my sarcastic tongue, cheat on you as often as I like, with whomever I like, and there's not a damn thing you'll do about it. Because you'll be so desperate to win even a scrap of affection from me, you'll put up with anything I throw your way.' There," she said, letting out a long breath, "that's what I think of your Jack Steele."

Matt was silent. He sat with his right hand under his chin, eyes open, mouth unsmiling. Maybe she'd been a little too honest.

She cleared her throat, searching for the words that would erase the damage she'd just done. Sometimes honesty needed a touch of diplomacy to make it more palatable. This was one of those times. "I'm sorry, Matt," she started. "But you asked—"

He held up a tanned hand. "I know I did. There's no reason to be sorry. I asked and you responded." He let out a short laugh. "Though I must admit, I'm not accustomed to such *brutal* honesty."

Sara winced.

"But I wanted to hear it from you." He rubbed his jaw. "I never thought about my stories from a woman's point of view. I was too busy having fun with Jack. He's a man's man. You know, rough kind of stuff. Thinks 'the other meat' means the blonde next to him. Belches when he drinks beer. Eats nothing but red meat and cheese fries."

"Sounds so appealing," Sara said, scrunching up her nose.

"Yeah, doesn't he? But women go nuts over the

guy. They send him fan mail and all kinds of gifts."
He lowered his voice. "Some are really bizarre. You
wouldn't believe it."

"Oh yes, I would." Some women had no pride
where a man was concerned. That's why they came
to her when they were all bled out.

"A lot of the women think I'm him."

"Ah-huh," she said, a hint of a smile playing
about her lips. "Are you?" she asked, trying to
keep the humor from her voice.

"Hell no!"

"Hey, don't get mad at me. He's your guy. *You*
make him walk, talk, and exert his machismo
style." She cocked her head to the side. "I can see
where some women might think Jack Steele was
living out Matthew Brandon's fantasies. Just one
time, I'd like to see him *not* get the girl. Just once.
Let old Jack feel the pain of heartbreak."

"But he's Jack Steele," Matt said. "Jack *always*
gets his man and he *always* gets the girl."

"That's why I don't like him."

"Not even a little? Not even in your subconscious
thoughts?"

"Not even in my sub-subconscious thoughts,"
she said.

"Tell me," he asked, "how many of my books
have you read?"

Sara smiled. He was determined to sell her on
his man, Jack. "I read *Cry in the City*. That was
enough of Jack Steele's escapades for me. But of
course, Jeff reads them all. And loves them. I told
him I wouldn't read another one until Jack is the
one who gets dumped."

"It would ruin his image," Matt protested.

"What image?" Sara countered. "Heartless bully or pompous pig?"

"Neither. Avenging hero was more what I had in mind."

"Well, Matthew Brandon, he's your man. You can do whatever you want with him. Have him sit in a tree and collect acorns, for all I care. But remember," she said, raising her voice a notch, "this reader isn't following Jack Steele anywhere until he takes the big fall. Not one baby step. Until he loses his heart."

Eight

"He'll never agree to it, Sara," Jimmy said, shaking his head. "Never."

She smiled and placed a hand on his arm. "Trust me, Jimmy. I'll handle it."

"Just because you got him to walk to the mailbox doesn't mean you can convince him to go to Dodger Stadium. There are a few more people there, Sara." He paused, running his beefy hand over his face. "Like thirty thousand."

"We've been talking baseball solid for the past three days. We listen to several games every day." Her voice rose with enthusiasm. "Jimmy, the Pirates are coming to town. You know Matt loves them. He even told me he used to wear his Pirates cap when he was writing as a sort of good luck charm. Do you really think he wouldn't want to see them?"

Jimmy looked at her, his brown eyes full of concern. "Sara. He doesn't go out in public. Period. Not since the accident."

She wasn't getting anywhere with him. He was determined to honor Matt's wishes, protect him from interlopers. Like herself. Sara added personal bodyguard to Jimmy's list of professions.

"Do you want him to get back to his old self?" she asked. "I mean minus the vision, because that's still an iffy thing."

"Of course I do." He looked so pitiful with his head bent forward and his big hands clasped together.

"Then get me the tickets. Upper deck, left field. Somewhere in the first five rows."

Beads of sweat popped out on Jimmy's wide forehead. "I don't know—"

She cut him off. "Just get them, Jimmy." The time for talking was over. Now came the action. Her no-nonsense voice left little room for argument.

"I'll make a few phone calls," he said, heaving a sigh. He reminded Sara of someone caught between two choices. Bad and worse.

"Good. And Jimmy, make that three tickets. You're coming with us."

Matt stuffed a handful of popcorn into his mouth. Five minutes to game time. Sara better hurry up or she'd miss the starting pitch.

"C'mon, Sara. Game's starting."

"I'll be right in," she called from the kitchen.

He smiled at the sound of her voice. Sara Hamilton was turning out all right. Considering she was a shrink. He took that last thought back. Sara Hamilton was all right. Period.

Too bad she was leaving in a few days. He felt a weight settle deep in his gut, like he'd eaten one too many of Rosa's enchiladas. And he hadn't touched one today.

There was no sense denying it any longer.

He'd miss her.

Ever since they'd discovered they were baseball soul mates a few days ago, he and Sara had fallen into a comfortable routine. At breakfast, over grapefruit and wheat toast with jalapeño jelly, they talked baseball. At lunch, with chicken fajitas or seafood supremes, they talked baseball. Sipping iced tea in the afternoon, with fat lemon wedges, they talked baseball. And at dinner, with grilled tenderloin à la chiles, or frijoles negros and rice, they talked baseball. Hell, two nights ago, they'd gotten into a heated discussion about right-handed versus left-handed batters. Matt felt the power was with the right-handed batter, but Sara argued that a left-hander had more versatility, greater ability to change the ball's placement and, therefore, keep the outfield guessing. After two glasses of cabernet and a midnight breeze blowing over their legs, they decided that a switch-hitter had the greatest advantage.

God, but the woman was everywhere, her voice, her scent, sinking into the stucco, the marble, filling their coolness with heat. But most of all, she was in his brain, in his thoughts, in his dreams . . .

And yesterday, they'd discussed more than stats and home field advantage. As stimulating as it was to debate right-handed versus left-handed batters, it had proven equally challenging to discuss the president's latest political blunder and the ramifications of oil spills off the coast. It seemed as though the subject didn't matter.

It was the woman who made the difference, with her fresh, honest perspective on issues that ranged from soul-provoking and morally responsible to light and inconsequential. For the first time in months, he looked forward to kicking the sheets off in the morning and getting out of bed.

He no longer desired to best her or dig beneath that impenetrable surface calm to excavate old wounds. Now, he just wanted to get to know Sara Hamilton, and if he discovered any hidden scars, he wanted to help heal them. That's what friends were for, he told himself.

And they were friends. Nothing more. He just liked to be around her. Nothing more. He had almost forgotten that night in his bedroom. As a matter of fact, he hardly thought of it anymore. Except when he was drifting off to sleep and his subconscious took control. Then, it consumed him. Every touch, every whisper, every sweet smell magnified itself tenfold, ending with Sara waking up naked in his bed.

"I'm coming. Just another sec," Sara said, breaking into his thoughts. He heard the clink of the icemaker followed by the hum of the machine dispersing water.

"Extra ice in mine," Matt hollered in to her.

"I know. I know." She padded into the room and walked over to him. Handing him a drink, she plopped down on the sofa. "I almost think I liked it better when you weren't talking to me," she said in mock irritation. "At least you weren't bossing me around all of the time."

He slid her a crooked smile. "Women! Just can't please 'em." His smile deepened. "Damned if I do and damned if I don't."

She slouched beside him, slumping into the soft white leather. "Right," she said. Her shoulder brushed his. "Something tells me most women would be pleased playing servant for you anytime."

"But not you." It was a statement, but there was just a hint of curiosity there. Would Sara Hamilton be interested? Would he want her to be?

"Not me," she said, her throaty little laugh rolling over him.

He couldn't picture her being interested in that position either. She leaned over and scooped a handful of popcorn from the bowl he held. Orange blossoms filled his senses. God, but she smelled good. Her bare leg touched his thigh. Soft, smooth. Enticing. Her breast brushed against his arm.

He turned rock-hard. *Shit! How had that happened?* Matt felt like a teenager on his first date. He did not need this bulge in his pants getting in the way of his friendship with Sara. He squeezed his eyes shut and willed the erection to go away.

"Matt?" There was that low, velvety voice. His penis pulsed.

"What?" The word came out like a growl. *Think of something else. Mother Teresa. The Virgin Mary. Joan of Arc.*

"Why are you squeezing your eyes shut? Is something the matter?"

"No." He forced the word out between clenched teeth. "Nothing . . . is . . . the matter." He edged the popcorn bowl closer to his stomach. Just in case there was any telltale evidence.

Don't inhale, don't listen, don't feel. Think of something else. Sister Mary Catherine. Sister Julia Angelina.

He jumped when he felt her fingers on his forehead. "What are you doing?"

"Relax. You've got a crease six inches deep. Right here," she said, smoothing out the lines on his forehead. He let his head fall back onto the cushions. Her fingertips felt warm and soothing. He could let her do that all night. She worked her way to his temples in long even strokes, then began circling. *Keep going. Lower. Lower.*

"Enough." He grabbed her wrists, halting them in midmotion. He had to stop this insanity now, before it got out of control. "I'm fine. Okay?" He knew he sounded too abrupt, but damn it all, she was pushing him. The hell of it was, little Miss Innocent had no idea what she was doing to him.

"I was just trying to help you relax a little." He didn't miss the defensive, hurt tone of her voice.

He wanted to reassure her that she'd done nothing wrong. He was the sick one who'd taken their new friendship and desecrated it with sexual fantasies. But he couldn't afford to be soft right now. If he did, she might forgive his rudeness and spend the rest of the night six inches from him, talking, laughing, sometimes touching, and never knowing that he'd been thinking about jumping her bones.

Talk about ruining a friendship.

"And would you mind sitting in that chair over there?" he asked, pointing to one of the matching leather loungers. He had to put some distance between them. Clear his head. And his nostrils of her sweet orange scent. "I need to spread out a little more."

"Sure," she answered in a clipped voice, telling him it was anything but okay. She bounded from the sofa and flopped into the lounge chair. "How's this? Do you have enough room now? Maybe I should go sit in the kitchen." Matt ignored the sarcasm. This was for her own good.

He turned his back to her, stuffed a pillow behind his head and lay down, propping his feet up on the armrest. "Yeah, this is great."

"Good. I'm glad." Her tone said she hoped he choked on his popcorn.

"Just one more thing, Sara."

"Yes, your majesty. What might I do for you?"

"Could you not talk so I can concentrate on the game?" When she didn't answer, he figured she got the message. He heaved a sigh and called himself a thousand kinds of fool. The erection was gone. Disappeared. Down the tubes. Unfortunately, the fragile new friendship they shared might have followed the same path.

Sara gnawed on her lower lip. He should be here any minute. Her fingers played with the edges of the tickets. Crisp. Hard. She flicked them back and forth with her thumb. Where was he? Rosa had gone to wake him up ten minutes ago.

Her stomach twisted and jumped. She had to tell him today. No more postponing. The game was tomorrow night. Sara sucked in a deep breath, swallowed twice, and wondered how she'd ever come up with such a lamebrain idea. Matt would never agree to it. Never. Especially after last night.

She still didn't understand it. He'd ruined the whole evening for both of them. Told her not to talk, so he could concentrate! The big oaf. Of course, she'd clamped her mouth shut for the rest of the evening, tighter than a size four dress. She would have ripped her tongue out before uttering another word. But he didn't even seem to notice her silence. He was intent on treating her like a piece of furniture.

Why had he acted that way? He'd reverted back to the old Matt, cutting and arrogant, nothing like the man she'd come to know these last few days. Why had he shut her out and gone to such pains to be rude? The question plagued her the whole night, wrecking any hopes of enjoying the ball game and stealing precious hours of early-morning sleep. Had she done something to offend him? What? It was a usual night, the same kind they'd shared for the last three days. Relaxing. Enjoyable. Intimate.

Intimate?

Where had that come from? She dropped the tickets onto the kitchen table. *Intimate?* Her mind replayed the events of last evening, leading up to Matt's strange behavior. She'd been fixing their drinks in the kitchen and enjoying his playful bantering. He kept telling her to hurry up or she'd miss the game. All perfectly normal. He wanted more ice. She got it for him and went to the living room, handed over his iced tea and sat down beside him. Nothing strange there. Then they'd joked about her being a servant or something. They'd both laughed, and Sara had grabbed a handful of popcorn. And a big whiff of Matt's cologne. Woodsy, with a tang of spice. Hmm. How close was she anyway? Then she'd noticed his tense expression and reached up to massage the lines away. That's when he'd gone a little ballistic.

Sara rewound the last part. His change in behavior had something to do with her touching him. She'd bet on it. Did he think she was coming on to him? Like the last doctor? A huge lump of dread settled in her stomach, weighing her down like a Double Whopper with fries. *Matt knew her better*

than that. Didn't he? He knew she'd touched him
with nothing but friendly concern. Knew she'd
thought nothing of her leg brushing against his
thigh. They were friends, bordering on becoming
good friends. It had nothing at all to do with romance. Nothing, she assured herself.

Didn't Matt know that? Was he still thinking
about that night in his bedroom? Hadn't she told
him to forget about it? Pretend it didn't happen?
Not that she'd been able to look at his mouth without remembering the feel of his lips on hers. But
she'd die before she admitted it to him. How could
she, when she couldn't even admit it to herself?

Her head started to pound. She needed to see
him right away, set his mind at ease, reassure him
that the last thing she wanted in this world or beyond was a romantic relationship with him.

Sara took a sip of lukewarm coffee and glanced
down the hall. What was keeping them? She heard
a door open and Rosa waddled out, carrying her
purse and a piece of paper.

"He be right out, Señorita Sara," the older
woman said. "I go to grocery store with Jimmy. You
need something?"

A badge of courage, she thought. "No, but thank
you, Rosa." She heard the back door close and
looked down at the three tickets in front of her.
First she'd talk to Matt about last night, then she'd
deliver the real blow. The Pirates were playing the
Dodgers tomorrow night. And they were going.
She hoped.

Matt ambled into the kitchen a few minutes later,
his dark, curly hair still wet from a recent shower.
His silver eyes scanned the room, honing in on
her like radar.

"Hello, Sara."

"Good morning, Matt."

He gave her a little half smile and walked to the coffeepot. She felt her stomach jump. She looked away. This wasn't going to be easy. She wiped her damp hands on her red-and-white sundress.

"About last night . . ." she ventured.

"I'm sorry."

He startled her with his closeness. She could feel his presence behind her, smell his cologne. Sara refused to turn around. "Actually, I think I might be the one who should apologize." Her index finger traced the flat edges of the tickets in front of her. "I think that maybe," she paused, "though I don't know how, I might have given you the wrong impression last night."

Silence.

He wasn't going to make this any easier on her. "Anyway, when I touched you last night . . . I mean, when I touched your *face* last night, you know, tried to massage your forehead and temples, well, I was only trying to help you feel better." She sounded like an idiot.

"I know."

"It's not what it might have seemed like," she continued, as though he hadn't spoken.

"What did it seem like, Sara?" His voice was low and gravelly.

"Well . . . you know . . ." she said, hoping he'd use his imagination to fill in the blanks.

"Why don't you tell me." He leaned forward, his breath fanning her hair. His scent filled her nostrils, pulsed through her veins, drowned out all other sensation.

Closing her eyes, she willed the words from her

lips. "It might have looked as if I were coming on to you," she whispered.

"Oh." He trailed a finger down the side of her neck. "Or maybe I was sending out some invisible signal that said I wanted you to come on to me," he suggested, making lazy circles along her collarbone. "Maybe I wanted you to, even as I was pushing you away."

Her breath caught in her throat. She found it hard to think with him touching her. "Did you?" She had to know.

He didn't answer right away. It was as though he were waging a private battle with himself over his next words. "I don't know," he said on a ragged sigh. "I just don't know. Last week I wanted to boot you back to Pittsburgh. But now . . . now I'm dreading the day Jeff shows up at my doorstep."

Heat washed over her like the desert sun. Vivid. Intense. Scorching.

"I know," she said. And she did. Sometime over the last few days, she'd forgotten she was on assignment. Forgotten it was temporary. Forgotten that she was never going to get involved again.

She'd forgotten a lot of things. All because of one man. One rich, famous, and very unattainable man.

"I think this is probably not a good idea," he whispered as his lips brushed over the back of her neck.

A small shiver ran through her. "No. Probably not." Even as she mouthed the words, Sara felt herself leaning forward to grant him better access.

Matt graced tiny kisses behind her left earlobe, trailing his mouth down to her collarbone. He pushed the sundress strap aside. "So soft. So silky," he murmured. "Good thing I'm not into but-toned-up psychologists from Pittsburgh." His rich, low laugh coursed through her, making her knees weak. "That could be dangerous."

"Very dangerous," she sighed. Logic crumbled with each of his touches, transforming itself into raw emotion. Pure and elemental. And needy. Nothing existed beyond this time. Beyond this man's touches. She reached back and ran her hands down his waist. The low rumble of approval spurred her to boldness. She let her fingers roam his thighs, feel the muscles beneath them.

"Sara," Matt groaned, grabbing her hands. "Too fast." He turned her around, circling her with his strong arms. "Too good." He took a deep breath, smiling down at her. "Too damn good."

She smiled back into unseeing silver eyes. Every part of her body was smiling. She wound her arms around his waist, anxious to be closer. He nudged her into the edge of the table, his legs on either side of hers. Their bodies melted together, flowing over and through each other, heat into light, strength into softness. Sara felt his arousal pressed against her womanhood. So good. So right. Liquid fire pooled low in her belly.

Matt leaned over, grabbing the soft flesh of her buttocks with both hands. He pulled her to him. "Ah, Sara." His words poured over her senses like warm honey. "Sweet Sara." His head dipped low, stopping mere inches from her lips. "I've got to taste you."

Oh, and she wanted him to taste her. *Now*, she thought as she tilted her face to his. Her eyes drifted slowly shut. Their lips touched, a light feathery promise of passion and desire swirling between them. Matt coaxed her mouth open.

She touched her tongue to his, stroking, probing, gently sucking. He growled low in his throat, an animal sound that intimated possession. Hauling her to him, he rubbed himself against her, letting her feel the hard ridge of his arousal. Sara moaned.

She wanted him. Wanted him with an intensity she'd never felt before.

He tore himself from her, burying his head between her breasts. "God, Sara," he rasped, running his hands under her dress and up her bare legs to cup her buttocks. "If you don't stop me soon, it'll be too late."

His hands teased the waistband of her silk panties, driving her crazy. "I think it's already too late," she said, tugging his polo shirt out of his jeans shorts. Her fingers crept up his back. *God, but he felt wonderful.*

"I think it was too late the day you walked through the door," he said, grabbing both sides of her panties and pushing them down her legs with one quick jerk. Sara stepped out of them, feeling strange and wanton.

Matt stroked the rounded flesh of her buttocks, his fingers working their way to her woman's heat. She was hot and wet. And dying for his touch. Just one touch.

His thumb flicked the swollen nubbin of her sex. She moaned.

One touch would never be enough.

He ran his fingertips along her clitoris and down to the very essence of her womanhood, moving in slow rhythmic circles. She grabbed his shoulders, trying to brace herself for the onslaught of emotions that poured over her. Nothing existed but those wonderful fingers doing incredibly wonderful things to the most private part of her body. Little whimpers escaped her. When he buried one of his fingers inside her, she let out a small cry.

"Ah, Sara," he murmured, working his magic with his finger and thumb. His free hand slipped the sundress straps off her shoulders, teasing her breasts through the silken fabric until her nipples ached.

Her breath came in tiny little gasps. His touch, his voice, his scent, drove her to the edge, pouring sensation into every fiber of her being, threatening to explode into hundreds of fragmented emotions, all centering on the flick of his thumb and middle finger.

She wanted to touch him, wanted to run her hand along the bulge in his shorts and make him as crazy as he was making her. Her right hand slid down his chest, hovered on his belt buckle, moved low to cup his penis.

He groaned deep in his throat, thrusting himself into her palm as he plunged a finger into her, and sought her mouth, his tongue letting her know what he planned to do with another part of his body. It was too much, too sensual, too intense for Sara to hold on and she exploded, crying into his mouth, her body filled with a hundred tiny convulsions that wouldn't stop.

She leaned her forehead against his chest and he pulled her close, stroking her hair.

Matt was the first to speak. "Was that a mistake?"

Sara squeezed her eyes shut. "I'm sure it was."

"Do you care?" he asked, his voice as soft as the caresses he'd given her a few minutes ago.

This was not the time to be untruthful. "No."

He pulled her closer. "Good. Neither do I."

She sighed and turned her head to rest on his chest, the thump of his heart beating against her ear. Strong and steady. Like the man.

"Rosa's usually gone for a few hours on shopping day. Why don't we go back to my room and finish this?"

And then what? she wanted to ask. But she didn't, because right now it didn't matter. She wanted to be with him. Needed to be with him. And for once in her very practical, extremely organized life, she was going to listen to her heart and not her head.

"Sara," he asked, "will you come back to my room and make love with me?"

Yes, her heart answered.

"Hey, anybody home!"

Nine

The words blasted them apart like dynamite in a quarry.

Adam.

Sara froze.

"Shit." Matt pulled her sundress straps up and ran a quick hand down her dress.

"My panties," she said in horror.

He knelt over and swiped them up just as Adam entered the kitchen.

"Hi, you two," he said, a big smile on his tanned face.

"Hi, Adam," Matt said, with a casual nonchalance that belied what he'd been doing a moment ago. Correction. What *they'd* been doing a moment ago. Together.

Was he always this smooth in these circumstances? she wondered. And how often was he in these circumstances? A lump of dread settled in her stomach, making her nauseated. Was she just the flavor of the month? And what was that? Triple Dipped Stupid? Dear God, she hoped not. Her gaze riveted to the swatch of balled-up pink silk in his right hand.

"Sara," Adam said. "What's the matter? You look pale. Are you sick?"

Sick? She was sick all right. In the head.

"I'm—"

Matt cut her off. "She's fine. Just stayed up too late last night watching the ball game. As a matter of fact, she just came to tell me she was thinking about going back to bed." His silver eyes settled on her. "Isn't that right, Sara?"

She stared at him, amazed at the finesse he employed as he twisted the truth, making it sound so believable. She'd been thinking about going back to bed, all right, but it hadn't been to sleep.

"Sara?" he repeated, tightening his hand around her panties.

"Yes," she said, dragging her gaze from his right hand. From the corner of her eye, she saw him stuff the panties into his jean's pocket.

"You two and your ball games," Adam said, shaking his head. "I don't understand how grown people can get excited about watching a guy hit a ball with a stick and run around."

Matt shrugged. "It's in our blood."

"Is it terminal?"

"Hard to tell yet," he said, digging his hand partway into his right pocket. "We both seem to be equally hooked."

Sara felt the color rush to her face. Was Matt talking about baseball or their mutual attraction for each other? She wasn't good at playing relationship games or throwing around double entendres. And she certainly hadn't considered what they'd been doing a game. Did he? Her head started to pound with unanswered questions.

"Well, I guess that makes me odd man out," Adam said, unaware of the truth of his words.

"Guess it does," Matt agreed, a hint of a smile on his full lips.

"How was New York?" Sara asked, eager to change the subject. Adam might be clueless to the double meaning of the conversation, but Matt knew exactly what he was saying. And she'd guessed he was even enjoying himself. Nothing like tormenting a "buttoned-up psychologist" with a pair of her own panties. Especially when they were stuffed in his pocket instead of where they should be, on her person.

"The trip was great. And productive. Looks like the merger is a go." He paused and settled his gray gaze on Sara. "But the company just wasn't the same."

Matt cleared his throat. "It's good to see you again, too."

Adam cocked a golden brow. "I wasn't referring to your company, big brother."

"I gathered that your target was Sara." His tone was dry, filtered with its usual blend of sarcasm and something else that she couldn't identify. Jealousy? Ridiculous. She doubted Matthew Brandon had ever been jealous in his life.

"You are so astute," Adam said, chuckling. He turned away and headed for the coffeepot, pulled a mug from the cupboard, and poured himself a steaming cup. "I really did miss you, Sara." His warm gray gaze flickered over her. "Watching the sunset on Dana Point, sharing a double fudge brownie sundae. Even the trips to those God-awful boutiques," he said, his smile deepening to reveal a pair of dimples and a flash of very white teeth.

"Did I miss something here? Is there something going on between you two?" Matt's voice broke through his brother's words like a medieval warrior with a battering ram.

"No!" Sara's denial filled the kitchen. "We're friends. Just friends."

Adam seemed undisturbed by her vehement denial of a more involved relationship. "Of course, we're just friends," he said, in a soft, soothing voice that reminded her of someone trying to calm a frightened child. "That's how all great relationships start." His lips curved up. "As friends."

She managed a weak smile. How could she tell him that they would never be more than friends? Not with his brother's touch still lingering on her skin. Her gaze skittered to Matt who had his eyes fixed on her, stone-faced. He didn't seem very pleased with his brother's words.

"I've got something for you," Adam said, getting up from his chair and walking toward the suitcase he'd deposited in the corner of the kitchen. He unzipped it and pulled out a square box wrapped in silver with an elaborate gold bow. With a huge smile on his face, he took three steps and extended the gift to Sara. "Here. For you. A little token from New York."

Guilt wrapped itself around her like a noose, pulling tighter and tighter, choking the breath from her lungs. "I . . . I . . ." she gasped, "can't accept this, Adam."

Because you think there's still hope for something other than friendship between us.

Because you don't know what your brother and I were doing in this kitchen a few minutes ago.

Because you don't know what I wanted to do . . .

"Open it. Please," he added, softening the command.

Sara hesitated a second longer, hovering between accepting or rejecting the gift, but the little-boy expression on Adam's face settled her decision. She sent him a reassuring glance and reached for the silver package. Out of the corner of her eye, she saw Matt tense. As though he had wanted her to refuse it. As though he had expected her to.

She eased the gold ribbon over the package, her fingers lingering on the fine satin. Saks or Bloomingdale quality, not the usual Kmart blue-light special she used for her own gift-wrapping needs. Another small but potent reminder of the different world she lived in. A world far removed from Matthew Brandon and his family.

Slipping a finger beneath the crisp, metallic folds of the paper, Sara lifted up on the tape and the wrapping fell away, revealing a plain white box.

"You don't get many gifts, do you?" Adam asked, his voice quiet, thoughtful.

Her head shot up. "Why do you ask?"

He shrugged. "Just by the way you're opening it."

"I like to savor my gifts," she said, brushing aside his question. She knew he was too much the gentleman to push her. Matt, on the other hand, was just the type to pry and probe until he dug out every last scrap of dirt. She just hoped he wouldn't. How could she tell either of them that Jeff was the only one who'd ever remembered her birthday? And that Christmas was a sad, lonely affair with nothing under her little Charlie Brown tree but a few small tokens from clients, and Jeff and Jessie?

"Just open the damned thing," Matt said, frowning.

She ignored him. He was getting into one of his moods. Again. Flipping the box up, she fished around puffs of white and gold tissue paper, uncovering a glass ball the size of a large grapefruit. It was painted in crimson, jade, and violet hues. She held it up to the light and watched the colors blend into one another, creating a muted kaleidoscope of design.

"It's beautiful," she breathed, fingering the violet cord attached to the ball.

"Handblown by one of those artsy types you seem to like so much," Adam said. "You can hang it up and 'contemplate the iridescence that envelops you.' " He laughed. "That's what the clerk told me."

Matt walked up to the table. "Mind if I take a 'look?' " He held out a tanned hand and Sara placed it in his grasp, her fingers brushing against his. She watched as he closed his hands around the ball, moved it between his palms and then traced his fingers over the textured work. His dark brows met over the bridge of his nose as he concentrated on the glass ball. Without looking up, he asked, "What color is it?"

"It's a blend of crimson, jade, and violet," she answered, watching his fingers run the length of the cord. "And the cord is violet."

He nodded his dark curly head. "And the pattern? Is there one?"

"Yes," she said, her eyes darting from the intense expression on his face to his fingertips trailing over the ball. "But it's very abstract. There's a mix of crimson, jade, and violet that repeats itself in soft swirls around the ball. That's about as uniform as it gets."

He smoothed his hand over the ball. Like a caress. "I can picture it," he said. "Almost as though I can see it."

"You *are* seeing it, Matt. In your own way." She couldn't hide her excitement. "You're piecing together the bits of information we've given you and mixing it with the history stored in your memory to formulate a picture." She looked at Adam. "Oh, Adam, isn't that wonderful?"

"Yeah, it is pretty amazing," he agreed. "Maybe I should have brought one back for my big brother, too."

They all laughed and Matt handed the glass ball back to Sara. She was careful not to touch him this time. Placing the gift back in its box, she looked at Adam and said, "Thank you so much. I'll treasure it always." On impulse she rose from her chair and walked over to him, planting a kiss on his cheek.

"Keep doing that and I'll bring you something every night," he teased.

"You'll have to do it on your own time," Matt interrupted. "She's mine from nine to five."

Adam laughed.

"Every day."

Sara's mouth fell open.

"You're kidding, right?" Adam asked.

"Saturday and Sunday, too," Matt said, his mouth flattened into a straight line.

"Matt?" Sara spoke his name slowly. What was he up to? Why the demands?

"What?" he snapped, turning toward her.

"Aren't you being a little . . ." she hesitated, looking for just the right word, "extreme?"

"I don't think so. Don't you want to provide me with every opportunity to adapt to my . . . condition?" he challenged. "After all, we've only got a few days left."

Now she knew he was up to something. Matt hadn't been interested in adapting to anything, let alone his blindness. Why the sudden change of heart? "What's going on, Matt?"

"I'm just seeing if the doctor is as dedicated as she says she is."

"I thought I wasn't a doctor to you." She remembered his words well. "No pads, no paper, no questions. Remember?"

His eyes narrowed. "I changed my mind."

Adam shot him a disgusted look. "Fine. Don't worry about it, Sara. Jeff should be here in less than a week. Why don't you think about staying on a little longer? In an unofficial capacity?"

"As what?" The chill in Matt's voice surprised her.

"As my *friend.*"

Matt snorted.

"Oh, I forgot, big brother. You've never known a woman who was just a friend." Adam's normal, easygoing demeanor vanished beneath his sarcasm.

Sara felt the tension swirling around her, thick and suffocating. She had to stop this verbal sparring. Now.

"Thank you, Adam, but I've really got to get back home."

"Don't say anything yet," he coaxed. "Just wait and see how things turn out."

Matt's silver stare fixed on her, cold and hard. He stood with his feet planted wide apart, jaw clenched, nostrils flaring, as though he were preparing to do battle. "You heard her, Adam." His lips barely moved. "She's got to get back home."

Was that sarcasm in his icy voice? And if it was, why?

Adam ignored his brother's words. "We'll discuss it later." His gray gaze leveled on her.

"Good," Matt's clipped voice filled the air. "Anytime after five." He stepped forward and took hold of her arm. "Right now, we've got work to do."

Sara threw Adam a helpless look and turned to follow Matt. But not before she swiped the tickets from the counter. If Adam thought his brother was being difficult now, just wait a few minutes, when she told him about the ball game. He'd hear some real fireworks.

Maybe strong enough to blast her back to Pittsburgh.

Matt practically dragged her down the hallway, his long strides eating up the distance twice as fast as her smaller ones. He surprised her by stopping in front of his study.

"In here."

She stepped inside, wondering why he'd chosen the study. Adam had told her he hadn't been there for months. Why now?

The door clicked shut.

"I want you to leave Adam alone."

Sara whirled around, unable to believe what he'd just said. "What are you talking about?"

He advanced on her, like a leopard stalking its prey. "He's falling for you. Big-time. I don't want you to encourage him."

She wanted to hit him with something, anything to knock some sense into his thick skull. But there wasn't anything big enough to do a half-decent job, so she settled for a verbal bombardment.

"You think I was encouraging him?" Her voice pulsed with anger. How could he even suggest such a thing after what had happened between them in the kitchen?

"Possibly," he said, rubbing his jaw. "Or maybe it was just a ploy to make me jealous."

"You think I would do that?" Did he really believe her capable of such subterfuge?

He shrugged. "You tell me."

It took every ounce of strength not to pounce on him and try to inflict the same kind of pain he was hurling at her. The deep visceral kind that scarred the soul and gutted the heart, leaving the flesh untouched. But a person had to care to be hurt like that.

And Matthew Brandon's casual accusations told her he didn't care.

Unfortunately, her reaction to his torture told her she did.

Sara closed her eyes for a brief second and drew in a deep breath. God, how had this happened? Hadn't she vowed to never open up to another man again? How had this one gotten through her defenses? More importantly, how could she get him back on the other side of the gate?

"Answer me, Sara," Matt demanded. "Would you use my brother to make me jealous?"

She stared at him, thinking him more a stranger now than the first day they'd met. "No."

He let out a slow breath.

"You're not worth it."

His silver eyes narrowed. "What the hell does that mean?" he asked through clenched teeth.

"It means," she repeated with an outward semblance of cool reserve that belied the roiling in her stomach, "that you aren't worth lowering myself to such base behavior."

His lips curved up in a smile that chilled her, sending frozen tentacles up her spine, gripping her with their icy manacles. "I see," he said, the smile still playing about his full lips. "And did you *lower* yourself to such base behavior with me a little while ago?"

"That was a mistake," she bit out.

"We've already established that fact," he said, taking a step closer and folding his large arms over his chest. "What I want to know is how the hell did you step off your pedestal long enough to experience some real *base* emotions?"

He was getting too close. And not just in proximity. She didn't like his probing questions. "Can't we just forget about it?" Sara asked, feeling the anger and frustration pulsing through her veins.

"I hate to admit it, but I'm finding it a little hard to just forget about it." He took another step and grabbed her wrists. "Before I only wondered what you tasted and felt like. Now I know." His smile faded. "And it's the knowing that I think is going to kill me."

He leaned in and brushed his lips against hers. Her breath caught in her throat. He laughed, a low masculine rumble that rang of challenge and victory. "Now tell me you can forget about it," he whispered, pulling her against him.

His lips caressed her cheek, her ear, nuzzled her neck, settled at the base of her throat. Reality dimmed, fusing past and present, meshing fact and fantasy, twisting truth and lies. In that moment, nothing and everything existed.

"No," Sara said, bracing her right hand against his chest. Her left clenched the forgotten tickets. "No," she repeated, strength seeping into her words. "This is wrong. I'm leaving in a few days. A week at most." She shook her head, wiping at a stray tear with the back of her hand. "Don't you understand? I can't do this. I can't just have a little fling and then catch my flight back to Pittsburgh like nothing happened. I thought I could, but I can't."

"And what about the electricity that's been flowing between us since the day we met? What do you plan to do about that?"

"Nothing." She didn't deny her attraction for him.

"What are you afraid of, Sara Hamilton? Why are you running away?"

"I'm not running. It's called self-preservation."

"Self-preservation?" He spat the word out. "You make me sound like some kind of beast."

"No," she said, her heart swelling with sadness. "It's not you. It's me. I don't go in for casual flings. Never have. " Another tear trickled down her face. "I couldn't just shake your hand and walk away when it was over, as though we'd shared nothing more than a cup of coffee."

"I don't make promises." The brackets around his mouth deepened. "Or commitments."

"I know." Her voice was whisper-soft. "But I do."

He swore under his breath. "Fine," he said in a tone that told her it was anything but fine. "If that's the way you want it, then *fine*. But don't tempt me."

"Tempt you?" She almost laughed. "How would I do that?"

"Even a lily-white Ice Queen like you knows about tempting a man, Sara Hamilton." His words were bitter, cutting. "Don't use that low, throaty voice on me."

"It's the way I talk."

"Change it. And stop using that lemon-orange perfume around me."

"Okay." Maybe she could find some skunk juice for him.

"And don't be so damned agreeable," he bit out.

"Fine." She knew how to be damned *dis*agreeable.

"And don't stand next to me, brush up against me, or touch any part of your person to mine."

Now he was beyond ridiculous. "I've got a better idea. Why don't we communicate through my door for the next few days? That way you won't run the risk of touching *or* smelling me."

"Don't be a smart ass."

She ignored his comment. "Better yet, we'll use Jimmy as a go-between. That way, you won't have to *hear* me either. Just in case you think I'm trying to seduce you with my voice."

"Stop it," he said, grabbing her hands.

"Let me go."

"What's this?" he asked, touching the tickets in her left hand.

She tried to pull away, but his grip was too strong. "Nothing. They're mine."

His long fingers traced them, feeling the raised lettering, the embossed surface.

"Baseball tickets."

"They're mine," she repeated.

"All three?" He raised a dark brow.

"Yes."

"Tomorrow night's game, I'll bet. Who's going?"

"Jimmy and I," she hedged.

"That's two. Who gets the third one?"

You were supposed to get it, you idiot. But I'm not up for a major battle. She opted for the smaller skirmish. "I thought I'd ask Adam."

"Like hell you are," he ground out. "Didn't I just tell you he's off-limits?"

"And didn't I tell you we're just friends? Period?"

"Not if he has anything to say about it."

"Well, he doesn't."

"Fine."

"Fine."

"I'll take the third ticket."

She blinked. Twice. "You?" It was hard to hide the disbelief in her voice.

He shrugged. "Sure. Why not?"

Why not? Because you haven't left the house in months, haven't walked down the street, let alone considered submerging yourself in a throng of thirty thousand screaming fans. "Because . . . you haven't . . ." She couldn't finish.

"Exactly," he said. "Because I haven't."

Before she could ask any more questions, he released her hand and turned away, leaving her gaping after him. She remained glued to her spot, staring straight ahead, long after the door clicked shut.

Ten

The black limousine maneuvered along the highway, winding its way toward Dodger Stadium. Matt could feel his pulse beating faster and faster as the miles ticked away. Soon, he'd be forced to reenter the real world. His palms grew sweaty.

He wasn't ready. He doubted he'd be ready a year from now. Or ten years. So why had he done it? Why had he opened his big mouth and said he was going to the game with Sara? He knew the answer, had known it from the beginning, but it didn't make it any more palatable. In fact, he didn't like it at all.

Anger. Hot, bold anger had spurred him forward to claim that third ticket. He hadn't liked the thought of Adam going. With Sara. That was another situation that had him bugged. Was something going on between those two? Sara denied everything. But was she telling the truth? Was she capable of groping around in the kitchen with him one minute and accepting his brother's advances the next? The thought gnawed at him, burrowing a hole straight to his heart, sickening him.

And just exactly what *had* been happening in the kitchen yesterday? He still couldn't figure it out.

Oh, he knew what they'd said to each other later that day. Her words had lain in his gut like a cold slice of pizza coated with congealed cheese and greasy pepperoni.

"Can't we just forget about it?" He'd heard the almost desperate sincerity in her voice. And she'd meant it.

Hardly. Not when just the thought of her soft skin under his fingers made him hard. What the hell was wrong with him? He'd touched a lot of women. With a lot more intimacy than their brief encounter in the kitchen. It didn't mean anything, he kept telling himself. She didn't mean anything. It was a physical thing. Period. His biological time clock was reminding him he was way overdue in the sex department. Time to get laid. That was it.

So why did the touches that meant nothing from the woman who meant nothing to him, continue to plague him?

"We'll be there in a few minutes, Matt." Sara's husky voice jolted him from his thoughts. She was sitting in the back with him, smelling like some sort of tropical concoction. Vanilla, maybe. There was probably a good three feet between them, but he could still smell her. At least it wasn't that orange-lemon scent that drove him wild. Unfortunately, this was a close second.

"Okay. Fine," he said, but he felt anything but fine.

She cleared her throat. "We may have one slight problem at the stadium."

His senses pricked to alertness. "Problem?" He'd thought of hundreds of "slight problems" since he'd gotten into the car. What if he fell? Got separated? Was recognized? Couldn't maneuver the steps? Bumped into something? Or someone? The *problems* went on and on.

"Someone is going to have to stay very close and help you negotiate your way around."

That was a problem? He breathed a sigh of relief. "Right. I know that."

"Well . . ." she dragged out her words, "that would be either me or Jimmy."

He let out a short laugh. "Sorry, Jimmy. If it's a choice between you and a beautiful woman, I'm taking the woman."

Jimmy snorted. "Some friend."

"But that will mean I have to *touch* you," she said, lowering her voice. He felt her move closer as though she were trying to keep the conversation between the two of them.

"So? Do I have leprosy?"

Her breath brushed against his ear. "Yesterday, you told me not to get near you or 'touch your person' again." She sounded irritated. Or was it hurt? "You were very specific about it." Those last words came out like a hissing cat. Pissed. That's what she was.

Of course he'd said those things. And he'd meant them. All of them. She was getting to him, making him think about her too much, want her too much. Time to put the wall up. Create some distance. But not now. He needed her now.

"I need you now, Sara," he whispered, ignoring her words. "I need you to help me get through this." It was as close as he would get to admitting he was scared.

Silence.

"Okay," she said.

"Thank you."

"I'll hold your hand and lay out a blueprint as we go," she said. "I'll be with you, every step of the way."

"Good," he said, laying his head against the back of the seat. He tilted his ball cap low over his forehead and closed his eyes, trying to shut out the road in front of him, the miles behind him, and the unpredictable, tempting woman beside him.

Matt didn't talk for the rest of the trip. He let the soft classical music and Jimmy's tour guide instincts fill the air. As for Sara, she seemed intrigued with Jimmy's elaboration on the glimpses of various locales they passed along the highway, questioning him about the scenery, history, and people.

Jimmy's loud voice and Sara's throaty responses bombarded Matt's quiet. It was impossible to ignore either one of them. Jimmy was a great guy, one of his most trusted friends, but damn the man had a mouth on him. Gregarious was an understatement. And Sara. Well, lately, it seemed she only had to breathe and his senses pricked with awareness.

"The stadium's over there, down to the right," Jimmy said in his usual voice, which ranked eight decibels louder than the average person.

"Oh, I see it! Matt, we're almost there," Sara said.

"Mmm," he grunted, pretending to be rousing from sleep. In less than ten minutes, he'd be thrust among a crowd of about thirty thousand people. And he'd bet he was the only blind man among the whole lot. His heart pounded in his chest so loud he was certain Sara could hear it. He drew in a deep breath, trying to calm the fear that had begun creeping up his spine. *Get a grip, Brandon,* he told himself. *Do you want to look like a coward? Do you want to let the fear grip you so hard, it'll paralyze you? Then you'll never be able to pull out of its clutches. It's time. Now.* Sweat beaded on his forehead as Jimmy slowed the car. *Don't fall apart. Don't lock yourself into it.*

You can do it. You can do it. His breathing came in rapid little spurts. *You can do it. Count the steps. Sara will guide you. She won't let you fall. Trust her.* His hands grew wet, clammy. *Open up. Just this once. Trust somebody other than yourself.*

"Okay," Jimmy said, pulling the limo up to the curve. "Here we are. Sara, you know the game plan."

"Right. Matt and I will get to our seats and meet you there. You've got your ticket. And we've got almost forty-five minutes to game time. Perfect."

"Good luck," Jimmy said, all traces of his usual casualness gone. His beefy hand grabbed Matt's. "You can do it," he said in a rough whisper.

Matt nodded but said nothing. Jimmy got out, walked to the other side of the limo, and opened the door. Matt unfolded himself from the backseat and planted his feet on the concrete. He stood very still. Noise, loud and overwhelming, buzzed around him like a giant bee trying to land. Some of the sounds he could identify: car horns, screeching brakes, crying children, shouting men, wailing sirens. Others were not as recognizable, but they blared in his consciousness just the same, tearing at his concentration, upending his orientation to time and place.

"Sara?" It was a plea. He felt like a drowning man sucking in his last breath, as the waves crashed about, battering him from crest to crest, pulling him under. He couldn't move. He could barely breathe.

"I'm here," she whispered her reassurance as she clasped his left hand and gave it a squeeze.

He let out a ragged sigh. He couldn't do it. Where was Jimmy? He wanted to get the hell out of here. Now. "I . . . I . . . can't, Sara." He admitted the defeat. "Maybe another time."

"No." Her words were firm, unbending. "You can do it, Matthew Brandon." She squeezed his hand. "And you will. We're going to turn around and walk to the gate." She hesitated just a second. "Put your arm around my waist and I'll do the same. It will be more secure until we get inside the gates."

"I don't know, Sara." He was probably a thousand steps away from his seat. How was he ever going to make it?

"Just do it, Matt," she persisted. "If you don't, you'll go back to that mansion of yours and spend the next several months tormenting yourself with 'if onlys.' " Without waiting for his response, she slung her arm around his waist and half dragged him forward.

Matt caught up with her, draped his arm around her waist, and hauled her against his hip. "Let's do it."

"Take smaller steps. There, that's it," she said, as he shortened his stride. "The turnstile is just ahead. About thirty of my steps." Matt started counting. "Swing left, there's a couple to the right." He moved to the left. "Almost there." They took ten more steps and she slowed. "We have to go single file through this thing. You go first.

Here's your ticket." Sara disengaged herself from him and thrust the ticket into his hand. "I'll be right behind you," she whispered.

He inched forward, the sound of the turnstile cranking back and forth in front of him. He felt Sara's hands on his waist, propelling him forward. "You're next," she murmured.

Holding out his ticket, he waited.

"And a good day to you, sir," a pleasant-sounding woman said, taking the ticket from him. "Enjoy the game." Matt passed through the clicking gate and turned to wait for Sara.

"You did great," she said, grabbing his hand and coaxing him along. "Do you want a program?"

He heaved a sigh of relief. He'd made it through the first blockade. "Of course," he said, daring a half smile. "I want it all today. Peanuts, hot dogs, beer, cotton candy. Everything."

"Including a barf bag for the way home," Sara said, stopping to get him a program.

"We're coming to the steps," she said in a low voice. "Lots of them, I think. You'll need to hold onto the railing."

"I would have to pick seats halfway to heaven," Matt muttered.

"Once you're in your seat, you'll think you are in heaven," she assured him.

He wanted to smile, wanted to take just a second and thank her for doing this for him, but he was too nervous. He'd thank her later. Once he was safe inside the car and heading home. Right now, he had to spend all of his attention trying to stay upright and clear of moving and nonmoving objects.

"It's another fifteen steps or so and then we turn right. And head up to heaven."

"Right," he said, pulling his cap lower over his forehead to meet the top of his sunglasses. He didn't want to chance anyone recognizing him. Not now, when he was being led around like some helpless child.

"Now we turn to the right. Slow down," she said, squeezing his hand. "There's a group of teenagers getting ready to cut us off." He slowed. "Good. I'm guessing another thirty steps or so to the usher."

He concentrated on Sara's directions. So far, she'd been pretty close to target. He shortened his stride to accommodate her smaller gait and counted thirty-three steps to her next tug on his hand, which he knew by now meant "stop."

"Up the stairs, second section, second row," an old man said in a mechanical voice.

"Thank you." Sara turned to Matt. He felt her breasts brush against his chest as she leaned up to whisper in his ear. "I'll go first. You hold onto my belt loop with your right hand and the railing with your left. I'll go slow. It'll all look very natural. Like we're a couple. Are you ready?"

Ready? If he weren't so damned worried about falling flat on his face, he'd be ready all right. Ready to bury his face between the valley of those firm, ripe breasts he'd felt a moment ago. Ready to stroke his hands up and down her legs. Ready to grab that tempting backside and haul her against him. Ready to kiss the breath out of her until she couldn't form one intelligent thought. Ready? Oh, yeah, he was ready.

"Sure," he said, amazed he could speak. "I'm ready."

"Good. Let's go." She turned and placed his right hand on her hip and headed up the stairs. Matt grabbed the railing with his left hand and followed her. One, two, three, sway. Four, five, six, sway. Seven, eight, nine, sway, all the way up thirty-two steps with the feel of her hips moving beneath his fingertips.

"Here we are. Second row, first three seats." Sara grabbed Matt's hand and sidestepped into the row. He followed, taking tiny paces. "You take the end. You've got the longest legs," she said.

"Good idea." He turned and felt the edge of the seat digging into his calf muscles. Feeling for the sides, he lowered himself onto the hard plastic. And let out a long sigh of relief.

He'd made it to his seat.

"Would you like something to eat or drink?" Sara asked, her vanilla scent teasing his senses. "Peanuts? Popcorn? A beer?"

"Sure," he said, laughing.

She laughed too. "Okay. It's your stomach."

"Hey, I told you, I was serious about tasting everything."

"And I'm serious about the bag for the ride home." There was a lightness to her voice that felt like sunshine on a winter day. Was Sara *his* sunshine come to warm his cold, lonely existence? Come to melt his heart?

The thought grabbed his chest like a fist, squeezing the breath from him. He pushed it away. She was leaving in a few days, he told himself. Then he'd never see her again. The fist sneaked past his defenses, pounding his chest like a two-ton hammer.

"So, you want a beer, peanuts and popcorn." Sara's words pulled him back. "That's it? No cotton candy? Hot dog with mustard? Lemon Chill? Maybe an ice cream?"

Matt smiled. He'd miss her sarcastic tongue. And that low throaty voice and soft laughter. Hell, he'd even miss her pain-in-the-butt persistence and dog-eared stubbornness.

The truth of it was, he'd miss *her.*

"Matt?"

"Huh? Oh, yeah." He needed a beer. Now. "That's it for this round." He grinned. "Do you want something?"

"I think I'll settle for a Diet Pepsi."

"How boring."

"That's me," she agreed. "Plain old boring. Keeps me out of trouble."

"You should take a walk on the wild side sometime, Sara," he said, leaning toward her. "Try a regular Pepsi," he whispered. "It'll change your life."

Her laughter rolled over him, warm and soft, like a summer night's breeze, making him laugh, too.

"Glad to see you two are all settled in," Jimmy's voice boomed from a foot away.

"Hi, Jimmy," Sara said. "You're next to me."

"No argument there."

Matt stood to let him squeeze by and felt Sara's arm brush against him as she did the same. "You can sit by her, but don't get any ideas. She's mine, Jimmy." It was a joke, meant as nothing more than lighthearted bantering. But once the words were out, they didn't sound funny to him. Not at all. Maybe because beneath the teasing attempt at humor, he'd been dead serious.

When had he started to think of Sara Hamilton as his? She was leaving, for Christ's sake. They were from two different worlds. It could never work. She'd want a commitment. Marriage. He wanted neither. Maybe he was experiencing one of those doctor-client things—even though she wasn't technically his doctor—when the patient falls for the doctor who helps him.

That was it. It had to be. It was nothing more than mild infatuation as a result of her relentless efforts to help him regain his life. Why hadn't he realized that sooner?

Today was a perfect example. A month ago, he wouldn't have even considered the possibility that he'd be sitting in Dodger Stadium, waiting for the opening pitch to hit off the game. Sara had made that possible. She'd given him hope, shown him a glimpse of life outside his iron gates, as a blind man. Shown him it was possible to see without his eyes, if he chose to.

It was natural to hold the giver of such a gift in high esteem, wasn't it? Of course it was, he told himself. Sara was *giving* him back his life. Not the life he'd had before, but a new one. Deeper, richer, more profound. One that he could carve out for himself, like a writer with a blank page, according to his own will and desire and not the demands and dictates of society. That in itself was a powerful aphrodisiac.

Matt smiled, relieved that he could find a reason for this intense, almost obsessive attraction to Sara Hamilton. Relieved that it wasn't terminal. He could relax now and enjoy her company, knowing his heart was safe. The more independent he became, the less he'd need her. The less he'd want her. And if he could do that in a week's time, then he could put her on that plane for Pittsburgh and wave good-bye.

He hoped.

"One beer," Sara said, jolting him back to reality. She handed him a large plastic cup. "Jimmy's got the peanuts. Popcorn's coming up the aisle and pop's coming down."

"Sounds like we're all set," Matt said, taking a healthy swallow. "Jimmy, did you remember the radio?"

"Sure thing," he said. "All ready to go." The sound of the local radio station buzzed around them as the broadcasters talked about today's game.

"I'll hold it for you," Sara said. "I think with all the food you're planning to stuff yourself with, you won't have any room left for the radio."

He grinned. "You might just have to roll me out of here."

"Now that would be a sight," she said, laughing.

"Would you please stand for the singing of our National Anthem," the announcer blared through the P.A. system. Matt stood and experienced a moment of panic when he removed his Pirates cap. What if someone recognized him? What would he say? What would he do? A gentle touch on his forearm was all he needed. The tension left his body. It was as though Sara knew his fear. And understood it.

The crowd cheered with the last words and the opening pitch signaled the start of the game. He plopped the cap back on his head and sat down, lost in the announcer's words as he gave a play-by-play. Soon, Sara had her own version of what was happening and he found her opinions more interesting and enlightening than the cardboard voice transmitting over the airwaves. Jimmy threw in his occasional perspective on a particular play, usually precluding it with a history of the player, including birthplace, family background, and number of children.

By the end of the seventh inning, they were all hoarse from yelling and cheering the Pirates to a narrow 5 to 4 lead. Matt had managed to gorge himself with two hot dogs; a bag of popcorn, which Sara helped him eat; peanuts, a beer, and a Lemon Chill. Another beer sounded awfully tempting, but that would mean a bathroom trip for sure. He'd save that adventure for next time.

Next time. A smile played about his lips. He was already thinking about the next game. It had been months since he'd considered "next times." Up until Sara came into his life, he hadn't even been interested in getting through the "first time."

But now he was. He wanted a life. Maybe it wouldn't be a traditional existence with two functional eyes, but he still had four other senses. And a hell of a lot of willpower.

"Take Me Out to the Ball Game," roared through the crowd, signaling the seventh-inning stretch. Matt joined in, bellowing out the verses with Sara and Jimmy.

"Thank you," he said, turning to Sara when the song was over. "This was a great idea."

She touched his arm. A feather-light graze against his skin. "You're welcome." Her words were warm, soft, genuine. "Now if they can just hold on for two more innings, everything will be perfect."

"Excuse me," a gruff voice interrupted, "but don't I know you?"

Dread gripped Matt, pounding his good mood like a sucker punch in the gut. "I doubt it."

"You sure do look familiar," the old man persisted.

Matt pulled his cap lower over his face and looked away. Had this guy recognized him?

"Don't you play for the Broncos? Second-string quarterback?"

Second-string quarterback? Matt laughed. "Sorry. Not me."

"But I could swear I've seen that face before. Maybe it's the Red Sox."

"Nope."

"Phillies?"

"Excuse me, sir," Sara said in a sweet voice. "But this is my husband." She paused. "Of four days. And he's nobody's star but mine." Her voice dropped to a throaty chuckle. She reached up and stroked his cheek, her fingers tracing his jaw. "I think I'd know if he were some big celebrity, don't you?" Her lips grazed Matt's cheek.

The old man coughed, almost choking on his next words. "Sure, miss, I mean missus," he sputtered. "Sorry for the mix-up."

Sara giggled. "He's gone."

"Nice ploy," Matt said, thinking he rather liked her tactics.

"It got the job done."

And then some. The kiss, the touch, the sexy voice left him rock-hard and throbbing. Again. At least he knew why this time. Nothing more than mere infatuation for the woman who was helping him regain his life. That was it. Nothing more.

Thank God.

Eleven

Sara closed her eyes and lay back against the soft black leather of the limousine. What a day. What a perfect day. He'd done it! Before twenty-eight thousand people, Matt had walked into Dodger Stadium and taken his seat among throngs of screaming, yelling fans. And become one of them.

Thinking of the mass quantities of junk food he'd inhaled made her smile. How could he stuff himself, when he had to be ready to burst? she'd asked. His answer was simple. With a wink and a lopsided grin, he'd crammed a handful of popcorn into his mouth and told her he had a lot of catching up to do.

It was good to see him smile. Good to see him laugh. He'd told her he wanted to start writing again tomorrow. With her as his typist. She'd agreed. Maybe she could work on reforming Jack Steele.

Matt was going to be all right. Day by day, step by step, he would find his way, fueled by willpower and sheer determination. She pinched the bridge of her nose. Thank God she was leaving in three days. Matthew Brandon functioning at full potential would be downright deadly. It would be too dangerous to stay a minute longer than necessary. Much too dangerous. The mere sound of his deep voice pricked the hairs along her neck. And the smell of his woodsy cologne made her heart do double time. And then there was his touch. She rubbed her temples. Better not go there at all. Better to pray for the last few days to fly by so Jeff could get out here and she could head back to her safe, predictable life.

"I have to tell you, Sara," Matt said, cutting into her thoughts, "I was a little concerned someone might recognize me."

She smiled and opened her eyes. "You mean other than 'Mr. Don't I Know You From Somewhere?' "

"Yeah. A second-string quarterback, for Christ's sake. At least he could've said I looked like a starter." He crossed his arms over his chest. "And the Red Sox? And Phillies? Good God."

"I knew nobody would recognize you."

He turned toward her, flipping up his cap. "How?"

She gave a quick little laugh that sounded more like a squeak. "In case no one has informed you, I don't fit the MO for Matthew Brandon's typical date."

He gave her a strange look. "Oh?"

"No, sad to say, I am only five-feet-five, several inches shorter than your mandatory five-nine, or ten, and am well over your standard ninety-two and one half pounds, with *natural* brown, not bottled-blond tresses." The hint of a smile on his full lips encouraged her to go on. "My fingernails are tapered and functional, sometimes sporting a clear gloss, not the three inches of acrylic red, magenta, or poppy pink that you seem to like. I opt for comfort, not spike heels. Too much like stilts. And spandex . . ." she gave a little laugh, "is a dirty word in my vocabulary." His smile turned into a full-blown grin.

"That's it. Nothing else?"

"Oh, there is one more thing. My name is Sara. Not a confection or a rhyme. No Candy, Sandy, Mandy, Dolly, Holly, Polly, Fawn, Dawn . . . or any other half-syllable vowel equation."

"I have never dated a Candy. Or a Dolly, that I can remember." Rubbing his chin, he asked, "Jimmy, have I ever dated a Dolly?"

"No Dollys."

"See? Jimmy remembers these things."

"How nice for you. Do you take him along on dates so he can take notes?"

Matt laughed. "Now there's an idea. Jimmy, the next time I have a date, you're with me. Not just as the driver. Sara's onto something. If I take a date to dinner, you come too and take notes. We go to a show; you write down the important stuff."

Sara rolled her eyes. He was going too far. Just to prove a point. The man drove her insane.

She was still thinking about how much he irritated her, when she felt his big hand reach out for hers. His first attempt landed on her hip. "Sorry," he murmured, in a low sexy drawl that made her wonder if he'd known his mark all along. He stroked her hand with warm fingers and spoke in a soft, soothing voice that reminded her of a lullaby. "I was honored that you asked me to go to the game with you."

"I didn't exactly ask you to go. If you'll recall, you *told* me you were going."

He shrugged. "Same thing."

It would be pointless to argue with the man about something so inconsequential. She knew what had been said. And so did he.

"I enjoyed being with you," he said, moving his thumb in slow circles along her wrist. "But I don't like to hear you knock yourself down like that."

She stiffened. "I was not knocking myself down. Only citing reality."

He stared at her, his silver eyes fixed on her face, as though he could see her. "Jimmy, I need a little private time. Excuse us?"

"Sure."

"Thanks." The dark-tinted glass divider whirred into place, separating driver and passengers. "Now," he said, "I have a little secret to confess about all of those beautiful women who flutter around me."

Flutter. Good word. Reminded her of butterflies.

"That's okay," she said, trying to pull her hand away. He tightened his grip. "I don't think I want to hear this."

"Yes, you do, Sara." His low voice moved over her, making her feel all soft and gooey inside, like melting caramel. "The reason I've dated the kind of women you mentioned—models, starlets, that type—is that they're not real to me. They're like hot fudge on a sundae. An extra. Gone long before the ice cream. They enjoy fun, know how to have a good time, and leave when the party's over."

"Sounds wonderful."

"No, it doesn't. Not to somebody like you. You, Sara Hamilton, are the ice cream, the flavor that stays on a man's lips long after he's finished."

Her mouth went dry. She'd never thought of ice cream as erotic. Until now.

"That's why your type is so dangerous," he continued. "Too dangerous. Men marry women like you, have babies, move to the suburbs, buy a van."

"But not you," she said, her heart aching with an emptiness she didn't understand.

"No," he whispered, moving closer, "not me."

She tried to inch away, but he caught her chin. "But by God, right now, I wish I were." He took her mouth with a fierceness that surprised her, hard, possessive. His hands were all over her, like a starved man who's just been led to a banquet and doesn't know what to sample first. He molded her breasts, her hips, her buttocks, dragging her onto his lap, never breaking the kiss.

He yanked her shirt from its waistband, running his fingers up her body to cup a lace-covered breast. She wound her arms around his neck, pulling him closer, pushing thought and reason out the window.

"I know I told you to stay away," he rasped, breaking the kiss to brush his lips over her eyes, her cheeks, her throat. "But I'm the one who can't stay away." He ran his tongue along the slender column of her neck, sending tiny shivers through her body. "God, but I need you, Sara."

Tears welled in her eyes. God, but she needed him, too. She pressed him closer, wanting to feel his strength against her, needing to feel it. If she made love with him, nothing would ever be the same. Not now or long after, when she was back in Pittsburgh. Living her safe practical life.

The choice was hers. A single tear escaped, fell down her cheek. No. Destiny had already made her choice. It had chosen its path from the first day she saw him on the patio. She placed a soft kiss on his stubbled cheek, whispered, "I need you, too."

Their mouths melted together, touching, teasing, needing. "I can't wait to get you home," Matt groaned.

"Oh?" She pulled the polo shirt out of his jeans, trailing her fingers up his chest.

"Yeah. Oh," he murmured, unfastening her bra, "to bed."

"Tired, huh?" Her hands glided down to his waist, toying with the belt buckle.

"Hardly." His fingers slid under her bra, cupping her breasts, urging them forward. To his mouth.

"Aahhh." The flick of his tongue on her nipple drove her wild. She pulled his head to her breasts, holding him there while he sucked and laved each one.

Neither noticed that the car had stopped. Or that the engine was off. Only when they heard Jimmy's baritone say, "He'll be out in a minute," did they spring apart.

"Jesus," Matt said, rifling a hand through his hair. His cap was long gone, lying on the floor somewhere.

Sara tried to scurry off his lap and adjust her clothing. She heard another voice outside. A woman's.

"No." Matt's firm voice stilled her shaking fingers. He brushed her hand aside. "We are not going to hide like two teenagers caught in the backseat of a car. Whoever is outside can wait. Let me help you." Reaching behind her, he fastened her bra with a little more expertise than Sara would have liked.

"I . . . I can get myself together," she mumbled, her voice a little shaky.

"I know, but I want to help." He ran his hands down her shirt, tucking it inside her shorts. *How could he be so calm? Had he been in this situation before? Of course, he had.* Her stomach hit the floor.

The voice kicked in again on the other side of the window. Louder. More demanding. Jimmy's muffled response followed.

Who was that person?

Matt jammed his shirt into his shorts. "Is my hat around here, anywhere?"

Scooping it from the floor, she placed it in his hand and ran all ten fingers through her hair. No time for anything as civilized as a brush.

"Ready?" Matt reached for her hand and gave it a gentle squeeze.

"Ready," she answered, trying to keep her voice steady. It was hard to concentrate on anything but what had been happening between them a few minutes ago.

"Let's see what all of the commotion is about. And how fast I can take care of it."

Before she could reply, he reached out and drew her to him, planting a hard possessive kiss on her mouth. It was over almost before it began. By the time she gathered her senses, the door swung open and Matt stepped out, taking her with him.

"Oh, Matt!" A woman with a tangle of red hair and long magenta nails flung herself at him. "I've missed you *sooo* much."

Sara's hand fell away like a dead weight as Matt reached out to steady the woman.

"Hello, Gabrielle."

"Oh, darling, have you missed me, too?" She ran her long nails through his curly hair, her red lips mere inches from his.

"Of course."

The woman named Gabrielle laughed, a low, sultry purr that exuded sensual promises. Then she pulled him to her and kissed him.

Sara stumbled back toward the limousine, sucking in air, trying to block out the sickening scene in front of her.

Matt and another woman. A beautiful woman wrapped in sex and the color red. Kissing each other. The images faded in and out like a disjointed picture, confusing her mind's eye.

She closed her eyes, blinked, refocused. The woman had her head resting on Matt's shoulder, eyes closed, a dreamy expression on her face.

Sara had seen enough. Gathering her tattered pride, she turned toward the house, away from the man she'd trusted and the beautiful woman named Gabrielle.

"Where is she?" Matt stormed into the kitchen, his expression grim.

"Who?" Rosa feigned ignorance. He hated when she did that.

"You know who," he said, trying to hold onto his last two shreds of patience. It was difficult. Very difficult.

"Ah, Señorita Sara."

"Yes. Señorita Sara."

"She no tell me where she goes." The old woman clucked her tongue like a chicken. "*Pobre-*

cita. Poor little thing. She come in with the big tears in her eyes." *Cluck, cluck, cluck.* "So sad."

Matt felt like he'd gotten punched in the gut. He had to get to Sara. Tell her it wasn't what it looked like. And what was that? He didn't need his eyesight to tell him. They would have looked like lovers reunited.

Without another word, he headed down the hall toward Sara's bedroom. Anger pulsed through his body as he thought of Gabrielle clinging to him like lint on a black sweater. Her overpowering perfume still filled his nostrils, worse than a stroll through the women's cosmetics at Bloomingdale's. Nothing lemon or orange scented about it. That was reserved for Sara. Light and fresh, like an early-morning walk before the world is awake and the sun sits high in the sky.

Sara.

He lifted his hand to knock on her door and hesitated. What could he say to her? Well, the truth, for starters. *Gabrielle is nothing more than a friend. She just forgets that sometimes.* Correction. Most times. *And if you think I could even consider touching her after being with you, then you don't really know me at all.*

He knocked.

"Who is it?" Her voice reached him through the door, sounding thin and strained.

"It's me."

Silence.

"I need to talk to you."

Silence.

"Now."

"It's open."

He turned the knob and stepped inside, closing the door behind him.

She was flitting around the room, making a lot of noise, expending a lot of energy. A closet door opened, then a drawer, then another.

"What are you doing?" he asked, tensing. He had a damn good idea what she was doing.

"Packing."

The word smacked him in the face.

"Why?" He took another few steps into the room. Closer to her.

"I'm leaving in three days. I wanted to get ready."

"Bullshit."

She said nothing.

"You're running away." *I don't want you to go.*

"I am not running away," she insisted. He thought he heard a tremble in her voice. Damn, but if he could only see her face, look into her eyes. Then he'd know if she was telling the truth. But he couldn't and so he had to depend on his other senses to guide him.

"Actually, I was thinking about asking you to stay a little longer. Say another few weeks or so." *Or months. Until I get you out of my system.*

"I don't think so." She slammed a drawer shut. He heard her walk into the bathroom.

He headed for the bed, located her suitcase and started pulling things out of it, tossing them on the bed. She was staying. Period.

"What are you doing?"

She was furious. Too bad. Once she calmed down, she'd see reason, understand there really was no other choice. She had to stay, had to ride this damn thing out, until it either crashed or landed. His fingers slid over a pair of silk under-wear. He smiled. "Helping you unpack."

"I said I was packing. And you heard me the first time." She yanked the panties from his hand.

"She doesn't mean anything, Sara." He figured he might as well get it over with. For a psychologist, she sure had a strange way of dealing with her own personal issues. She avoided them.

"Who?"

"Gabrielle."

"If you say so."

Her nonchalant attitude irked him. "I do say so," he ground out. "We're just friends."

She let out a hard, short laugh. "You must have an interesting definition of 'friend.' "

Matt grabbed her arm, jerked her toward him. "Stop it, Sara." His fingers closed over her soft skin. "Stop trying to avoid this conversation. She may want something more, but I don't." He paused, lowered his voice. "Not with her."

Her body relaxed a little. He loosened his grip.

"She's very beautiful."

"Yes, she is." *Was that jealousy rearing her ugly green horns?*

"And tall."

"Yes." *It sure sounded like it.*

"And thin."

"Yes." *Yep. That was her all right. Jealousy. In all her green glory.*

"Did you sleep with her?"

"What?" That threw him. He was still basking in her jealousy.

"Did you sleep with her?" she repeated as though he were deaf *and* blind.

He wasn't going to lie to her. "It was over a long time ago."

"Not from what I saw," she said, pulling free from his hold.

"Sara—"

The phone rang, loud, shrill.

"You can't just ignore what happened between us."

"You mean what almost happened between us," she said, escaping to a far corner of the room. She was making sure he couldn't get to her again.

"Señor Matt?" Rosa's voice called to him from the other side of the door. "The phone, it is for you. It is Señor Jeff."

"I need to talk to him," Sara said, hurrying toward the phone.

Matt took two steps and picked up the receiver.

"Jeff? Hi. How's it going?" It was an innocent question with a gut-wrenching answer. "Christ. I'm sorry." He felt Sara hovering close by, trying to make out the conversation. Pinching the bridge of his nose, he listened to his friend's tormented voice on the other line.

"Sure. No. Fine. I'll tell her." The words came out in tiny intervals, helpless responses to helpless words. If only there was something he could say that would make a difference.

But there wasn't. Not a damn thing.

And so he clutched the phone tighter, anger bubbling deep in his gut, threatening to boil over like hot, molten lava. Why in the hell did life have to be so goddamned unfair? Matt rubbed the back of his neck, listening to his best friend's voice choke on the word *baby*.

This is what love did to a man? he thought. *Tore at*

his humanity, shred by shred, emasculating him, clawing away his dignity, until nothing was left but a tragic desperateness in a black hole of hopelessness?

Well, no thank you. He was not interested. Not one bit.

"I'll talk to you in a few days. Call me if there are any changes," he said into the receiver. "Okay. Take care." *Click.* He blew out a long breath and hung up, thanking God he was immune to that kind of heartache. You had to love somebody to hurt like that.

And it wasn't worth the trip.

"What is it, Matt?" Sara's voice trembled, full of concern. And fear.

He turned toward her, rubbing the back of his neck. "It's Nina. She's bleeding again."

"Oh, no," she whispered.

"They put her in the hospital." He paused. There was no nice way to say the rest. Straight out would be best. "But they don't know about the baby."

A small sob escaped her lips.

"It's fifty-fifty right now."

She sniffed.

"Jeff's taking it pretty hard."

Another sob.

"Looks like you'll be here awhile."

Silence.

"Three, maybe four weeks."

Nothing.

"Or longer."

Why wouldn't she say something? Anything?

"Sara?"

"I can't," she whispered. "I can't stay."

"Why? I'll double what Jeff pays you. Name your price."

Her voice quivered. "It's not about money."

In his experience, somewhere, buried beneath all the protestations, it was always about money. "I'll triple it."

"Didn't you hear me? It's not about the money."

"What then? Your clients? He said they're fine."

"No."

What was wrong with her? She was acting like a scared chicken. What was she so afraid of? He ran a hand through his hair, determined to get to the bottom of her fear.

"No, what? No, they're not fine? No, it's not about them?" Frustration crept into his voice, threatening to take over and make him lose his temper. "What is it, Sara?"

"I have responsibilities to my clients—"

"Who are *fine,*" he cut in.

"And I have a responsibility to myself." She let out a weary sigh.

"Would you care to explain that?"

"I have to leave *now*, Matt." Her words were soft, low, like crumpled velvet. They tore at his heart. "Before," she paused a second, "we get any more involved. Before I don't want to leave."

"Can you honestly tell me it's not already too late?" he asked, reaching out and grabbing her arms. "That you can turn around and walk away? Just like that?"

"I have to." Her words brushed over him like needles, pricking open wounds, drawing blood.

"No, you don't, Sara." His voice was thick, gravelly. "Stay. With me." It was as close to a plea as he had ever come.

"And then what, Matt? You'll send me back to Pittsburgh when you're through with me?" He heard the pain in her voice. "When I've fallen so deeply, hopelessly in love with you that I can't bear the thought of life without you?" She let out a little laugh. "No. I don't think so."

How could she be talking about love in one breath and have her suitcase half out the door in the next?

"Why are you so afraid of caring about someone?" he asked, beginning to think she had just as big a problem in the commitment area as he did.

"I care about people," she said, her tone stiff and defensive. "I care about a lot of people."

"Not men, I'll bet. Except for Jeff and he's a friend." Something wasn't right. "Are you afraid of men?"

"Of course not, for heaven's sake."

"But you don't like to get involved with them," he ventured.

"Too many complications."

"Is that how you see me? As a complication?" This was a side of Sara he hadn't noticed before. Not to this degree. Scared. Vulnerable. Defensive. With a wall around her a mile high. Even he, athlete that he was, couldn't scale it.

Not unless she threw him a rope.

And for some ridiculous, insane reason he wanted her to. Very much.

Was that part of this whole doctor-patient infatuation thing? He doubted it. Deep down, he doubted the whole concept. At least for him. But he didn't dare explore his real feelings any deeper. That would be like jumping overboard without a life jacket. And Matt wasn't about to do that. The waters would be too muddy, too deep, too dangerous.

"Answer me, Sara," he persisted. "Am I just a complication to you?"

"No," she breathed. "But I'm scared."

"Of me?"

A small tremor ran through her body. "Of everything. Scared of caring too much. Scared of getting hurt. Scared. Period."

He pulled her to him, coaxing her head to his chest, one hand running through her hair, the other stroking her back. It wasn't a sexual thing. He wanted to protect her, comfort her, heal her.

"I'm scared, too," he whispered.

She buried her face in his shirt and sighed.

"I don't make promises. You know that. But I think there's something going on between us that can't be ignored." His voice dropped to a whisper. "We'll go slow. You set the pace." His hand worked up and down her back in slow, lazy circles. "Tomorrow, we'll start working on my book. And maybe we can venture out again. I'd like to take a walk on the beach." He brushed his lips over the top of her head. "Just the two of us. Okay?"

Her silky head moved up and down.

"Good," he murmured, closing his eyes and inhaling her scent. Vanilla. He'd told her to get rid of the citrus smell because it distracted him too much. Made him think of her luscious body and what he wanted to do with it. Vanilla was no better.

"If and when our relationship goes any further, it'll be your call. No pressure from me." Those words were probably going to kill him, especially if they spent much time holding each other, like they were now. He was hard, ready, and aching.

But he had to gain her trust.

"Thank you," she whispered, lifting her head from his chest. Her fingers stroked his cheek, trailed along his jaw, settled on his chin. As soft as a caress.

Matt held himself still, trying to think of something other than her warm fingers and firm breasts. Sister Catherine Angelina. Sister Margaret Esther. Thank God for Catholic school. He'd promised Sara she could move at her own pace. Damn his big mouth. If it were up to him, he'd throw her suitcase off the bed and take her right now.

Then he'd do it again. And again. And again.

A groan escaped his lips.

"What's the matter, Matt?"

Her breath fanned his jaw, her fingers stilled on his chin. "Nothing. Nothing at all." He circled her wrists and removed them from his person, stepping back to put space between them.

"Matt?" He heard the question in her voice.

"Look, Sara," he said, running a hand through his hair, "I'm not a saint. I'm just a flesh-and-blood man trying to keep my promise. But I want you so damn much, I can't think straight." He took another step back, raising his hands as though to ward her off. "So don't get too close right now. And don't tempt me."

"Are we going to go through that again?" Exasperation trickled over her words.

He shook his head. "The vanilla's just as dangerous as the citrus."

"It's only a fragrance."

"And nitro's only a liquid. Until you light it. Then *kapow!*" He slapped his hands together. "It explodes."

She laughed then, a rich, clear sound that warmed his heart and put a smile on his face. "Thank you, Matt," she said, taking his hands and placing them in her own. "Thank you for caring."

"Do you really mind staying?" It was a silly, almost childish question and he could have kicked himself as soon as the words were out of his mouth. Nothing like exposing insecurities. But he had to know. He didn't want her to feel like he'd coerced her into staying. She needed to be here because it was where she wanted to be.

With him, he hoped.

Her hands tightened around his. "No, Matt," she said, her low throaty voice transmitting sensual signals straight to his groin. "I don't mind staying." Her lips brushed his cheek, moved along his jaw, settled on his mouth for a whisper-soft kiss. "Not at all."

Twelve

"Does anyone have any idea how much starch is in this stuff?" Gabrielle asked, lifting a single strand of angel hair pasta onto her fork.

Adam rolled his eyes. Rosa huffed. Jimmy snickered and shoveled a forkful into his mouth. Sara stared and Matt ignored her.

Gabrielle Jontue seemed unaware of their behavior. She was too involved in her nutrition lesson. Starch, grams of fat, calories, sugars, protein. The words flowed out of her red-lipped mouth like a child reciting a nursery rhyme. Did they know how many grams of fat lurked in their pasta and rolls, just waiting to latch onto some unsuspecting celluloid victim? And butter? "An absolute no-no," she'd told them in her most exaggerated French accent. "Do not even look at it.

"You have to be very careful about starches," she continued, twirling a lone strand of pasta on her fork. "They break down into sugars that just kill the body." She lifted the fork to her mouth and munched on half the strand. "Matt, it would be much healthier to eat pasta made from wheat flour." She tipped her red head to one side and

looked at him. "Haven't we had this discussion before?"

He took a sip of wine before answering. "You've
told me all about it," he drawled. "Several times."

A little huff escaped her lips. "I'm only trying
to help you improve your dietary habits."

"I like my dietary habits," he said, tearing off a
chunk of bread slathered in butter.

"I'll bet you still eat potato chips."

"With dip."

"Disgusting."

"He had three beers the other night," Adam
chimed in.

Matt?" she wailed. "How could you do that to
your body? Water. That's what you need. It flushes
out the impurities."

"I like my impurities," he said, "especially the
thoughts."

He flashed a grin around the table, settling on
Sara a fraction of a second longer than the rest.
She felt the heat rush to her face.

"I don't understand why you insist on making
fun of this." Gabrielle twirled two more strands of
pasta around her fork. That left approximately ten
on her plate. "If everyone were just a little more
observant in their dietary habits, we wouldn't have
so many overweight people crowding out the rest
of us." Her green gaze glittered across the table,
landing on Jimmy's slight paunch.

He smiled at her. "Gabrielle, would you please
pass the pasta?"

She glared at him. "Certainly."

"And the meatballs? Can't have pasta without
meatballs."

"Of course not." She edged the platters toward him. "How about some bread? And butter?"

"Sure," he said, around a mouthful of meatball. "Why not?"

"Why not, indeed?" She raised a well-sculpted brow. Rosa passed the bread and butter, a little smile playing about her lips.

"One piece will do me," he said, reaching for a thick hunk of Italian bread. "Gotta save room for Rosa's cheesecake."

Sara hid her own smile. It was obvious that Jimmy was goading her. He seemed to be the only one paying Gabrielle the slightest amount of attention, even if it was derogatory. Everyone else was ignoring her. Especially Matt.

But the woman didn't seem to notice. Her attention was focused on Matt. And herself, of course. She was beautiful. Almost surreal, with her high hollowed cheekbones and thin straight nose. Her lips were full and pouty. And her eyes were the color of emeralds gleaming in the sunlight. Her tousled flame-red hair lay heaped atop her head, like a glowing crown. Sara felt awkward and dowdy beside her, like an evergreen standing next to a willow. Everything about the woman spoke of elegance, though, whether born of breeding or hours in front of a mirror, Sara wasn't certain. She *was* certain that Gabrielle Jontue was obsessed with herself. And the man beside her.

"How long will you be staying?" Adam asked, his voice cool, impersonal. He'd spoken very little during the meal and Sara got the distinct impression that this redheaded beauty was not one of his favorite people.

"Well," she cooed in a long drawl, "that depends

on your brother." She leaned over, her full breasts brushing against Matt's forearm. He flinched but didn't pull away. "I'd like him to come to Venice with me."

"Venice?" Matt yanked his arm out of her grasp and turned toward her. "What the hell are you talking about?"

She let out a low throaty chuckle. "I meant to discuss this with you when we had a little more privacy," she said, her green gaze shooting around the table before coming back to him.

"Out with it, Gabrielle."

"Really, Matt. Sometimes you can be so cruel," she pouted. When he didn't respond, she gave a little sniff and said, "Well, all right. If you must be such a spoilsport about it, I'll tell you." Her voice dropped to a sultry whisper. "I was planning a little surprise for you. Back to Venice. Just the two of us." Magenta nails stroked his biceps.

Back to Venice? As in they'd been there before? Together? Sara drew in a deep breath, trying to ward off the sudden rush of jealousy that gripped her. He may not be involved with her anymore, but he once was. Intimately. And from the way she was rubbing herself against him and touching him, odds were that Gabrielle was doing her darnedest to rekindle the relationship.

"I don't think so."

"Why?" She edged her red silk-clad body closer. "Is it because of . . . your condition?" She stumbled over the last word.

Sara saw the left side of his jaw twitch. And twitch again. "No. It is not because I'm *blind.*" He hurled the last word at her.

"Then why won't you go?" she whined, crossing her arms over her ample bosom.

He shrugged, forking a chunk of meatball. "Other commitments."

"What *kind* of commitments?" Her gaze narrowed to green slits.

"Personal."

"Oh," she said, pulling her slender frame into a ramrod-straight position. "I see." The words were stiff, forced, colder than a chunk of ice.

Sara doubted she saw anything, other than her own desire to get what she wanted.

There was very little conversation during the rest of the meal, with the exception of an occasional comment on the food or a casual remark about the news. Gabrielle Jontue remained quiet, toying with the last strands of pasta on her plate. It was obvious from her silence and the sour-lemon expression on her face, that she was not pleased.

What *had* Matt meant by other commitments? Was he just trying to give her the brush-off or had he been referring to something else? Someone else? Herself, perhaps?

Jimmy broke through her speculation. "I'm stuffed," he announced, pushing his plate aside and patting his belly. "It was delicious, Rosa." He winked at her. "Especially the jalapeño bits in the meatballs." He brought his hand to his mouth and kissed his fingers, making a loud smacking sound. *"Magnífico."*

Rosa beamed at him, nodded. *"Gracías."*

"I second Jimmy's compliments," Sara said. "Everything was indeed, *magnífico."* She smiled at the older woman. *"Especially,* the meatballs."

It was one of the few comments she'd made during the entire meal. She'd been too busy trying to analyze Gabrielle Jontue and her motives. Sara felt the other woman's green eyes on her, watching her as though she were some kind of bug who'd just flitted into the light.

"How long will you be here, Dr. Hamilton?" Gabrielle asked, leaning back against the chair, her hand under her chin.

"Well, I'll be staying a little longer—"

"Until I don't need her anymore," Matt cut in.

Talk about truth in words. They hadn't discussed the real length of her stay. Or her eventual departure. Her stomach twisted in a huge knot, making her feel as if the pasta she'd just eaten were balled up in a stringy heap, topped with jalapeño-laced meatball bits.

Gabrielle's eyes widened a fraction at the firmness in his voice. "What exactly will you be doing?"

Sara fought back the heat that crept into her cheeks. What indeed? She cleared her throat, met the other woman's level stare. "I'll be helping Matt adjust to life outside of these walls."

"And she's going to help me work on my book," he interjected.

"Oh." Gabrielle insinuated plenty with that one little word. "I thought you never let anyone but your editor read your books before they were finished."

He shrugged. "Don't have much of a choice. I need a typist. Sara volunteered for the job."

That wasn't quite true. She hadn't volunteered for anything. But now wasn't the time to bring it up. Not when the woman across the table was studying her every move with the stealthy intent of a lioness trapping her prey.

"Well, I don't care what Sara's doing," Adam said, laying his napkin down. "I'm just happy she's staying."

"I'll second that," Jimmy's baritone filled the room.

"*Sí,*" Rosa chimed in.

All eyes turned to Matt. His silver gaze settled on Sara, looking past her, into her, sending chills up her spine. When he spoke, his voice was low and soft, as though they were the only ones in the room. "I'm happy, too."

She wanted to smile, wanted to reach across the table and squeeze his hand. But she didn't. Whatever was happening between them needed time to grow and flourish, gather strength before the outside world bombarded them with all of its demands and expectations. *Take it slow. Wait and see.* Incredible, that a few short weeks ago she'd have agreed to almost anything, a root canal, Chinese torture, anything, that would have gotten her out of coming to California and dealing with Matthew Brandon. Incredible, too, that she'd believed every tabloid, every article on the man and his many women, permitting no leeway, no margin for error or misrepresentation on the part of the publisher. Her gaze settled on his mouth. *Very incredible.*

"Well," Gabrielle purred, "how nice that you all are so happy. Now if you'll excuse me . . ." Her words hung in the air as she rose and clipped away on her three-inch red heels.

"Somebody's in a mood," Jimmy whispered.

"We've got about fifteen minutes before she explodes," Adam said, looking at his watch. "Let's get out of here."

"I stay. To protect Señor Matt," Rosa said in a half-joking voice.

"Wait a minute," Matt said. "I don't want to be around her when she blows, either. I'm coming with you."

Adam's gray eyes crinkled at the corners. "Sorry, old man. She's your guest. You find a way to detonate her. We're outta here."

"Sara?"

"Sorry, Matt. She *is* your guest." She smiled at his obvious discomfort. The woman might be a porcelain image of perfection, but she was a witch, a rich, spoiled witch. So much for professional objectivity. Might as well admit she didn't have any where Gabrielle Jontue was concerned.

"Fine," he muttered. "I'll take care of this situation myself."

"I know you can do it," Adam said, suppressing a laugh.

Sara walked around the table and gave his shoulder a light squeeze. "Good luck," she murmured.

"Right. Don't be too late. We've got a lot of work to do tomorrow."

"I know. Good-bye." Her fingers skimmed the back of his chair, trailing along his shoulders.

"Later." The word tumbled over her like warm molasses, heating her insides.

"Grab a jacket and let's go," Adam said, breaking the intimate moment.

"Just give me a minute." She headed down the hall to her room, pulled open the closet doors and began rummaging through her clothes until she located her black-and-white jacket.

"Have a good time."

The voice startled her. Sara swung around and

met Gabrielle's inquisitive green gaze less than five feet from her.

"I didn't hear you come in."

The other woman stood with her arms crossed under her full breasts, making them appear even larger. Her smile was cool, assessing.

"What you're trying to do for Matt is commendable," she began, shifting from one stiletto heel to the other. "Truly commendable." She paused a moment, tilting her head to one side, exposing a long, graceful column of creamy neck. "I just hope you're doing it for the right reasons."

When Sara didn't answer, she gave a little throaty laugh and continued. "I understand Matt. We've been through a lot together. No matter our differences, he always comes back to me." Her full red lips curved at the corners. "Always."

The words hit Sara like a bullet in the chest. Hot, searing, fatal. She drew in a deep breath, fighting to remain calm. "What does that have to do with me?"

Gabrielle smiled again, tapping a magenta nail against her chin. Her green gaze glittered from Sara's brown hair to her white sneakers. "Well, I think you know, Dr. Hamilton. I think you know exactly what it has to do with you."

"I've got to go," Sara said, anxious to get away from this woman's hard stare and cold insinuations.

She headed past her, yanking her jacket on as she passed.

"Only a fool would fall in love with Matthew Brandon." Gabrielle's words struck her like a blow, slowing her step. "And something tells me, Dr. Hamilton, you're no fool."

* * *

"He watched her from across the smoke-filled room, his eyes scanning her every move. Cataloging for future reference. Her thick sable hair swirled behind her, rose-tinted lips sipping the straw of her fancy pink drink, long slender legs crossed at the ankle. He could only see her in profile. And it wasn't enough.

"But he was a patient man. It wasn't that she was beautiful in the classic 'skin' sense, because she wasn't. The woman wasn't even his usual type. He normally opted for a bustier, brassier female with a beautiful face and well-rounded curves. The kind who turned heads and made men drool. And liked it, too.

"This one seemed quiet, almost demure in her mannerisms. She kept her eyes down, ignoring the questioning gazes of the regulars. There was a paper spread out in front of her. Reading? He wanted to laugh. Didn't she know she didn't fit in a place like this? Someone should tell her she didn't belong. Someone should tell her that the inhabitants of Charlie's Grill only came here for two reasons. To drink or get laid.

"She didn't seem to fit into either category. Now on the occasion when he felt the serious need for a drunk, then Charlie's Grill was the only place for him. It afforded him privacy, the best bourbon in town, and Charlie's willing ear. As for the other, well, getting laid was not something he usually had to worry about. Women found him.

"Take the blonde in the corner. She'd been eyeing him for the past twenty minutes. He knew all the classic signs: the unwavering stare, the slight tilt of the head, the forward thrust of an already big bust, the shimmying of material to expose a little extra thigh. Yeah, he knew it all. That one was on the make, all right. It wouldn't take more than a flick of his finger to have her next to him, panting in his ear.

"But not the other one, he thought, as his gaze shifted back to the brunette. She was like sunshine after a hard rain, all fresh and serene. And he wanted her. Badly."

"Well, she better not give in," Sara's loud warning filled the room, interrupting Matt's next words. "Why is he going after this innocent woman when he has a ready-and-willing one waiting for him?"

Matt laughed, adjusting the bill on his Pirates cap. Only Sara would say something like that. "You're the psychologist, Dr. Hamilton. You tell me."

"I thought Jack Steele was interested in anything with breasts, the bigger the better."

"Not true. You don't really know Jack. He's not the marauder. It's the women. They're always after him, throwing themselves at him." He shrugged. "What's a man to do?"

"What, indeed? Perhaps he could try to have a relationship with one of them."

He didn't miss the sharpness in her voice. "Jack's not good with relationships."

"Hmmm."

He hated it when she did that, as if she had a lot to say on the subject and mere words would never suffice. "Can we continue? Or do you need to dissect Jack Steele's motives first?"

She sniffed. "I know *exactly* what his motives are."

"Good," he said, annoyed with her snide comment. He was edgy this morning, and it had little to do with Sara bashing his hero's character and more to do with the time she strolled in last night. With Adam. One o'clock, if Rosa hadn't fooled with the chimes again.

What the hell was she doing with his brother for all those hours? Matt was dying to know, but damned if he'd ask. He shifted in his chair, crossed his arms behind his head and leaned back, trying to get his mind on Jack Steele and the brunette. The innocent, tantalizing brunette with rose-tinted lip, long legs, and eyes the color of—

His thoughts slammed into his consciousness, scattering ideas like dummies in a crash test. Matt shot up from his chair. "Describe your eyes to me."

"My eyes?" Her voice sounded guarded, uncertain.

"Yeah. What color are they? What shape?"

She didn't answer at first, as though she were weighing the options of fight or flight. When she did speak, there was a hesitancy that he didn't understand. Was she embarrassed? Uncomfortable? Self-conscious? What? What was making her so skittish?

"I guess they're a kind of mix between green and amber."

He remembered Adam's words. *And I can't forget her eyes. You can get lost in them when she looks at you. . . .amber green . . . kind of tilted at the corners . . . When she's passionate about something, they turn this rich amber color . . . like old whiskey . . .*

"Which is dominant?" Matt asked, wondering if she agreed with Adam's observations.

"Green, I guess. How do I know?" There was an edge to her words. "I don't stand in front of the mirror and stare at myself all day."

"Don't get testy. I was just curious." He laughed. "It's the writer in me working overtime."

"Well, the writer needs to take a break."

"What shape are they?" *Kind of tilted at the corners . . .*

She made a disgusted sound. "Matt, stop—"

He held up both hands. "Okay, okay. No more questions. Truth is, I thought the least I could do to show my appreciation for your assistance would be to write in a character with your eyes."

"Let me guess. The big-busted blonde with the come-hither look is going to have *my* eyes."

He laughed. "Would I do that to you?"

"Yes. You would," she said, her voice short and huffy. "Especially when you know I can't stand a woman throwing herself at a man."

He decided to string her along a few more seconds. "Even if he wants her to?"

"Even then," she said, with the primness of a nun who's never known passion or desire and is appalled by the very thought of it. He knew differently.

Sara Hamilton was a flesh-and-blood woman with enough heat to burn him and half of Laguna Beach. And if he were lucky, he wouldn't have to wait much longer to feel her fire.

"Actually, I thought I'd use your eyes for the mystery woman."

"Oh."

"She seems more your type. Elusive. Compelling. Unaware of her own sensuality."

He paused, waiting for a response. Nothing.

"You are, aren't you?" he prompted. Delving into the psyche of this woman was becoming his greatest challenge.

"What?"

He laughed. "You're good. And elusive. Or maybe, evasive is a better word." Matt rubbed his jaw. "Yeah. Evasive would be my pick. You dance around most questions about yourself, and I'm starting to think there's a big dark secret hiding under that velvety skin."

"I'm not evasive. Or elusive. There's just not much to say when compared to a celebrity like yourself."

Something in the tone of her words didn't ring true. She was hiding something, he'd bet his favorite Pirates cap on it. But what would a hometown "I believe in God and country" girl be hiding?

"And I don't suppose you consider yourself compelling either?"

She laughed. "Compelling? As compared to what? Saturday night reruns or fried baloney sandwiches? I'm just ordinary. No frills, no extras. Just plain old ordinary."

"I like fried baloney sandwiches. And I'd say you're anything but ordinary."

"I've driven the same way to work for the last three years."

"So you like the scenery."

"And I've eaten at the same restaurant." She paused. "In the same booth."

"Must be good food with a good view."

"At the same time every day."

"Hmmm. And the food? Is that the same too?"

"I usually pick the special of the day."

"How daring of you."

"I told you. Just plain old ordinary."

"That's not plain old ordinary, Sara. That's plain old weird."

She laughed, a light trickling sound that coursed through him like wildfire, heating his blood, making him realize once again how far from ordinary she was. At least compared to the women who usually occupied his time. They all came with agendas, timetables, and expectations, their words calculated down to the smallest preposition. They were hunters, all of them, armed with insincere praise and bright red smiles, aimed directly at him.

The hunted.

He knew the game, knew how to play it, even got a certain amount of perverse pleasure twisting their psyches into knotted cords of confusion.

But Sara was different. Her open honesty and sincere words bore no signs of entrapment. She made him relax, feel comfortable with her and with himself, despite his blindness. He'd spent half of last night plotting his book and his life, something he wouldn't have considered possible a month ago.

A month ago, he'd had no life.

Sara had given it back to him. She'd paved the way, led him through anger and despair to the other side, where hope and new beginnings dwelt.

She'd pierced his heart with her genuineness. No facades. No gimmicks. No ploys.

Just Sara. Intoxicating. Exhilarating. Fresh. Unique. Sara.

Brimming with sensuality, yet refusing to acknowledge the word.

"Matt?" Her voice broke through his thoughts. "Are you stuck on my 'weirdness' or is Jack Steele running through his come-on lines?"

He laughed. Add sense of humor to her attributes. "Relax. You're a cute weird. And as for Jack," he rubbed his chin, "he's about to get the shock of his life."

"Let me guess. His former conquests close in on him, choking out his space, red nails poised and ready for clawing."

"Better." He grinned. "The brunette turns around and he finds himself staring at the most arresting pair of amber-green eyes he's ever seen. His mouth opens, but the words won't come."

"Jack Steele left speechless?" Sara laughed. "Now that's a first."

"Oh, yeah. This little lady's gonna give him a lot of firsts."

"My heroine." He heard the humor in her voice. "Does this wonder have a name?"

"Of course."

"Well? Shall I start with A and work my way through the alphabet or do you just want to make it a little easier and tell me?"

Matt crossed his arms over his chest and leaned back in his chair, a slow smile spreading over his lips. He'd give just about anything to see her face right now. "Well," he began, his voice low and soft, "considering the fact that this woman is going to challenge him at every turn, test every bone in his body, and drive him absolutely wild," he paused, "I thought I'd call her Sara."

Thirteen

"No, I don't mind staying, Jeff." Sara gripped the receiver, trying to ignore the sudden pang in her chest at the mention of heading back to Pittsburgh. It was too soon. Much too soon. She couldn't think about leaving. Not yet.

She forced the next words past her lips. "Yes, we're working quite well together. Uh-huh." She blinked hard. "Yes. He's a pretty special guy." A flash of silver darted through her mind, tugging at her senses with memories of Matt's slow steady smile and deep rich laughter.

No. She couldn't leave yet.

"Another month? Sure. That would be fine." *How about another two months? Two years? Two lifetimes? Maybe that would be enough. Maybe. But probably not.*

"I'm so happy Nina's doing well. Just a little while longer and you'll be holding a baby in your arms." Her voice was soft, encouraging, hopeful for the unborn child who'd already claimed his parents' hearts and dreams.

Jeff spent the next several minutes informing her of the baby's preferences. He or she, as it were, kicked harder when Bach was playing as opposed to Beethoven, but Mozart seemed a soothing second choice. Pasta Primavera won over Fettuccine Alfredo every time and Beatrix Potter was more relaxing than the Brothers Grimm.

Sara nodded, her lips tugging at the corners as she pictured Jeff reciting the tale of Squirrel Nutkin. "I'm so happy for both of you. Give Nina my best and let her know she's in my prayers." *Dear God, keep this child safe.*

"Hey, California girl, how's it going?" Jessie's voice boomed into the receiver, a sharp contrast to Jeff's low, controlled timbre.

"Hi, Jessie. How are you?"

"Great. Just great. Things are really moving here, Sara. You'd be proud of me. Guess what? April got the job!" Jessie's words bubbled over the phone, her enthusiasm grabbing hold, spilling through the line. "She can't believe it. Administrative Assistant to the V.P. of Marketing at Alltron!"

"That's wonderful," Sara said, thinking of the meek little horn-rimmed woman, who, six months before couldn't maintain three seconds of eye contact, let alone promote herself or her capabilities for employment. Six months before, April Pearson didn't know she possessed worthwhile, marketable qualities.

But now she did.

She was the latest success story of determination winning over degradation. Perseverance championing humiliation. Honesty and integrity triumphing over deceit and denial.

April had done it. She had stripped away the cloak of inferiority bestowed on her by a bitter abusive mate and armed herself with a shield of positive affirmations that repelled doubt and self-recrimination.

She had won.

"And Heather?" she ventured, hoping for the same uplifting news. "How is she?"

There was a pause at the other end of the line, followed by a long sigh. "No good. She's back with that jerk."

"I was really hoping she'd make the break this time."

"Not with the way this guy's been after her. He's been giving her the works. Flowers, dinner, love notes. The whole bit." Jesse's next words dripped disgust like a leaky faucet. "Said he'd never look at another woman again."

"And she believed him," Sara said, sickened by the string of empty meaningless words slapped together like a day-old Band-Aid on an open wound. There just wasn't any stick.

"Of course."

"Of course," Sara echoed, her voice a mere whisper, her mind fast-forwarding to the inevitable pain that awaited Heather the next time her husband cheated.

And there would be a next time. There always was.

"I'm just sitting tight, waiting for her world to come crashing down, like it does every six months or so," Jessie said.

"That's all you can do. Maybe one of these days, she'll get hit in the head with a little common sense and realize she can't build her future in the path of a tornado that levels everything twice a year, like clockwork."

"I'd like to level *him*. The jerk."

"Me, too," Sara agreed.

They spent the next several minutes discussing other clients. Most were on the right path or at least getting off the wrong one.

"So tell me," Jessie asked, when the last client's method of care had been strategized, "how's Matt?"

"Fine." *Very fine.*

"I'll bet." There was unmistakable female interest in her voice. "Did he lose the glasses yet?"

"He did, as a matter of fact," Sara said, trying to downplay her answer.

"And?"

"He has very nice eyes."

"*Nice* eyes?" Jessie squeaked. "Either you're the one who's blind or you need to take a better look. He's got *incredible* eyes."

Like a sliver of moon on a black night, Sara thought. "I have to admit I've never seen anyone with that shade of silver-gray." She tried to make her voice sound matter-of-fact. "I wonder if he gets it from his mother or father."

Laughter tinkled through the line. "Oh, Sara. Only you would be thinking about genealogy when you looked at him. The rest of the female population would be oohing and ahhing over the man, studying every delectable inch of him."

"For heaven's sake, you make him sound like a dessert."

"Hmmm. And I'll bet he'd be quite a tasty one, too. Kind of like a big piece of chocolate cake with sprinkles on top."

"Well, I wouldn't know." *Liar. You know exactly what he tastes like. And he's much more tantalizing than plain old chocolate cake. More like a double fudge brownie, smothered in chocolate sauce, with a glob of whipped cream surrounding it. And a maraschino cherry on top.*

Jessie sighed. "That's why it's a good thing you're there and I'm not."

"What are you talking about?" Sometimes Jessie made about as much sense as an infant trying to mouth his first words.

"You're so unaffected by Matt Brandon. You can look at him every day and not get lost in the pure magnetism of the man, like I would."

Right.

"I mean, if it were me, I'd be head over heels for him."

I'm afraid I'm halfway there. Sara squeezed her eyes shut. "You don't know that."

"Yes, I do." She spoke with the confidence of one who's spent long hours contemplating the matter. "I couldn't resist him, Sara. Not like you. You can be so intellectual about everything, remain so detached."

If you only knew.

"That's one of the reasons why you're so perfect for him."

Perfect? "I don't know about that."

"Yes, you are. It's *so* obvious. And then," she paused a second, "there's the big reason."

"Which is?" Sara held her breath. What else was there?

"You'd never be foolish enough to fall in love with him."

The phone slipped from her hand, crashing against the desk with a loud thwack. Sara gasped, scrambling for the receiver. "Oh, Jessie, I'm so sorry. The phone . . . it fell."

"That's okay. My hearing will never be the same, but I'll forgive you, if you get me an autographed copy of one of 'Mr. Beautiful's' books."

"Which one?"

"Dangerous Secrets is my favorite." She sighed. "It's got the best picture of him." Her voice lowered to a whisper. "Those lips are something else. Full. Firm. Sensual. If I close my eyes I can almost feel them on mine."

Sara shook her head, chasing images of Matt's mouth from her brain. "You're crazy."

"I know. See why it's a good thing I'm not there? He needs someone like you. Steady. Strong. Immune."

"Sounds like a new vaccine."

Jessie laughed. "You know what I mean. Your heart is safe. You're much too sensible to fall for someone like him."

That's what I thought, too. "You're right."

"Well, gotta run. April's stopping by to fill me in on her first week at Alltron."

"Take care. And give her my best."

"Will do. Toodles."

The phone clicked on the other end. Sara placed the receiver in its cradle, and sank back in the leather chair, rubbing her temples.

What was she doing? Was she crazy? Jessie's words buzzed in her head, making her dizzy. *You'd never be foolish enough to fall in love with him.*

She was right, of course. She *wasn't* that foolish. Was she? Her fingers worked the dull ache on both sides of her head, trying to smooth away the pain, erase the words she didn't want to hear.

Getting involved with a man, especially one like Matt Brandon, was not something Sara had ever planned to let happen again. Men had their uses. In small defined doses. And at designated distances. They provided pleasant companionship at infrequent intervals, occasional dinner conversation when desired, and rare accompaniment to necessary functions. As long as they stayed within those parameters, she felt comfortable. In control. Almost relaxed.

But Matt played like a pinch hitter with a full count in the ninth inning of a tied game. He went for broke, slamming the bat against the ball, sending it careening into the stands with the force of a small rocket.

He played for keeps.

And word had it he usually won.

So, how did she fit in? If she scraped away the ten-dollar words and pawed through the deep, soft articulation that made most women swoon, what was left? Was there truth and depth of feeling underneath or was it just more empty calories on an already too sweet confection?

And if the words were sincere, then what? Could she risk opening herself up to the hurt and the pain of loving all over again, risk having her self-respect torn to shreds if he tired of her? Love carried no guarantees. She'd learned that harsh lesson when Brian had stuffed a piece of paper into her hand and walked out of the hospital room and out of her life.

It had been his new phone number. *To be used only in case of extreme emergency,* he'd scrawled in the corner. She'd torn it into tiny pieces and threw it in the air like confetti. That was the last day she cried for "what might have been."

Was she capable of even *thinking* about that kind

of pain again? Something told her she was on the brink of exposing herself to that same kind of brutal heartache if she became involved with Matt.

Did she really want to do that? Did she have a choice or was it already too late? She ran her fingers through her hair, closed her eyes, heaved a sigh. Why couldn't she be like the millions of people who engaged in casual sex? Why did she have to *care* about the other individual?

Lots of women dabbled in recreational sex without regret. Why couldn't she be one of them? Settle for being the pinch hitter, scoring once in a while, but with no real identity, other than filling in when the big guns weren't hitting?

Why? Why? Why?

Sara knew the answer, even if her brain didn't want to register it. There was no sense imagining herself any different, because in the depths of her soul, she knew that her reality existed in the strong, steady, committed relationship between a man and a woman. All or nothing.

There had been no men since Brian. Not even in her dreams. But now, Matt Brandon invaded not only her sleep, but great pieces of her waking moments, in both thought and human form.

If she were honest with herself, she'd admit that she was getting used to, even looking forward to, their time together. And she wanted more. He'd told her five days ago that she would set the pace and he'd been true to his word. There had been no overt caresses, no insinuations. He'd been polite, courteous, proper.

And it was driving her absolutely mad.

She wanted to feel his fingers on her skin, taste his mouth on hers, his tongue searching, exploring, conquering. But that wasn't all. There was a longing, deep inside, to touch *him*, to feel the warm, welcoming strength of his body beneath her fingertips as she pulled him to her. Closer. Closer. Until he blanketed her, covering every inch of her like new-fallen snow.

And then she wanted to feel him sink into her, join their bodies in one perfect union.

She wanted him to make love to her.

The admission hit her like a hard ball crashing home plate. For the first time since her husband, she wanted a man in a very elemental, physical way. And it scared her to death.

Giving her body to Matt was a pledge, a promise on her part, that went much deeper than the flesh. But would he share those sentiments? Would he consider her anything more than a willing, convenient pastime?

Of course, he wanted her now. But what about tomorrow? And all of the tomorrows after that? Could she have a relationship with him that had no boundaries? No rules? No commitments? Her head throbbed with indecision, ached with the other question that loomed like a dark shadow.

Could she walk away from the heat that smoldered between them, walk away from the finger-curling, breathtaking, heart-stopping passion that she knew lay just beneath the surface of civility she and Matt shared?

And what of other women? Gabrielle was long gone, shooed away five days ago on her stiletto heels with Jimmy toting her Louis Vuitton bags behind her. Not a pleasant sight, but a most gratifying one. A small smile crept to Sara's lips. It lasted a space of about three seconds as she recalled the appraising female looks that seemed to follow Matt wherever he went. Since the ball game, they'd been to Dana Point twice, taken a walk on the beach and eaten lunch in an open-air café. Each time, women poured over him like maple syrup, thick and sweet.

There would always be women; of that, she was certain. But would there come a time when the smile he gave them would turn from polite to inviting? When he would reach for the plastic-shaped, silicone-stuffed, scarlet-dressed Barbie dolls of his past?

And if that time came, then what? Sara leaned forward, burying her head in her hands.

Then she would die.

"I can't wait to see you," Adam said. "Have you missed me as much as I've missed you?"

Sara clutched the receiver, grasping for a response, hovering between a blatant lie and the bald truth. She settled for a lukewarm half truth.

"I'm looking forward to seeing you, too, Adam." *But not in the way you think.*

"Great. My flight's getting in around four. Be ready to go at six."

"What?"

He laughed, a lighthearted sound that filled the receiver. "I'm taking you out. We're celebrating the completion of the merger. And," he added, his voice lowering, "the end of my time away."

Great. "Great." She decided to play dumb. "I'll make sure Matt's ready by then."

"Matt? He's not invited. It's just you and me."

Time to hedge. "I don't think he'd like the idea

too much. You know he's very territorial with his time."

"He's just being a pain, as usual. Besides, it's after five. Free time, remember?"

Somehow, she didn't think Matt would look at it that way. "I . . . don't know."

"Come on, Sara," he coaxed, "it's not like he has any claim on you after-hours. You're free to do whatever you want."

Am I?

"Say yes."

She took a deep breath. Maybe she should go out with Adam and give him the news in private. They were friends. Good friends. But it could never be more than that.

Not when she might be half in love with his older brother.

But that was another issue and she had no intention of disclosing that information. To anyone. Not even Matt.

"Okay," she found herself saying. "I'll be ready."

"Great. See you then."

"See you then," she echoed, replacing the receiver with a quiet click.

Time to tell Matt. Her palms grew sweaty just thinking of the confrontation. She hadn't seen him since her phone call from Jessie. Hadn't seen him since she admitted her feelings for him might run much deeper than casual concern or companionable friendship.

A quick glance in the mirror told her she looked as frazzled as she felt. Her thick hair stuck out in random tufts from one too many overanxious finger rakings. The deep furrows on her forehead were almost as numerous as the creases in her cot-

ton shift. Using all ten fingers, Sara tried to smooth
out her hair, face, and clothes. Not that Matt would
know, but looking neat gave her a sense of control.
And she needed all the control she could muster
to tell him she'd just accepted a date from his
younger brother.

"Absolutely not."

"I wasn't asking for your permission. I was *informing* you I wouldn't be here for dinner."

Matt's fists clenched like a fighter ready to strike.
Damn her! How could she sit there and spout off
her plans when she knew damned well what his
reaction would be? He'd warned her to stay away
from Adam, told her not to encourage him in any
way. For Christ's sake, the guy had been falling all
over himself trying to get her attention from the
day she walked through the door.

But had she listened? Of course not. And why?
Hell if he knew. Maybe she was going to play him
and Adam against each other, watch them duke it
out, see who came out on top. Sara didn't seem
like that type of person, but life was full of sur-
prises. The stakes were high and she could do
worse than to end up with one of them. Who
knew? Maybe she was getting tired of life in Pittsburgh and wanted to coast along the sunny shores
of California for a while.

Of course, there was always the second possibility, the one that made his blood boil. She might
be trying to make him jealous by using Adam. The
mere thought drove him wild. Little Red Riding
Hood from Pittsburgh had no idea what she was
up against if she was trying to hoodwink him. He'd

make the Big Bad Wolf look like a kitten. After all, more skilled women had tried, using much more sophisticated tactics.

And failed.

But this one had him on the ropes and it annoyed the hell out of him.

"Why do you want to make a fool of him?" he asked.

"I'd never do that."

Matt rubbed his jaw, settled his gaze in the direction of her voice. Time to go for pay dirt. "If you're trying to make me jealous, it won't work."

She gasped. "Jealous?" He heard her move toward him in quick even steps. He guessed she was less than a foot from his bent knees. Her citrus scent swirled around him. *Damnit, hadn't he told her not to wear that perfume again?* "Why would I do a thing like that?"

"Why, indeed?" he asked, his voice smooth and silky. "Maybe you're looking for some kind of commitment from me, before we," he paused to emphasize his next words, *"intensify* our relationship."

"That's ridiculous."

"Is it?" The more he thought about it, the more plausible it seemed. "We both know we've been dying to get into each other's pants, almost from the beginning. You, because of some uptight morality, want it tied up nice and sweet in the name of pledge or commitment or whatever in the hell else will let you sleep with me and not feel guilty about it."

She didn't respond, but he could hear her breathing, hard and heavy, just a few steps away.

Of course she wasn't talking. What could she say? "You found me out?"

"Well, it won't work, Sara." The vein in his forehead throbbed. "Your little ploy to have me crawling at your feet just backfired." His lips curved into a cold smile. "I don't crawl for anybody, no matter how good they feel in my hands." He settled back in his chair and locked his arms behind his head. "Understand?"

"Perfectly." One word, carved out of ice, as frigid as the North Pole.

"Good."

"Is that all?" A second glacier, bigger than the first.

"There is one more thing," he said, trying to keep his voice calm. Quite a remarkable feat, for a man whose anger threatened to explode any second in one violent attack. "I don't care what you do, or who you do it with, but don't you dare make a fool of Adam or you'll answer to me."

He heard her footsteps, heavy on the carpet, turn and walk away. The door clicked and she was gone, taking with her the joy and sunshine he'd felt since she'd come into his life.

Cursing her, himself and the world in general, Matt worked his way to the small bar at the far side of the room and poured himself a Scotch. He downed it in one healthy swallow, enjoying the burn.

And then he poured another.

Fourteen

"It was incredible, really. The whole deal went better than I ever anticipated."

"Hmmm," Sara murmured, only half listening to Adam's soft voice recounting the details of the merger.

How could Matt say such a thing? Accusing her of trying to make him jealous? It was ridiculous, beyond ridiculous. She speared a piece of meat and brought it to her mouth. What the heck had she ordered, anyway? Tuna steak or chicken? Popping it into her mouth, she let her taste buds decide. Tuna steak. At least some of her senses were still working.

"And I thought since I'll be in town more often . . ."

"Hmmm." What was that bit about *intensifying the relationship?* Hah. If he thought he'd *ever* get within five feet of her again, well, he could just think again. And if he tried, she'd sock him but good, blind or not.

". . . we'll be able to see each other on a more personal level."

"Hmmm." The tuna steak was superb. Matt was right. Pacific tuna was much better than the East

Coast variety. Matt, Matt, Matt. Why couldn't she get the man out of her head? She was through with him. For good.

She stabbed another piece of tuna. *Take that, Matthew Brandon.*

The sound of Adam's laughter brought her out of her dark musings. "And here I always thought attacking one's food was a figure of speech."

Sara looked at the fork in her hand and the impaled fish on the tines. Heat climbed to her cheeks as she forced a little laugh. "It's good," she said, plunking it into her mouth.

"What's wrong, Sara? You haven't heard a word I've said all night." His tone was gentle, encouraging, like a priest ready to hear confession. It took every inch of reserve not to spill the whole sordid story.

"Nothing's wrong," she lied, jabbing a green bean. "I guess I'm just a little preoccupied tonight."

His eyes narrowed. "A *little* preoccupied? I've asked you to go to Hawaii, New York, and London with me three times in the last three minutes and all you could do was say 'hmmm.' "

"Hmmm? I mean, I did?" Her face grew warmer. Damn Matthew Brandon. It was all his fault. "I'm sorry."

"What's going on, Sara?" He took a sip of wine, studied her.

"Nothing," she said, taking a sudden, avid interest in the length and symmetry of the six string beans remaining on her plate. Three long and lean, the rest short and plump. And then there were the scattered bits of tuna. She'd massacred them pretty well, but they formed an intriguing pattern of sorts if one studied it closely enough. And she was doing just that.

Anything to avoid Adam's watchful stare.

"Look at me, Sara." It was a command, a departure from his usual soft-spoken manner.

She looked up, met his gaze. He wasn't smiling. His face looked serious, determined. No wonder he had such success in the corporate arena. In his own quiet way, he could be as forceful as his brother.

He smiled then, a warm boyish grin that wiped away his earlier sternness, reminding her of the first time they'd met. This was the Adam she knew and liked. Easygoing, with a ready smile and a quick wit. Fun. Free. Undemanding. Unlike his older brother.

"Is it me? Have I moved too fast?" His tone was gentle, concerned.

Sara shook her head. "Of course not. You've been nothing but kind to me." *Unlike your brother.*

"Kind?" He ran a hand through his blond hair. "Kind is reserved for friends. I think you know I want to be more than your friend."

She swallowed. Hard. "I . . . I don't know what to say."

"Say you'll think about it. Say I have a shot. Say you're thrilled, but not quite ready." His lips curved up. "Say anything, but don't say no."

"Adam—"

He put a finger to his lips. "Don't say anything right now. Just think about it. Okay?"

What was there to think about? What was there to say? *I've fallen for a jerk. Again. And this one's your brother.* She couldn't do that. Not to Adam.

There had to be another way without stripping him of his pride. It was the least she could do.

Sara fastened her gaze on his and spoke the words she hadn't said in over three years. "I was married before."

It all spilled out after that, the pitiful tale of the cheating husband and the abandoned woman, beaten down and left to dig her way back to humanity. The lost child, buried, but never forgotten. The weeks of depression, lying in a bed where hours stretched into infinity and day ran into night with no hopes, no dreams, no possibilities. And the recovery, one step at a time, leading to a pledge to help all women survive similar abuse and go on to carve out healthy, productive lives.

"I had no idea," Adam said when she finished.

Sara gave a little half smile and shrugged. "Not many people do. Just Jeff and a few close friends. And my clients of course. They're all women who've been in battered relationships, like me. That's why they come to me." She toyed with her spoon. "I guess you could call me a 'work in progress.'"

"Do you have family?"

"Just an older brother in the military. I see him once or twice a year when he's on leave."

"I see."

He looked at her and she saw the sympathy and compassion on his face.

"Please don't feel sorry for me. I believe in destiny, no matter how painful. And it was beyond painful; it had to happen. I couldn't have lived that kind of life, never knowing if my husband would come home at night. And if he did, where he'd been."

"The bastard," Adam said under his breath.

"Yes, he was. But I've gotten on with my life. I've forgiven him." Her eyes misted. "And as for Rebecca . . . it just wasn't meant to be." Her voice was full of whispered pain. "But not a day goes by that I don't think of her."

"I'm so sorry, Sara." He reached across the table and grasped her hand. "I really am."

She sniffed, swiped at her eyes. "Thank you."

His grip tightened. "I would never do that to you." His gray eyes bore into her. "Never."

She remained silent, watching the open honesty on his face. She believed him. He wouldn't hurt her. Most likely, given the opportunity, he would spend his life trying to make her happy. There was just one little problem.

She wasn't in love with him. Not now, not ever.

"All I'm asking for is a chance to show you that love doesn't have to turn out that way. It could be good between us." His warm fingers stroked her hand. "Once you learn to trust me, you'll realize I'd never hurt you. Never," he whispered. "And then you'll be able to open up and care again."

"Adam—" she started, determined to steer him away from seeing them as a couple.

"Just think about it," he said, cutting her off. "I've got a long list of credentials." He held up five fingers, ticking them off as he spoke. "Dependable. Trustworthy. Honorable. Good sense of humor. Picks up after himself." Laughing, he said, "That's my whole hand, and I've got a lot more. Let's see. Generous. Likes good restaurants. Knows how to cook. Will clean, on occasion."

Sara stifled a laugh. "You're crazy."

"Thank you. That's another quality. Crazy when

needed." Scratching his head, he pretended confusion. "That's all? I know there are at least two hundred more."

"Make sure you add modest to that list."

"Ah, yes, modesty."

"Thank you, Adam."

"For what?"

"For making me smile. I needed it. Especially tonight."

"It's all part of the package." He winked at her. "Just remember that when you consider my résumé."

"Crazy and persistent," she said, laughing again.

"Hey, it could be worse. You could be considering Matt's résumé." Adam closed his eyes and placed a hand on his forehead. "Let me think a minute. Attributes . . . attributes. Hmmm. He's a little light in that area. How about plain old character traits? Or should we say flaws?" He chuckled. "Let's see. Moody, forceful, opinionated, gruff." He laughed again. "Actually, it's all just an act. Underneath, he's a big teddy bear, with a soft spot where his brain should be when it comes to the less fortunate." He shook his head. "That's why he hires help he doesn't need. He can't say no."

"He doesn't let many people see that side of him," Sara said. But she'd seen it, glimpsed the real Matthew Brandon beneath layers of arrogance and disinterest. And liked what she'd seen. Very much.

"Women would attack him if they knew he was such a nice guy. The tabloids paint him as a crazed, self-absorbed womanizer. Yet, would you believe women still flock to him, desperate for a crumb of affection or a scrap of acknowledgement?"

It was a rhetorical question, intended for no one, spoken as a matter of course. But the words hit Sara, as though he'd looked into her heart and dug out the truth, like a scavenger on a hunt.

"Who would be foolish enough . . ." His words hung in the air, suspended, threatening to drop like a lead weight, right in the middle of her heart. She squeezed her eyes shut, trying to get past his words. When she opened them, he was staring at her. ". . . to fall in love . . . with that miserable . . . tyrant?" His voice drifted off, over the brink of recognition, into silence.

She clamped her mouth shut, her heart beating in her throat. Had he guessed? He was looking at her, with an odd sort of light in his eyes. His fingers moved from her hand to cup his chin in a pensive sort of way.

Beneath the table, Sara balled her hand into a tight fist, waiting for his next words. She prayed he hadn't guessed. Prayed he didn't know what a fool she'd been. And now he would feel like a fool, too. Maybe, just maybe, he hadn't seen the shock on her face when he'd started talking about Matt's love life.

"I see," he said.

She drew in a deep breath, trying to still her nerves.

"Does Matt know?"

Three little words that told her Adam knew. She shook her head, unable to speak, unable to tell him how sorry she was.

He blew out a long breath. "I see."

She hated herself at that moment for hurting this kind, gentle man. Hated herself for not loving someone as noble and good as he was. And she hated Matthew Brandon, too, for not playing by the rules, for not being kind and noble, like his brother.

But most of all, she hated him for not loving her back.

Adam steepled his fingers under his chin and stared at a space behind her left ear. "Guess this makes me the number one fool of the century." He tried to laugh, a short little sound that ended on a flat rumble.

"I'm so sorry, Adam," Sara said, pinching the bridge between her nose. "You're a wonderful man and I wouldn't hurt you for anything in the world."

"But I'm not my brother, am I?" His words were tight, filled with traces of bitterness and something that sounded an awful lot like resignation.

Sara said nothing.

Adam shrugged. "As you said before, 'everything happens for a reason.'" He rubbed his hand over his face and sighed. "But you were so different. So real. So unlike his other women."

"I'm not his woman. At least not the way you mean."

He ignored her denial, swatting it away like a bothersome fly. "I've never wanted any of Matt's women before. Never." His eyes met hers then. They were full of hurt and sadness. "And if I didn't love him so much, I'd hate him."

Sara swallowed. "I think I know the feeling."

"He's never had a woman like you before."

"He doesn't have me, Adam. And I don't think he really wants *me*. Not the me who would expect a commitment, require absolute fidelity . . . and love." She shook her head as the reality of her own words filtered through her brain. "That's not his style. We both know that."

"He's a damn fool if he lets you get away."

"Maybe. But only if he's looking for the same thing I am."

"I don't want to see you get hurt again."

A faint smile played about her lips. "I'm already hurting, Adam. The minute I opened myself up to care about him, I started hurting. I guess that's why I refused to get involved with anyone for so long." She picked up a spoon and stirred her coffee, watching the brown liquid lap the sides of the cup. "I liked living in my own little world. There were bars on the windows and an iron gate protecting my heart. Nobody could get in and no feelings could get out." A splash of coffee sloshed over the sides of her cup. "Until Matt."

"God, what a mess."

"Life usually is."

"So, now what? Are you going to let him know how you feel?"

Sara let out a small laugh. "Of course not. Things could never work between us."

"I see," he said, using that little phrase she was beginning to recognize. It really meant, *I see more than you think I do*. He rubbed his jaw. "So . . . you're not going to say anything to him. And you plan on working beside him . . . every day, guarding your emotions like a mother hen so he'll never guess your true feelings. And then, when your job is done, you'll run back to Pittsburgh with your broken heart leaving a bloody trail behind."

"Well, kind of. I hadn't really thought about the incidentals, or the analogies," she added, raising a brow, "but, yes. I guess that about sums it up."

"Not that I would venture to advise you, seeing as I haven't been too successful in my own love life, but don't you think he deserves to know how you feel?"

"No!" The word flew out of her mouth in a big *whoosh*. "No," she repeated, in a calmer tone, ignoring the rapid-fire beat of her pulse, "I don't."

"Mind if I ask why?"

"Because he made his feelings toward me very clear the last time I saw him." *I don't care what you do or who you do it with. . . .* The words still stabbed at her, tearing at the wound, ripping it open for a fresh bleed. Brushing a stray lock of hair from her forehead, she met Adam's gaze and said, "There's no hope for us. None at all."

Where the hell was she? And what the hell was she doing at this hour in the morning? Matt's fingers whisked over the watch on his left wrist, calculating the hour for the tenth time in as many minutes. One-thirty. He'd ring her neck when he got ahold of her. Then he'd tell her that her silly schoolgirl attempt to make him jealous hadn't worked.

Not at all.

He was just feeling edgy right now. Very edgy. And furious that she'd try such a childish ploy to trap him into admitting he cared. Of course, that's what she was doing. Why else would she be out with Adam half the night? It wasn't as though she was interested in him. Was it? That thought hadn't even entered his mind until this second. *Could* she be interested in Adam? Matt raked a hand through his curly hair. No. Of course not. He and Sara had an understanding. Sort of. Didn't they?

Shit. He was so goddamned tired of her games. She was driving him crazy with all of her psychology mumbo jumbo, making him think about his feelings, instead of just acting on them, as he was used to doing. He'd survived on gut instinct for thirty-seven years. Why all of a sudden did one woman have him second-guessing himself?

Hell if he knew. But it was going to stop. Now. Tonight. As soon as she walked through that door. His fingers flew over his watch again. One thirty-five. He cursed under his breath.

Just as soon as she walked through that door . . .

He'd wait here, in her room, for as long as it took. All night if necessary, but he would have answers.

Matt slouched down, resting his head on the back of the overstuffed chair and kicked his feet out in front of him. He closed his eyes and crossed his hands over his stomach, trying to concentrate on his breathing. *Relax,* he told himself. *Breathe. Just breathe.*

The familiar, tantalizing fragrance of orange and lemon filled his nostrils. He'd smelled it the second he sneaked into her room, but now it was stronger, more powerful. Turning his head toward the scent, he felt the soft caress of silk across his cheek. He reached out and pulled the swatch of material from behind his head. His fingers ran over the fabric. There wasn't much to it, but it was bathed in oranges and lemons. He brought the material to his nose and inhaled, breathing in the essence of the woman who wore it.

Mesmerizing.

Like the woman.

He traced two thin straps and a scant edging of lace. Sara's nightgown.

Uttering a foul curse, he sat up, wadded it into a small ball, and heaved it across the room.

Witch! Even now she was trying to exercise her power over him. But he'd show her that she had no control over him *or* his feelings. None. He couldn't even smell her citrus scent in the room anymore.

Not at all.

And he wasn't going to spend one more second analyzing his recent, semi-irrational behavior. He didn't want to try to figure out why he was really sitting in Sara's bedroom waiting for her to come home. Nor did he want to delve into the intricacies of his agitation over her being out with his brother. Or why the mere whiff of her scent tripled his pulse rate.

And there was no way he'd even think about the gnawing twist in the pit of his stomach. So what if it had manifested itself after his blowup with Sara? It didn't mean he cared about her. Or that he was sorry for blasting her.

It didn't mean anything.

Did it?

Jesus, he must be losing his mind. He couldn't even formulate a single thought without doubt casting its shadowy finger on him.

Sara Hamilton was doing this. He pinched the bridge of his nose with his thumb and forefinger. She was making him crazy. Totally crazy.

And he was going to put an end to it.

Tonight.

Just as soon as she walked through that door . . .

At ten minutes after two, he heard the low hum of Adam's Mercedes. A year ago he wouldn't have noticed it. But the loss of his sight had kicked his other senses into overdrive, enabling him to experience everything with much greater clarity.

That's why he heard the back door open and the subsequent murmur of hushed voices moving down the hall. Two pair of footsteps . . . stopping in front of Sara's room. Matt strained to hear the whispered words but they were too faint.

The click of the doorknob pricked his nerves, sent his pulse racing, slamming his heart into his throat. He heard the flick of a light switch and a second click.

She was in the room.

Any second now she'd turn around and . . .

Her sharp gasp filled the air.

Matt's lips curved into a humorless smile. "Miss me, sweetheart?"

Fifteen

"What are you doing here?"

Matt's lips curled into a snarl. "I live here."

"You know what I mean. What are you doing *here*, in my bedroom?"

He gave a short hard laugh and muttered something under his breath. "I wanted to make sure you got home safe."

Sara moved a few steps closer, sensing the anger coiled just beneath the surface, waiting to unleash itself.

On her.

"Well, here I am. You can leave now."

"I could," he agreed, rubbing his stubbled jaw. "Or I could wait and tuck you in." He paused. "Or get in with you."

"Get out."

"Would you say that to Adam?" His words were bitter, cutting.

"That's sick." She folded her arms across her middle, trying to protect herself from his cruel words. What was wrong with him? Why was he playing the jealous lover when he'd made it very clear that he wasn't capable of such an emotion?

"Where were you?"

Sara clamped her mouth shut. She'd had about enough of his high-handed manner.

"I said, where were you?" he repeated, loud enough to be heard down the hall.

"Shhh. Everyone will hear you."

He dropped his voice several octaves to a menacing growl. "You've got exactly ten seconds to tell me what you were doing tonight."

She took two small steps backward. And then two more. Just to make certain he couldn't get her if he lunged in a fit of madness. He looked half crazy, teetering on the brink of insanity, with his dark hair sticking out on all sides, his silver eyes steady, staring right at her. As though he could see her.

"Adam and I went to dinner." One more step back.

"And?" A tiny muscle on the side of his jaw twitched.

"We talked."

"You talked." She ignored the mocking tone. "For *seven* hours?"

"We had a lot to say."

"I'll bet." Pause. "Do you realize you could have traveled to Pittsburgh in less time than that?"

Sara stared at him, wondering if he'd just taken the big dive into insanity. "I hadn't thought of that, but yes, I guess I could have done that."

"Yes, you could have."

She waited for him to elaborate, to make some kind of sense out of his garbled musings, to draw a parallel or two, but he didn't. Silence followed on long tentacles, enveloping, capturing, holding them prisoners in its web.

Sara was the first to break through the barrier. "Why are you here, Matt? What are you after?"

She was bone-weary from lack of sleep and mental exhaustion. Matt Brandon could do that to a person.

He leaned forward, elbows resting on his knees, hands clasped before him, and blew out a long breath. "Hell if I know."

"Exactly. You don't know." Her chest felt heavy, filled with heartache for a man who couldn't even tell her why he was in the same room with her. "Please . . . just go."

"I can't," he said, his voice hoarse, unnatural. As if in slow motion, he unfolded himself from the overstuffed chair and stood. "I can't go. I've been sitting in this chair for two and a half hours. Waiting. Asking myself why, at least two hundred times. Why I was in that ridiculous chair, counting the seconds until you walked through that door?"

Sara couldn't move. She hardly dared breathe. The man who'd been the cause of tonight's red eyes and swollen nose sounded as though he'd been having his own share of torment.

Matt raked both hands through his rumpled hair and shook his head. "I cursed you, told myself I was going to lay into you the minute you walked through that door." He let out a harsh little laugh. "And I tried. But now all I can think about is feeling your soft skin beneath my fingers and tasting those sweet lips."

"What . . . what . . . are you saying?"

He took a step forward. Slow. Cautious. As though he feared she might bolt. He ventured another two, and then one more. His words brushed over her like crumpled velvet. "I'm saying I didn't like how I felt when you were out with Adam."

Her heart skipped a beat.

He reached out, found her shoulder, ran his fingers down her bare arm. "I'm saying I was jealous, knee-deep in the green stuff and hating every minute of it."

She swallowed. "You? Jealous?"

His lopsided grin made her stomach do a flip-flop. "I guess there's a first for everything."

"I guess there is," she said, watching his fingers stroke her skin.

"Sara?"

If only she could wrap herself up in that voice, lose herself in the touch of those long lean fingers.

"Sara?" His tone was lower, more intimate.

"Yes?" She dragged her gaze from his fingers.

"I'm sorry for the things I said earlier today. I was trying to punish you instead of dealing with the situation."

That got her attention. "What situation?"

His fingers trailed up her arm, brushed her cheek, settled on her shoulder.

"Me. You. Us. The fact that I was half out of my mind thinking I'd driven you right into my brother's arms."

She reached up to stroke his stubbled cheek. "You didn't."

He crushed her against him, his large hands wrapping around her, pulling her into his warmth. "I care about you, Sara," he murmured, burying his face in her hair. "Very much."

"And I care about you. So much that it hurts," she whispered, blinking the moisture from her eyes.

He pulled back and found her lips, claiming her mouth in a searing kiss that promised what words could not. His tongue stroked and mated with hers, pleading, asking, demanding that she respond in kind.

And she did.

Sara wrapped her arms around his neck, sinking her fingers into the silky curls that brushed his nape. She rubbed her body against his, her nipples hardening as they touched his chest. His low growl made her bolder, made her want to please him, made her want to please herself. Drawing in his tongue, she sucked with long even strokes.

He groaned, cupping her buttocks with his hands and lifted her against his arousal.

It was her turn to groan.

They worked their way toward the bed, touching, teasing, tasting each other, anxious to have more, frustrated over not having enough. When her leg bumped the foot of the bed, Matt guided her, his hard body covering hers as he pressed her into the mattress.

His hands were everywhere. In her hair, on her shoulders, covering her breasts, stroking her legs. He couldn't seem to get enough of her. His fingers found the top button of her black cotton sundress and flipped it open. Then they attacked the next button. And the next, until the fabric fell aside, exposing scraps of lace and bare skin.

"You feel wonderful," he murmured, planting a kiss along the hollow of her throat. Sara smiled and eased the bottom of his shirt from his jeans.

"And you smell wonderful," he said, nuzzling his face in her hair. Her fingers inched the shirt up, found bare skin and muscle beneath.

"And you taste wonderful," he groaned, sinking his tongue into her mouth. She ran her nails down

his back and around to the front, circling the flat
planes of his stomach.

"Keep those hands moving like that and this will
be a very short night," he growled.

"I want to touch you." The need in her voice
surprised her.

"And I want you to touch me," he assured her.
"But not that well."

She laughed, a low throaty rumble filled with
desire. Her hands roamed over his thighs, moving
in long firm strokes, anxious to feel the flesh beneath the heavy material.

He seemed to know what she wanted, even if she
wasn't quite certain herself. He leaned up and tore
his shirt off, then went for his belt buckle.

Sara's hand shot out to stop him. "Let me."

His hand fell away and she leaned up, working
the buckle with jerky fingers. She should have been
nervous. She should have been filled with doubts,
reservations, and every other imaginable concern
possible. She should have been petrified to enter
into a relationship with this man.

But she wasn't.

Nothing had ever felt so right.

She slipped the leather through the buckle and
the belt fell open. Her hand slid over to touch the
metal button at the top of his jeans. His hips
jerked, telling her what he wanted. What he
needed.

Emotion took over then, coupled with raw physical desire, propelling her forward, making her
bold. Sara traced his arousal with one finger, learning the shape and feel of him. He sucked in air
like a man deprived of oxygen.

"Stop," Matt said, grabbing her hand. Small

beads of sweat broke out on his forehead. "Just . . . stop."

She watched him, confused. Maybe she wasn't pleasing him the way he liked. Brian had always accused her of not knowing how to take care of a man. Had he been right?

Pulling her hand away, she spoke in short choppy phrases. "I'm . . . sorry. Guess I'm not . . . very . . . good . . . at this sort of thing."

He let out a strangled laugh. "Honey, if you were any better, I'd be embarrassing myself right about now."

"Oh." Heat crept into her cheeks.

"Yeah. Oh." Easing himself off the bed, he took a step and reached out to locate the nightstand. He pulled the door open, fished around a few seconds before pulling out a handful of colored little packets and dropping them onto the bed.

Condoms.

So many of them.

"Personal inventory?" The sight of them hit her like a punch in the stomach. How many other women had been privy to Matt's private stock of brightly colored latex?

He shook his head. "No. I stuck these in here after that morning in the kitchen." He flushed a dull shade of red. "I . . . just in case."

"Oh."

"Jimmy got them for me."

"*Jimmy?*" she squeaked. "You sent *Jimmy* out for these things?" Her gaze shot over the labeling. " 'Good fit, great feel?' 'Extra ribbed for heightened pleasure?' 'Just like the real thing?' "

She'd never be able to face Jimmy again.

"It's okay," he assured her. "Jimmy's been bet-ting we'd get together from the minute you walked through my door."

"But does he have to know about 'great feel and heightened pleasure'?" She picked up a purple packet and read, "Passion's Plum—exotic, erotic, endless." Tossing it aside, she chose a yellow one. "Love's Lemon—tart, tasty, titillating." She threw it across the room and hung her head. "How humiliating."

"I'm sorry, Sara." Matt's deep voice reached through her mire of self-pity. "I wasn't sure . . . there were so many. . . ." He stumbled, started again, "I wasn't sure what you might . . ." His voice trailed off into awkward silence.

She lifted her head, saw the dull flush on his cheeks. Matt Brandon, embarrassed?

"It's okay," she said, touched that he would go to such lengths to consider her preferences. Not that she had any in her limited, one-dimensional, "I hate latex," experience with her ex-husband.

"How about Paradise in Pink?" she asked, picking up a light scarlet-rimmed foil packet.

"Sure," he said in a low sensual drawl that sent tingles through her. "Sounds good. For starters."

He smiled down at her then, that broad white-toothed smile that made her forget her next word and every one after that for a solid thirty seconds. Her lips curved upward in response, even though she knew he couldn't see her. He'd be able to feel it, sense it in the gentleness of her touch, hear it in the softness of her voice.

He'd know her heart was smiling.

"I'm tired of talking, Sara," he said, hooking his thumbs in his belt loops. "I've got another form of communication in mind."

"Oh?" The little breathy voice didn't sound like her own.

His fingers settled on the fly of his jeans. "Yeah. It's especially useful when the words . . . just won't come." His lips turned up in a little half smile. "No pun intended." He inched the zipper down.

She tried to swallow, think of some witty response, but the words got caught in her throat. Her gaze shot to the spot of white cotton beneath his fingers. And the trail of dark hair tapering to a vee into his briefs. With casual grace and not a hint of self-consciousness, Matt pulled his jeans over his narrow hips and kicked them aside.

His smile was gone, replaced with desire, need, and determination.

For her. For what they were about to do.

Before her brain could register his actions, he slipped his thumbs in his briefs and pulled them off.

Matt Brandon in clothing was an appealing sight. But a naked Matt Brandon was simply overwhelming. The muscles of his arms and thighs, the flat plane of his stomach, the dark whorl of hair narrowing from his abdomen to his groin, all made him an objet d'art. As well as every woman's secret fantasy.

And then there was that *other* part of him, the one Sara's eyes kept flitting around and pretending she didn't notice. That part could keep a women's imagination well fed for a long, long time.

Matt sat down on the bed and reached for her. "I love your skin. Like brushed velvet, all soft and warm." He eased the dress from her shoulders. "I want to feel you beneath me." He slid her bra straps down.

His hands found her breasts, rubbed her nipples hard against his palms. She let out a low sigh. "And I want to hear you moan with pleasure when I suck you." He released the front clasp of her bra. Her breasts spilled into his hands. "When I lick you and take you into my mouth," he whispered.

His tongue found her nipple.

She moaned.

"Yes," he murmured, sucking and laving the swollen peak.

His hands were all over her then, stroking her breasts, her stomach, her thighs, stripping her of the silk underwear that provided the last barrier between them.

And then he touched her. *There.*

He caught her moan with his mouth, branding her with a fierce kiss of possession.

His fingers played over her mons, flicking her clitoris, tormenting her with desire. When he sunk a finger deep into her, she bucked against him.

He laughed, low in his throat, a deep husky sound that promised sensual pleasure. Her hips arched to meet his touch, slow and even at first, then faster in quick jerky thrusts. Every nerve in her body centered on the feel of his finger inside her, the flick of his thumb on her clitoris.

She sucked on his tongue, pulling him closer.

Deep inside, she felt the slow pulse building, threatening to explode with the heat of the next stroke. Sara rose to meet it, desperate to feel the explosion that could send her spiraling outside of herself.

One more flick. Two more strokes.

And she was airborne, convulsing beneath his touch. She tried to scream, but Matt stifled the sound with his mouth. Her hips flew off the bed, twisting against his hand, her body throbbing, pulsing with the swell of her climax.

When he released her mouth, she gasped for breath, panting and sucking in air. She pushed a damp strand of hair from her face and turned to look at the man who'd just given her such extreme, ultimate pleasure.

Matt.

He was resting on his elbow, a smile sliding across his lips.

He'd touched her.

Deep inside.

Touched her heart.

Touched her soul.

"Hello, beautiful," he whispered, stroking her cheek.

She turned her face into his hand, planted a small kiss there. "Hi."

"That was pretty fantastic."

"Yes, it was." Reaching beside her, she pulled out the pink-foiled packet and stuck it in his hand. "But it's far from over."

"Would you do the honors?"

"Of course," she said, taking the packet and ripping it open. She looked at the shiny pink ring of latex in her palm. Hmmm. Just because she'd never had occasion to use one before didn't mean she couldn't figure it out. After all, she was an educated woman. How difficult could it be?

Her left hand grasped his erection at the base while her right positioned the condom over the tip of his penis. She tried to unroll it, her fingers slick with lubricant. The condom didn't budge, but her fingers did. All the way down Matt's hard penis.

He groaned.

"Sorry. Let me try again."

She did. Three more times, with no success and a lot of manipulation.

"Sara."

"Yes?" She'd get this blasted thing on if it killed her. One inch at a time. Her fingers tried to roll it back up and start again.

"Stop." His hand grabbed her wrist, stilling her movement.

"But I think I figured out what I was doing wrong." Just one more time . . .

"I can't make it through another 'attempt,' " he said, gritting his teeth. "I'm a man, not a machine."

She looked at him then, saw the deep frown etched on his tanned face, the clenched jaw, the flaring nostrils. Signs of a man in pain.

He pulled the condom through her fingers and tossed it aside. "Get me another one."

They were scattered all over the bed. Sara grabbed Remember Me Raspberry, and handed it to him. He tore it open, fitted it, and smoothed the crimson latex into position in less than five seconds, making her wonder how many times he'd done this before.

She didn't think she wanted to know. Not now. Probably not ever.

"Now," he murmured, stroking a finger over her nipple, "can we continue? Intermission's been much too long."

Sara leaned over, placed a whisper-soft kiss on his mouth, and said, "Make love to me, Matt."

That was all the invitation he needed. He moved over her, positioned himself between her open thighs and entered with one deep thrust.

"Oh, God," he groaned, moving slowly inside her. "You . . . feel . . . wonderful."

His fullness invaded every inch of her body, coaxing with small strokes first, then demanding and possessing with deeper ones. She met each thrust, her hands gliding down his back, settling on his buttocks. Closer, she needed him closer. She wrapped her legs around his hips, drawing him to her, giving what he commanded.

Giving him her love.

The feel of him moving inside her, so deep, so consuming, so powerful, sent her over the edge and beyond, splitting her world apart in a flash of fire and feeling.

"Sara. Sara." Matt's breathing was hard, heavy, as he grabbed her buttocks and thrust into her. Deep. Deeper. Her body still pulsed with the aftermath of her climax when a fresh wave of sensation rolled over her. God, but she was coming apart, one stroke at a time. The feeling . . . the fullness . . . Matt thrust one last time, let out a groan of pleasure and joined her.

Heaven, Sara thought. *This is heaven. Now I know. I've seen it, touched it, tasted it . . .*

Matt was the first to speak. "Tell me about the condom," he said working a path down her arm with his fingers.

"What?" The request surprised her. She'd been hoping he wouldn't notice, or at least, not comment if he did. But she should have known he'd want to scrutinize the situation, investigate the details.

"You had no idea how to use it."

Because my ex-husband didn't like them. And he was my only lover. Until you. "It's been a long time."

"How long?"

"Long enough."

His mouth flattened into a thin line. When he spoke his voice was tight, controlled, determined. "Well, we'll just have to see that you get more practice, now won't we?"

She wanted to tell him he had nothing to be jealous of, that her experience was limited to one man who'd used her and tossed her aside with about as much concern as an old condom. But that would mean more questions, more probing into things she didn't want to talk about right now, not when she was still trembling with the aftermath of their lovemaking. Later. She'd tell him later.

Besides, it would show her extreme inexperience against a man who'd probably be able to use every one of the twenty-something foil packets littering the bed and floor on his lovers.

At a limit of one per woman.

Sara tried to push the thought aside. She didn't want to be just another statistic, didn't want to think about the others before her, or the possibility of others after her.

But with a man like Matt, who had women sticking to him like bubble gum on a hot sidewalk, it was hard not to imagine those things. Especially, when she herself was the sugar-free nonstick kind who wouldn't dream of clinging to a man.

"What are you thinking?" His deep voice broke into her thoughts.

About you. Losing you. "Nothing really."

"You got quiet all of a sudden." He reached out to touch her hair. "You're not regretting this, are you?"

"Of course not. Why would you think that?"

He shrugged his big shoulders. "I don't know. Maybe because more than anything, I don't want you to regret it."

"I don't," she whispered, snuggling against his chest.

A slow smile curved his lips. "Then why don't we try out Blast Me Away Blue?"

Sara giggled. "I think it's on the floor beside Orgasmic Orange."

"Better yet. Let's try them both."

A long while later, they slept in each other's arms, three discarded foil packets at the foot of the bed. Blast Me Away Blue, Orgasmic Orange, and Say Yes Silver.

Sixteen

"Hey, Rosa," Matt said, walking into the kitchen and tossing a workout towel around his shoulders, "when Adam gets here, will you tell him I'm in the weight room?"

"Sí, Señor Matt. I will tell him."

"Thanks." He flashed her a grin. "What's that I smell? Spaghetti with chilies? Frijoles in sauce? Pork lo mein?"

Her laughter tinkled around him. "No, no. Is Señorita Sara's favorite. Spanish rice with corn bread."

"Hmmm. Any meat tucked away in there?"

"Sí. Chicken with pork."

"Good job, Rosa. I might just have to marry you yet," he teased.

She tsk-tsked him. "Not me, Señor Matt. But perhaps it is time you settle down, find nice wife, have few *niños* . . ." Her singsong voice trailed off, leaving a range of possibilities dangling in her unspoken words.

He sighed. Rosa on a roll was relentless. She'd been dropping discreet little hints regarding his marital status for the last five days. Jimmy was no better. He'd offered to drive him and Sara anywhere, even suggested Las Vegas as a nice starting point. According to Jimmy, a person could play a couple hands of Black Jack, eat a lobster dinner, get married, and be back in the casino by seven o'clock. His delivery was so smooth, Matt almost missed the marriage part.

The only one who hadn't joined in on the Marry Matt and Sara campaign was Adam. Maybe because he just plain hadn't been around. He'd said something about business in San Diego. Or was it Seattle? Damn if he could remember.

She was doing it to him again. *Witch,* he thought, a faint smile tugging at his lips. Sara had her claws in him but good.

And she hadn't even been trying.

They'd made love the past five nights and it had been incredible. More than incredible. Almost ethereal. When they were together, she gave everything, her heart, her soul, her delectable body. And it was that total selflessness that made him want to give back. Made him want to keep giving. He'd never known that feeling before with any other woman.

But she wasn't just any other woman.

She was Sara.

His Sara.

The sound of the back door opening jarred him from his thoughts.

"Anybody home?"

"Hey, Adam," he called out. "In here."

"Hi, Rosa," Adam said. "Hey, Matt. What's for dinner? No. Don't tell me. Let me guess." There was a long pause. "I think it's one of my very favorite meals. Turkey with stuffing and mashed potatoes."

She laughed. "You are silly man."

"Okay," he teased. "Then it must be pork and sauerkraut."

That made her *tsk, tsk* again. "Silly, silly boys. Is Señorita Sara's favorite. Spanish rice with corn bread."

"Oh." Pause. "I see." Another pause. "It smells wonderful." Matt didn't miss the way his voice slid downhill from upbeat and happy to dejected and monosyllabic at the mention of Sara. She'd told him they were just good friends. So what was going on?

He intended to find out. Soon. Very soon.

"Dinner's a long way off. We've got some weights to lift."

"I'm right behind you," Adam said, sounding more like his old cheerful self.

The first hour went as usual. Free weights first, followed by universal. Neither spoke much, which wasn't unusual. They preferred to focus on the workout and save the talk for later. Forty-five minutes into the second hour, Matt finished his cooldown and dragged his tired legs from the treadmill to the weight bench. He plopped down, ran a towel over his sweaty face, and waited for Adam to finish with the rowing machine.

"Almost done," Adam huffed.

"Take your time." It would give him a few more minutes to decide how he wanted to approach the subject. There was just one thing that needed to be said: Don't waste your time brooding over Sara, because she's mine. Of course, he couldn't be so blunt about it. That would only hurt Adam's feelings, damage their relationship. In all of their years together, through all of their women, they'd never let one come between them.

Matt refused to let it happen now.

"Done."

Swiping the towel over his face and neck, Matt smiled. "Not bad, for an old man."

Adam laughed. "Right."

No sense stalling any longer. "Where've you been these last few days?" He tried to keep his voice casual. "I know you must've told me, but I can't remember."

"Working."

"Out of town?"

"No."

"Oh." So they were back to the monosyllables again.

"Yeah."

Something was definitely wrong.

"Okay."

"Look, Matt, I've been staying here since your accident. You're doing fine." Frustration filtered through his next words. "You don't need me here anymore. It's time I got back to my own place."

"Fine." *Is that the real reason?*

"I thought I'd pack up my stuff this afternoon."

"No rush. The room's yours. For whenever."

"Thanks."

"Thank you. I know I wasn't the easiest person to be around these past several months. I appreciate you sticking by me."

"We're family," he said.

"That's right." *And family talks to one another. And asks questions. Uncomfortable questions.* He drew in a deep breath. "What's going on between you and Sara?"

"Nothing."

Let's try again. "She said you were good friends."

"We are."

Okay. Time to toss out a feeler. "But you'd like more."

"I didn't say that."

"We're not in a courtroom. Or a boardroom. Can't you just answer the damn question?"

"It wasn't a question. It was a statement."

"Thank you, Attorney Brandon. Let me rephrase my statement. *Would* you like it to be more?"

"It doesn't matter what I want," he answered, sidestepping the question. "Sara isn't interested."

"No?"

"No. She's interested in someone else."

So he knew. How much had she confided?

"He'd better not hurt her."

"He won't." *I mean, I won't.*

"If you say that, then you don't know him as well as I do. He never *intends* to hurt any of his women. But he does. Eventually, he tires of them or something about them. Their company, their voice, their choice of shoes. It doesn't matter. When he's had enough, he sends them away, usually with an expensive gift to stop the tears."

"Sounds like a great guy." *Is that how he sees me? As an arrogant, uncaring, self-centered user?*

"Actually, he is. Except when it comes to his love life." Adam sighed. "But you can't blame it all on him. Women use him, too."

"What about this one?" He knew the answer, but there was some part of him that needed reassurance.

"This one's the only one who could care less how many gold cards he has or that he can walk into any restaurant without a reservation. She cares about *him*. Period."

"And he cares about her, so what's the problem?" And why the hell were they still talking in third person, when they both knew they were referring to him?

"She's not a short-timer. This woman's a keeper."

"I don't think he's making plans to get rid of her."

"She's the marrying kind."

Silence.

"And we both know he isn't," Adam said.

More silence. Matt had always told himself he'd never get married, never get boxed in. Better to ride on the outside of commitment, bob and weave in the relationship arena; kept things fresh, fun, fast. Impersonal. Get in; get out. Why would he put himself in a situation where another person could take potshots, peck away at his character, thrust expectations and values on him that were not his? Demean him? As his mother had done to his father. He'd watched the old man withdraw, one year at a time, until he'd erected an armor that shielded him from everything: his wife's dissatisfaction with him, her cruel words, her separate bed. Even his children's love. He rarely spoke or gave an opinion, even when solicited. The only time the old man came alive was in Three Rivers Stadium watching the Pirates. A few hours a week or month, at best. A sad, pathetic existence. Who needed it? Till death do us part? Right. His father had to die to get a little peace. *So, who needed that?* Not Matt. No way.

And then came Sara with her soft husky voice and fresh innocent ways.

She was messing up his frame of reference, dammit, throwing curve balls, confusing him. Making him question his own beliefs.

"She's been hurt before."

That got his attention. "What do you mean?"

"Just what I said. She's been hurt before. Really badly."

By a man? The thought of some other man's hands on her body made him sick. "Who?" It was the only word he could push out of his mouth.

Adam didn't answer at first. "Maybe you should ask her."

"Tell me. Who was it?" His heart pounded in his chest like a kettle drum preparing for the grand finale. Or the death march.

"Her ex-husband."

If Adam had said an ax murderer or a man with three heads, he wouldn't have been more shocked. *Ex-husband?* His hands balled into tight fists. *Ex-husband?*

"I wasn't aware she had one of those." *Damn right I wasn't aware.*

"She does. He left her to move in with his girl-friend the day she lost their baby."

Baby? "Good God, Adam," he said, plowing a hand through his hair. "Are we talking about the same woman? Sara? *My Sara?*"

"It's Sara."

"Jesus." It was just too much to comprehend. He hadn't felt this overwhelmed since he'd lain in a hospital bed, listening to the doctor talk about Seeing Eye dogs.

Or this angry.

"Why didn't she tell me herself?" His voice hardened. "And why'd she tell *you?*"

"She told me because we're friends. As for why she didn't tell you, I guess you'll have to ask her yourself."

"Friends." He couldn't get past the word.

"Yeah, friends." The challenge hung in the air.

And what was *he* to Sara? A plaything? A recreational sport? Her second favorite pastime? His breathing quickened. What the hell right did she have keeping something like an ex-husband and a dead baby from him? She'd had plenty of opportunities to tell him. He could even recall a few instances where he'd taunted her, accusing her of not knowing real pain and loss.

And she'd said nothing to dispute his claim.

Well, she'd sure made him look like a fool, getting him to spill his sad tormented story to her and giving nothing in return. Or very little. And then, she'd told Adam. *Because he was her friend.*

The pain, slow and insidious, tugged at him, wrapping itself around his heart. Squeezing, squeezing, until the hurt was so excruciating, he thought his heart would burst.

But it didn't. It kept beating. Damn it all, it just kept beating, one miserable ache at a time.

"Don't be too hard on her."

Matt ignored his brother, wanting to stay adrift in the pain and anguish of Sara's betrayal. "Are there any other little secrets I should know about?"

"Not that I know of."

"Well, I'll consider that a plus." He could feel the muscle twitching on the side of his jaw. A dead giveaway for the rage boiling within. And it was boiling. Threatening to explode, given the right provocation.

Correction. Given *any* provocation.

"I'm sure she was going to tell you," Adam said.

"After she told *you*, of course," he said, annoyed with the knowledge that left to her own devices she still wouldn't have revealed the truth. "Tell me, little brother, when do you think she might have mentioned that little fact to me?" *After we slept together a dozen times? Two dozen?*

"I don't know."

"Neither do I. But I intend to find out."

Sara was already in the study waiting for Matt. Her eyes scanned the computer screen, reading over the material they'd worked on yesterday. She smiled to herself. Jack Steele was working his way into her heart. Under that arrogant chauvinistic armor he wore, there was a tender caring side that showed itself every once in a while. Not often, but on rare occasions, the reader got a glimmer of it.

And if her instincts were correct and her powers of persuasion forceful enough, this macho, love 'em and leave 'em guy just might realize he'd fallen for the innocent brunette with the big amber-green eyes.

And maybe, just maybe, another macho, love 'em and leave 'em guy, might realize the same thing about her.

She hoped.

The past five days had been filled with long walks on the beach, visits to the local market, hours of committing Jack Steele's escapades to disk, and . . . talking. Real talking. About attitudes, perceptions, ideas. There were also great gaps of silence, when just being together, holding hands, was communication enough.

And the nights . . . Heat crept into Sara's cheeks at the thought of the intimacies they'd shared. The nights had their own form of communication, unlike any she'd ever experienced before. Matt might not be able to identify her by sight, but his hands knew every inch of her body.

Very well.

And she was learning every inch of his. . . .

The door opened, interrupting her thoughts. Matt. Sara looked up, a smile on her face.

"Why the hell didn't you tell me you had an ex-husband?" he roared, slamming the door behind him. He advanced on her, fury etched in every line on his face.

Oh, God, no. Not now. She sat there, stunned and staring, unable to speak or move. Or formulate one scrap of plausible explanation in her frozen brain.

"Answer me, damn you," he demanded, towering over her, hands on hips, nostrils flaring like an angry god from ancient times come to seek his vengeance on his betrayer. "Tell me why you could *sleep* with me, let me explore every inch of you, and not tell me you'd been married and lost a baby?"

Her eyes glazed with tears. "It was too painful."

He cursed under his breath. "But not too painful to discuss with Adam." The calmness in his voice didn't hide the hurt and anger harboring just below the surface.

"It just happened."

"It just happened," he repeated, throwing her

words back at her like daggers. "And it couldn't just *happen,* with me, could it?" he ground out. "Of course not. You don't trust me enough with something as personal as your real feelings. I'm just for sex." He turned away from her and stalked across the room.

Sara bit her lower lip to stop the tears that threatened to pour out at any second. *He must hate me right now, really hate me.*

"That's not true. I should have told you," she managed, her gaze trained on the back of his dark head. "I was wrong."

He didn't turn, didn't even acknowledge that he'd heard her.

She tried again. Stumbling over her words. "I'm sorry, Matt. I . . . didn't want our relationship . . . to . . . be marred with the past. It means too much to me." Drawing in a deep breath, she whispered, "You mean too much to me."

He flinched. "But not enough to trust me with your past. That privilege was reserved for Adam." Bitterness dripped from his mouth, spilling into the air, contaminating them both.

I'm losing him . . . "I don't care about Adam the way I care about you." Tears spilled down her cheeks.

Matt threw back his head and laughed. *"Do* you care about me, Sara? Really care?" He swung around. "Or have I just proved a convenient case study? Or should I say 'case stud'?"

"Don't." She swiped her cheeks with the back of her hand. "Don't let your anger diminish what we share."

"What we share? What *do* we share, Dr. Hamilton? Enlighten me. Analyze it please, because I'm way off base." He took a few steps toward her. "I thought we were building something, based on *trust* and caring."

"We were. We are."

"Then why would you shatter that trust by confiding something to my brother that you should have come to me about?" He stood there, fists clenched, jaw set, feet planted wide. A warrior readying for battle.

She pinched the bridge of her nose with her thumb and forefinger. "Adam made a few comments that led me to believe he held out hope for a more . . . personal relationship with me. I didn't want to hurt him by telling him I could never care about him that way, because of you, so I told him about my ex-husband. It just kind of came out . . . as an avoidance tactic." Sara sighed. "But it didn't work. It took him about two seconds to figure out there was something going on between you and me."

"You still should have told me."

He wasn't going to give her a break. Not even a little one. "I realize that," she snapped. "I realized that ten minutes ago."

"You should've realized it before you spilled your heart out to Adam."

Anger, slow and seething, boiled to the surface. "Since when did you become an expert on relationships?"

"I never claimed to be an expert, but I sure as hell know what destroys them."

"Speaking from experience, I presume."

He ignored the snide comment. "I never wanted one to work before. And I'm starting to think I'm damn crazy for wanting one to work now."

Had she heard him right? She forced the breath out of her lungs. "What did you just say?"

"I said I think I'm damn crazy," he muttered, shaking his head.

"No. Not that." Her voice shook. "The part about wanting this to work."

"Nothing." He looked in her direction and she wondered once again how a blind man could see so much, could look into her heart, tear aside the curtains of her soul, and peer inside.

"You said something about wanting to make this work. Do you, Matt? Do you want to make this . . . us . . . work?" She held her breath, waiting for his answer. Praying for the words that would make her heart sing.

"Yes," he said, on a sigh, the anger draining out of him. "Even when we're arguing, I want you by my side." He shook his head. "I must be crazy."

She walked to the side of the desk and put her arms around his neck. Leaning up on tiptoe, Sara planted a light kiss on his full lips and whispered, "If it's any consolation, I feel the same way."

He smiled and bent his head to deepen the kiss.

"If you . . . if you want to talk about my ex-husband—"

"No," he said, pulling her to him. "Not now."

She welcomed him, pressing her body into his.

"I want you," he groaned against her lips.

"What about your book?" she murmured, brushing her breasts back and forth against his chest.

His laugh rolled over her, low, sensual. "Time for research," he said, cupping her buttocks in the palm of his hands.

Sara moaned. "The bedroom?"

"Too far away." He took her hand and led her to his leather easy chair. Matt sat down and pulled her onto his lap. "Just right." His strong hands skimmed her bare legs, maneuvering under the thin cotton summer dress she wore to settle on the triangle of silk between her thighs. "These have got to go," he said, shifting her hips and working the pale pink material down her legs.

His fingers found her heat, stroked, plunged inside, making her squirm with desire. Sara tugged at his shorts, dipping her hand inside.

"Take these off," she whispered, fingering his briefs.

With her still on his lap, Matt lifted his hips from the chair and pulled his shorts and briefs down. Just enough to free himself. Sara smiled. Just enough to touch him.

Just enough to drive him wild.

She gave his penis three long strokes. "Wait," he rasped, reaching over to open the drawer of the small side table next to them. He pulled out a gold foil packet and held it up.

"What? You have these things all over the house?"

He grinned. "Every nook and cranny."

"You horrible man."

"Not horrible man. Horny man."

Sara snatched the foil packet from his fingers. "Glow in the Dark Gold. What if Rosa found one of these? I'd never be able to face her again."

He laughed. "Don't kid yourself. If Rosa, the matchmaker, came across one, she'd probably stick it on your lunch tray, right next to your napkin and say, *'You take care of Señor Matt.'*"

Sara laughed. "You really are horrible."

"No." He trailed a finger over the cotton covering her nipple. "I really am horny."

"I think I've got a cure for that," she whispered. She ripped open the packet and fit the gold shimmering latex on his penis. Then she stroked him again.

"I can't wait any longer." He grabbed her hips and repositioned her body over his. "Not one second longer." The tip of his penis touched her, teased her.

With a low groan, he impaled her, filling her with raw pleasure and wild need. She moved her hips, sliding up and down his length, slow at first, then faster, riding him, giving herself up to pure sensation.

"It's too good. Too damn good," he ground out, pushing against her, hard and fast. Sara felt his need pulsing through his body in quick jerky thrusts, his rapid shallow breathing fanning her ear. He was at the edge of his control.

At the very edge, teetering and about to plunge into the netherworld of sensual ecstasy.

She rode him harder, nails digging into his shoulders, leaving little half-moons on his tanned skin. "Come with me, Matt," she pleaded. "Come with me."

He grasped her hips, pumping into her with long determined strokes, eyes closed, head thrown back, mouth set in a firm line of concentration. Sara closed her eyes and gave herself up to the feel of him possessing her body.

Possessing her soul.

"Sara," he groaned, jerking against her. Heat filled her body, sharp and intense.

It sent her shattering over the edge, free-falling

and fragmenting into oblivion. She collapsed against him, burying her head in the crook of his neck.

Matt pulled her closer.

This is where she belonged. Here, in his arms, with his slow even breathing washing over her like a lullaby, the beat of his heart thumping under her hand. Forever wouldn't be long enough to lay, just like this. Cradled. Protected.

Loved.

Loved? Did Matt love her? Could he ever love her? Just her? Forever? Her chest squeezed with pain. And if he didn't? If he *couldn't?* The questions pulled at her, gnawing away hope and possibility like buzzards pecking their prey. *Foolish, foolish, foolish,* they nipped. *So foolish to give your love. Again.* They ripped a chunk from her heart.

Just like he's going to do.

"Sara?"

Matt's low voice touched her, soothed her. Made her ache with the pain of loving him.

"No more secrets," he said, stroking her hair. "Okay?"

"Okay," she murmured, knowing even as she made the promise she couldn't keep it. Not until she knew whether Matt would view her love as a blessing or a curse.

Seventeen

"Yes! Yes! Yes!"

Matt smiled, thinking that the words Sara had just yelled out in front of twenty-five thousand fans, were the same ones she'd used last night. In bed.

"He got a double. Winning run's at the plate."

"Then I did better than him," he whispered in her ear. "I scored a triple last night." He nuzzled her ear.

"*Matt.* Someone will hear you." Her low throaty voice shot straight to his groin.

He had to stop thinking about last night. About how incredible it had been. Again. But then, with Sara, every time was a new, wonderful, *incredible* experience. Better than the last.

"Keep your fingers crossed," she instructed, lacing her fingers with his.

"I have my good luck charm right here," he said, squeezing her hand.

The radio in his right hand blared the batter's statistics. The crowd cheered.

"Do you think he can pull it out?" Sara asked.

"He's capable, but he's been known to choke."

"That's what I'm afraid of." The words weren't

out of her mouth before the announcer on the radio blared, "Strike one."

"Darn. Come on," Sara yelled. "Pull it together."

"Strike two."

"Let's go, Pirates!"

Matt squeezed her hand, listening for the crack of wood on leather. He heard it, half a second before Sara jumped from her seat.

"Yes!" she yelled.

His gaze shot instinctively to the outfield. Flashes of light assaulted him, shocked him, paralyzed him. He stared, eyes wide open, as hundreds of balls of light blinked at him, beacons in a sea of darkness. *What the hell?* Squeezing his eyes shut, he rubbed his hand over his face and looked again.

Blackness.

He blinked twice, tried again.

More blackness.

What the hell had happened? He hadn't seen anything, not so much as a thin ray of light, since the accident. But what he'd just experienced, this bombardment of visuals, had been real. Hadn't it?

"Matt? Can you believe it?" Sara's voice reached him through his confusion. "Wasn't that incredible?"

"Incredible," he murmured, setting his gaze toward the outfield. "Absolutely incredible."

He was going crazy. That was it. What other possible explanation could there be for the events of the past four days? Matt slouched low in his lounge chair, ball cap pushed down on his forehead, shielding his eyes from the sun.

One. Two. Three. He took a deep breath. *Four. Five. Go!* He flipped the cap up and turned his gaze to the sun. And darkness.

"Damn." He'd been playing this little game for the past two hours. Ten times, he'd tried to "see" the sun's light. It had worked on six attempts. Bright rays of light had seared his lids, making him recoil from its brightness.

To say he'd become obsessed with his situation was an understatement. Since the day at the ball game, when he'd looked into the stands and seen balls of light, he'd fostered hope of seeing again. Something was happening. He was certain of it. Something big.

And he was petrified.

What if he did regain his vision? What would happen? His world was different now. He didn't want the glitz and glamour of public life. Not the notoriety, or the pressure of insincerity, or the women. He only wanted one woman. And one life.

But what if he could regain his sight and have a life with that one woman? Wouldn't he have everything he'd ever wanted? Didn't he owe it to them both to try?

From the first night after the game, he'd been testing himself, experimenting with light and vision. Crazy little schemes, like sitting in the bathroom, flicking lights on and off. Or having Jimmy take him and Sara for a drive at night, just to stare at the headlights. Sometimes he saw them grabbing him, flashing before him in the breadth of a second only to disappear into darkness. Other times there was nothing but a steady stream of black.

It was this torment, this agonizing torture of seeing, and not seeing that was the worst. He'd just about come to terms with his blindness, even considered using the walking staff Sara gave him a few days ago. Hell, he'd even been toying with a dog. Sara loved animals, so he thought he'd make her happy and get an extra pair of eyes in the bargain.

So why did he have to be tossed about, thrown into purgatory, when he'd just about clawed his way out of hell and had his foot on the first rung of heaven's ladder?

Damned if he knew.

"Matt? What are you doing?"

Sara. He jerked his head away from the sun, and pushed his hat low on his forehead. How could he not have heard her coming? Too engrossed in his experiments, that's why.

"What are you doing?" she asked again, her voice mere inches from him.

He reached up, found her hand. "Nothing," he said, trying to sound casual. "Just getting a little sun."

"Well, you looked a little strange with your face all scrunched up. Kind of like the sun was bothering your eyes."

"Now that would be a trick, wouldn't it," he laughed, pulling her toward him for a kiss. Her lips were warm and inviting.

"We have work to do, remember?" she murmured against his lips. "Another chapter today."

"Jack can wait." He ran his hand down her bare arm. "I can't."

"You'll have to," she said, laughing and pulling out of his grasp. "He needs to get out of disaster and hooked up with his woman."

"So do I," he teased, reaching out, trying to find her. His hand snatched gobs of air.

"Right now, all you're going to get is an iced tea. Rosa just made a fresh pitcher. Would you like some?"

He blew out a sigh, pretending disgust. "If that's all you're offering, I guess it'll have to do."

She planted a light kiss on his mouth. "You'll get dessert later."

"It's my favorite part of the meal," he said, rubbing his lips against hers.

"Then you can have seconds," she whispered. "Or thirds."

He groaned and she laughed, a low husky sound. "Be right back."

Matt took a deep breath, his nostrils filling with orange and lemon. He sighed and looked toward the patio door.

His breath slammed against his throat, threatening to choke him. He shot up in his chair, eyes wide open, staring at the indistinct gray shape moving away from him.

Sara. He'd just *seen* Sara.

"What's wrong, Matt?" Sara asked, cuddling next to him. "You've been fidgeting all night." She smoothed a curl from his forehead. "And you've been squinting for days. I'm starting to wonder if you shouldn't see a doctor."

"That's probably not a bad idea."

His words startled her. Matt Brandon, agreeing to see a doctor? He wouldn't do that unless he thought something was wrong. Very wrong.

"Are you having any symptoms that are causing

you concern?" She doubted he'd admit to anything outright; but maybe if she were gentle and less obvious about it, he might open up.

"Now you sound like a doctor." His voice was gruff, but she heard the warmth underneath, soft and cozy like a fleece blanket.

"Just concerned."

"Don't be," he said, taking her hand in his, and stroking her fingers. "I just think it's time for the good old doc to let me know if anything's changed. That's all."

"Honest?"

His hand stilled a half second. "Honest."

"I'll go with you if you like."

"I'd like that very much."

Sara scooted down on the leather couch, resting her head on his broad shoulder. She felt safe, protected, loved. She smiled.

"It doesn't matter if the doctor says things are the same," Matt's deep voice broke into her thoughts. "I just want to know."

Why did he want to know now? After all these months of fighting doctors? Had something happened to change his mind?

"Why don't we plan a trip to Pittsburgh in a few weeks," he said. "Stay six or seven days, take in a few ball games, visit Jeff. What do you think?"

"Sounds great. After all, Pittsburgh is my home and Jeff is my boss." She tried to make a joke of it, but the words fell flat, dead, like a bug splattering a windshield.

"That could all change," he said.

How? she wanted to ask him. *How could it change? What are you offering?* But she was too chicken. Maybe because she was afraid he wasn't offering anything. Sara squeezed her eyes shut, forced back the sudden threat of tears. *She had to know. Might as well say it.* "But sooner or later, I have to go back for more than a visit."

"Why?"

Was he serious? "Why?"

"Yeah. Why do you have to go back at all? Why can't you stay here?" He ran a hand through his rumpled hair. "I thought that was the plan."

Her heart pounded in her chest. *Just stay? No promises? No commitments?*

She sat up, turning toward him. She needed to look at his face, see his expression, try to read between his words. "We've never talked about anything . . . on a long-term basis."

A muscle twitched on the left side of his jaw. "I assumed you'd stay with me. See how things worked out."

And if they didn't? She'd be right back where she was three years ago when Brian dumped her. No. She couldn't do that again. Not even for Matt.

"I'm sorry, Matt. I can't do that."

"Can't?" She felt his whole body tense. "Or won't?"

"It's the same thing, isn't it? I have another life, a job, other responsibilities . . ." her voice trailed off. He'd never understand.

"I'll double your salary."

"To do what?" Each word felt like a dagger, piercing her heart.

"Be my assistant. Type, go on tour . . . just . . . be with me."

"Oh." Her voice was a mere whisper of sound. "A paid companion."

"Kind of."

"No better than a whore." Pain seared her soul, carving out a huge gaping hole.

"No! Why would you say a damn thing like that?" His voice shook with fury.

Because somewhere between that first shared kiss and now, she'd assumed they were building toward something, forging a bond that was stronger than "just for today." Foolish as she might have been, she actually dreamed of being with this man, loving him, maybe bearing his children.

But obviously, he hadn't shared her dream. She'd been nothing more than short-term parking—easy access, convenient, temporary.

Sara regained some of her calm. Or was she just numb from the pain? It didn't matter. She felt dead, either way. "I said it because if I stay with you under those conditions, then I'm no better than a paid whore."

His fists clenched into tight balls. "I want you to stay. You know that."

"I know."

"But you want a ring," he spat out the words, as though he'd tasted something vile.

"I want a commitment," she corrected, feeling the distance between them growing. "A promise to love, cherish, be faithful."

He let out a harsh laugh. "You've been reading the wrong kind of books. No wonder you don't like mine. They deal in reality. Betrayal. Pain. 'For now' not 'forever.' "

Sara straightened her shoulders. "I'm looking for real-life people who love each other and aren't afraid to make a commitment."

"You're looking for a fairy tale with a happy ending," he bit out. "I'm no Prince Charming. And if that's who you're looking for, you should've picked Adam." His words struck her like a dagger.

He would not see the pain pouring from her wound. No matter the cost to her, he would not know how his words ripped her heart open, bleeding the very life from her. She took a deep breath, gathered the last vestiges of pride and strength around her, like a well-worn cloak in winter, and threw her own weapon. "God, but I wish I had."

His face contorted with anger at her words. "Goddamn you," he hissed, heaving himself from the couch. "Goddamn you." He turned on his heel and stalked out of the room.

Sara laid her head down, closed her eyes and let the tears come.

How much longer was he going to be forced to sit here, with his ass hanging out of this ridiculous gown? Where was that damn doctor? He needed answers. And he needed them now.

He was tired of waiting. It had taken three days to get an appointment. That was his first annoyance. The receptionist had told him the doctor usually had a three-to-four-week wait, but considering the circumstances, she'd adjust the schedule. What she meant was considering who he was, she'd bump him up a few days. What if he'd said he was Robert De Niro? Or Al Pacino? He'd probably have gotten same-day service.

Matt had insisted on having the MRI done the same day as his doctor visit. He wanted answers. The lights and shadows came to him daily, assaulting his senses, threatening to drive him mad. He needed to understand what was happening. Was he on the path to seeing again or was this quasi-sight God's way of punishing him for the early months he spent cursing Him for his blindness?

He'd been cursing a lot these last few days. Not that anyone would have noticed, because he wasn't talking to anyone. The words were all in his head, long hyphenated phrases, with colorful expletives.

All because of *her*. Sara Hamilton had finally done it, pushed him over the edge of sanity. He hoped she was happy. They hadn't spoken more than twenty words to each other in the past three days. Other than a perfunctory "Hello," or "Please pass the salt," they'd treated each other like pieces of furniture.

And as for sharing the same bed . . . Well, that was a subject better left untouched.

Why couldn't she have just left things alone? Why did she have to go and start spouting words like *commitment*? Next she'd be talking about picking out silver patterns. He didn't need to hear that right now. Didn't want to hear it. And now she was talking about leaving? Just because he wouldn't say some ridiculous, overused words? Didn't she know he cared for her, wanted to be with her, would take care of her?

Why couldn't that be enough?

The door opened, intruding on his thoughts. *Thank God*. He welcomed any diversion to take his mind off of *her*.

"Hello, Matt," Dr. Myers's gruff voice filled the room.

"Doc." He nodded in greeting.

"I've got good news. The swelling is gone. There is some scar tissue, but that shouldn't hinder your sight."

"Meaning?" Matt held himself still, not daring to breathe, not daring to hope.

"Meaning there's no reason your sight shouldn't be restored."

Matt let out a long sigh. "Really?" Could it be true, that after all these months of darkness, he might see light again?

"The lights you've been seeing, along with the shadows are normal. Your vision will return in stages."

"How long?"

"That's uncertain. You need to be patient and just let your body follow its own course."

Matt ignored the advice. "Patience has never been one of my virtues, Doc." He ran a hand through his hair. "At least, give me a guess. How long until I really see again? One month? Two? A year?"

"I'd only be guessing."

"I'll take it."

"Well, the rapidity with which you progressed from blinking lights to moving forms suggests your vision may return within a matter of a few months. Two to three, perhaps."

"And then, I'll see normally, no more flashes or blurs like I'm underwater?"

"You should see as well as you did before."

Matt closed his eyes, trying to digest the doctor's words. A month ago, he'd lived in darkness, thinking he'd never see again. Ten days ago, he was considering a Seeing Eye dog and a walking staff. And today, he had just learned that the lights and shadows that haunted him daily would, in time, reshape themselves into real things, like people and objects.

"So, what do I do now?"

"Now comes the hardest part," Dr. Myers said, his gruff voice softening. "You wait."

Matt stepped out of the office, looking much the way he had when he'd entered it over an hour ago. Stoic. Unreadable. Grim. Deep lines bracketed both sides of his mouth. Had he received bad news? Sara wondered. Had the doctor squelched his last hope to see again?

She guided him to the elevator, her hand resting in the crook of his arm. She wished he'd worn a long-sleeved shirt. Then she wouldn't have to touch his bare skin. Wouldn't have to be tortured by the feel of him, tormented with what had been and most likely would never be again. For a short space in time, they had connected, become one.

And it had been a beautiful, glorious ride, glimpsing a slice of heaven. Before they'd spun out of control and crash-landed, leaving no survivors. But oh, what a ride it had been. Who would have believed that she, who hadn't been on a date since Brian left, with the exception of dinner meetings and the occasional social function where an escort was required, would have fallen headfirst for a man she'd once half detested? The myth of Matthew Brandon had turned out to be far different from the flesh and blood man; him she hadn't been able to resist and that was proving to be her ultimate demise.

As they entered the elevator, she pushed the lobby button and glanced at the man who'd given her joy mixed with equal torment. He was staring straight ahead, like a statue carved out of granite. Cold. Silent. Rigid. As though she weren't there.

As though she didn't even exist.

Sara sucked in a breath and faced him. "What did the doctor say?"

There was a long expanse of silence, so long that she thought he might ignore the question, altogether. When he did speak his words were clipped, void of all emotion. "He said everything seems to be healed. With time and patience, I'll see again."

Tears filled her eyes. The lump in her throat felt the size of a baseball, but she pushed past it, forcing out the words. "That's wonderful, Matt." A single tear trickled down her cheek. "I'm so happy for you."

And so sad for us, she wanted to add. *So sad that we couldn't find a common ground to work through our differences. So sad that soon I'll be less than a faint memory for you. So sad that you won't ache for me the way I'll ache for you.*

So sad . . . Another tear fell. Then another. She swiped them away with the back of her hand. Jimmy would be waiting. Mustn't let anyone see tears of sadness. Only tears of joy. . . .

"You've achieved your mission, Sara. And then some. You should be proud. I'll be back to my old self in no time." He paused. "And you'll be back in Pittsburgh."

Had she sensed a slight crack in that stony facade, perhaps a speck of emotion, when he'd mentioned her leaving? She thought his voice had wavered, if only a little, and the harsh lines of his mouth seemed to soften. But his next words made her certain she'd only imagined it.

"In six months' time, we'll have our lives back.

Just as they were before," he said, enunciating the last word.

Before. Before they met. Before they touched. Before they shared. Before they loved.

Did he really believe that? Could he just erase her, like water washing away footprints at high tide? That was it? Gone? As if it had never been?

Of course he could. He was Matt Brandon, King of the Uncommitted.

God, what a fool she'd been. What a complete, ridiculous fool. She had to get away, had to leave, before she humiliated herself any further.

Before there was nothing left but the tattered shreds of a woman, who had once again chosen the wrong man to love.

Eighteen

Matt paced the bedroom, one foot in front of the other, just like he'd done for the past, what was it, hour or more? He had no idea what time it was. At midnight, disgusted with himself and his cowardice, he'd yanked his watch off and thrown it on the bed.

He should just go to her and apologize for being such an ass these past few days. He could do that, couldn't he? Of course. And then he could say he'd treated her like dirt because he'd been so preoccupied with seeing Dr. Myers. A half truth, but a nice segue into what he really wanted to tell her.

The real truth.

He'd been miserable since their damned argument. And he missed her. Not just in bed, but in the routine course of every day. Silly things like fixing her coffee, a drop of cream with a hint of sugar, listening to her *ooohh* and *aaahhh* over Rosa's fried ice cream, feeling the strength of her fingers laced through his. But Sara would never guess that. Not after the way he'd been treating her. Like week-old leftovers headed for the garbage disposal. And if she'd had any doubt, he'd taken care of that when he slammed her in the elevator. *In six months' time, we'll have our lives back. Just like they were before.* Who the hell was he kidding? His life would never be the same. Not since Sara.

And not without Sara.

But he'd said the words to inflict pain. Make her bleed. Just as he was doing. Only, instead of giving him even a small modicum of satisfaction, it had made him feel worse, more the monster.

Did she really believe he could just go on as though she'd never happened?

He hoped to God not.

Plowing his fingers through his hair, he looked up at the ceiling in silent supplication. Light glared into his eyes. He blinked them shut. Damn, but he should be thrilled that brightness sliced into his black night several times a day. It was a reminder that some day soon he'd see much more than fuzzy blurs and flashing lights. He'd see everything with precision and clarity.

If only he could see his life that way. Then he'd make the right decisions. Do the right thing. For a man on the brink of regaining his sight, he'd never felt so out of focus, so blurred, like he was swimming underwater with his eyes open, confused and disoriented.

Only one certainty pushed through the murky depths of his heart. One certainty in an ocean of uncertainties. He'd needed Sara in the beginning to be his eyes, his guide, to give him courage and direction, to "see" without sight. But not anymore. That was all changing. Soon, he'd have his vision back.

And then he'd have to admit that he *still* needed her. Very much.

Before he could analyze his actions, or the ramifications of them, he threw on a pair of shorts and headed toward the door.

The soft knock roused Sara from shallow layers of sleep. Only one person would be standing out there at this time of night. Her heart skipped a beat. Should she ignore him? Pretend she was still asleep? Maybe not. Maybe she should just tell him to go away.

"Sara?" His soft low voice reached her, stroked her, folding its warmth around her.

She swung her legs over the side of the bed, flicked the bedside lamp on and padded to the door. Her fingers reached up to touch the knob, hesitated.

What could he possibly have to say that could make any difference? *I'm sorry?* That wasn't a big phrase in his vocabulary. Had he thought of just one more way to jab her, make her bleed, and it was so good, he couldn't wait until morning? Hadn't he done enough damage already? Hadn't he made certain he'd strangled the last bit of breath from their relationship with his cruel words?

"Sara?" The soft insistence made him sound almost desperate. Matt Brandon desperate? Hardly.

She grabbed the knob and opened the door.

"What is it, Matt?" she asked, trying to keep her voice steady. That proved to be a full-time job, especially with him standing bare-chested in front of her, his hair rumpled either from sleep or agitated fingers, she couldn't tell which. But what tugged at her heart most was the look of vulnerability on his face. There were no demanding lines bracketing his mouth, no clenched jaw or flaring nostrils. Not even a slight furrow between his brows.

He just stood there, hands at his sides, like a tired warrior coming home after a long bitter battle. "I'm tired of fighting."

Her heart jumped. She beat it down. "So am I."

He took a step forward, reached out a tanned hand, stroking her cheek with his fingers. Light soft whispers of longing fluttered along her skin. "God, but I've missed you, Sara."

"And I've missed you." The words were out before she could stop them.

He reached for her then, took her in his strong arms, and crushed her to him. Their mouths found each other, drank of need and longing. And forgiveness. Sara wrapped her arms around his neck, flattened her body against his, feeling the beauty and power of the man. One more time . . . She needed to be with him . . . *just one last time.*

Matt took another step into the room and closed the door behind him.

"I've got to be inside you," he rasped. "It's been too long."

She answered him with a long slow kiss, her tongue mating with his. They worked their way toward the bed, unbuttoning and removing clothing as they went. When Sara landed in the middle of the bed, she was naked with Matt on top of her.

He reached for the nightstand drawer, pulled it open and dug around for a condom. She watched the muscles of his body stretching. Anything he wanted, she would give to him. Desire coursed through her as she watched him rip open the foil packet and fit himself.

There was no bantering or joking words tossed about this time. Neither cared about the condom's color or distinction. They wanted each other. Desperately. Now.

Matt plunged into her, filling her, possessing her. She drew him to her, moving with him, pulling him closer. There were no words, no sweet whispered endearments, no hushed murmurings. Only heat and sweat and need, wrapped in groans of pleasure. And in between it all, swirling in the final moments of release, there was forgiveness.

Sara closed the latch on the suitcase and shot a quick glance toward the bed. Matt was on his stomach, his head turned to the side, one arm tucked under his pillow, the other flung out over an empty space of sheet. She'd been in that space an hour ago, lying in his warm embrace.

He would call her a coward when he found out she was gone. And he might be right. But she had to get away. Now. Before it was too late. Before she traded self-respect and self-esteem for long nights of sensual pleasure. Again. And they had been pleasurable, the intimacy they'd shared, climbing to new heights of sexual fulfillment.

But what had it proved? That she couldn't resist him? Not now? Not ever?

There had been no words, no attempt to work things through, find a common ground. And certainly, no promise or commitment of any kind. She'd allowed him to berate her, ignore her, and then, when he felt so inclined, bed her. But Matt wasn't the only one at fault. He'd only had to whisper a few words, brush his fingers over her skin, and she was shedding her clothes *and* her self-respect.

He'd needed her, maybe he'd even really cared about her in his own way. But her usefulness was short-lived. Another month, maybe three. It wouldn't be long before he would sit in Dodger Stadium and watch fly balls zoom by, gaze at the sunset from Dana Point, look in the mirror. See. Really see. And he wouldn't need a junior typist to transcribe his book. He could do it all himself. Matt wouldn't need her at all.

And when he tired of her? What then? When his sight returned and the women started flocking around him again? Adam had already deflected six phone calls from reporters this afternoon inquiring about Matt's visit to Dr. Myers. How had they found out so quickly? Two of the calls claimed Gabrielle Jontue was flying back from Greece to be with him. Matt didn't seem interested in the beautiful model anymore, but what about the next one? And the next?

What would happen when those silver eyes saw her for the first time? Really saw her. Would he be disappointed? Could he stay *interested* in "ordinary"? She doubted it. He might be nice to her, even sympathetic, but then what? Then he'd wish her back to Pittsburgh.

Well, she'd save him the trouble. Let him off the hook. There was an envelope on the nightstand with his name on it, brief, impersonal, informing him that with Dr. Myers's good news, her assignment was complete. She thanked him for his hospitality and asked him to say good-bye to Adam, Jimmy, and Rosa.

That was it. Her association with Matthew Brandon culminating in five short sentences.

Sara grabbed her suitcase and briefcase. She'd send for the rest later, the ceramic butterfly mobile, the iridescent blue and green globe, the seashell picture frame. Or maybe she wouldn't. The fewer reminders of this trip the better. Tangible objects could be disposed of, left behind, or put in a drawer, out of sight.

But what about the memories? The slow half smile, the gentle lingering touch, the warm deep voice? How would she ever be able to erase those from her mind, strip them from her heart, tear them from her soul?

She hurried across the room and opened the door, stepping into the dark hallway, before she changed her mind. A tiny finger of light stretched toward her from the kitchen. Thank God, Rosa always left the stove light on. It made everything much easier for her. First, she'd have to call a cab, then she'd probably spend the better part of the next several hours trying to get a flight back to Pittsburgh.

"Going somewhere?"

Sara whirled around. "Jimmy! What are you doing up?"

He pointed to the fridge. "Couldn't sleep, so I thought I'd grab a piece of Rosa's cherry pie." He frowned, his brown eyes taking in the suitcases. "What's going on?"

She looked down, avoiding his gaze. "I'm going home."

"Now? At three o'clock in the morning?"

"There's never going to be a good time."

"But . . . I don't understand," he said, scratching the back of his head. "Why are you running away?"

"My job's done. And I am *not* running away." Drawing in a deep steadying breath, she added, "I'm walking. Very fast."

"But, you two are made for each other. Perfect."

Sara shook her head. "No. We're as different as night and day."

His mouth curved upward into a grin. "That's what makes you so right for each other. *Contrast.* Light and dark. Like taking a picture. Who would want something that blended into itself, so you couldn't tell where one ended and the other began?"

"It's not that simple." Jimmy was a sweetheart, but he was way off base here.

"You two love each other," he said, shrugging his big shoulders. "What's more simple than that."

"Jimmy. *Please.*" She'd fought every battle with herself already; she didn't need someone else to take up the sword. "That word has never been mentioned between us. Besides, he doesn't want commitment. Matt likes things the way they are between us." Her voice wavered. "I can't live that way. Not forever. And he doesn't believe in forevers."

"He could change."

"Why should he? He's going to have his sight back. Then he can pick up right where he left off last November. Do you really think he's going to want me here, expecting love, trust, and fidelity, when he can have ten women who'll take him with no demands?"

Jimmy looked at her, long and hard. "Yeah," he said. "I do."

"No." She dashed the spark of hope in her heart. "No." Sara turned away, not wanting him to see her pain. "I've got to go. I was just getting ready to call a cab."

"Don't call a cab," he said. "If you really want to go, I'll take you."

"Thank you, Jimmy."

"I just wish you'd give him a chance."

"Look," she said, turning to face him. "If by some outside chance I'm wrong and Matt can't live without me, he knows where to find me."

"But why can't you just wait? At least until you've talked to him."

"And have him feel obliged to ask me to stay? No." She let out a harsh little laugh. "I don't think so. I'm making it easy on him." She forced a smile. "In six months' time, he won't remember my name."

Matt rolled over, the smell of orange and lemons filling his senses. Sara . . . He'd missed that the last few nights. Missed her smell, her touch, her voice. Missed everything. But last night she'd more than made up for her absence in his bed. She'd clung to him and loved him, her touch rolling over him like fire unfurling its flames, hot and searing. Almost as though it were the last time for them.

It was anything but that, he thought. And it was time to tell her.

Time to commit. Say the words, take the risk, because she was worth it. Because without her, he felt dead, empty inside, like someone had carved a big hole in his heart and she was the only one who could fill it. He needed her.

And he loved her, had for a very long time, even though he'd been too thick-headed to realize it before last night. He opened his eyes, squinting at the blurred space in front of him. It was empty.

"Sara?" No answer. She was probably in the kitchen talking to Rosa. Well, he'd just go find her there. Flinging back the covers, Matt reached for his shorts, humming a little tune under his breath. Life was good. Life was very good and he was the luckiest man in the world.

He couldn't wait to find Sara, tell her he loved her, wanted her with him.

Forever.

As his wife.

Ten minutes later, Matt left the room and headed toward the kitchen.

"Hi, Matt."

"Adam? What are you doing here? Why aren't you at work?"

"I needed to talk to you."

His voice sounded strained, unnatural, not like the easygoing brother he was used to hearing.

"Sure," Matt said, heading toward the coffeepot. "Just give me a minute." He reached for his cup and opened the carafe, pouring with great care. "Where's Sara?"

A sniffling sound in the corner got his attention. It grew louder, ending on a hiccup. "Ay, Díos mio."

"Rosa? What's the matter? Why are you crying?" He started moving toward the crying gray shape at the end of the table, but Adam put a hand on his arm.

"She's fine. Just a little upset. I have to talk to you."

Matt pushed his hand away. "Rosa? Are you okay?"

"*Sí, sí.*" She sniffed. "Go." The clicking of rosary beads mingled with her quiet sobs.

"Come on, Matt." There was an edge to Adam's voice this time.

"Okay, okay."

"I'll meet you on the patio in a minute. I have to get something first."

"Fine." The sun's rays greeted him as he stepped onto the patio. Maybe Sara was in the hot tub. "Sara?"

"She's not there," Adam said from behind him.

"Where is she?"

There was a long pause, but no response.

"What's the matter with you, Adam? This is not a trick question. Where's Sara?"

"Gone. Back to Pittsburgh." The words were low, flat, emotionless.

"What?" He couldn't have heard that right. She couldn't be gone. He loved her. He was going to *commit*, for God's sake. He wanted to marry her.

"She's gone, Matt." Adam drew in a deep breath. "Jesus, I'm sorry. She left you a note."

"A note?" His chest felt tight, like a three-hundred-pound weight was sitting square in the middle of it. "Read it."

" 'Matt, Dr. Myers's prognosis is excellent. Soon you'll be seeing again. I think it's time to end this assignment and get back to the clients who really need me. Thank you for your generous hospitality. Please say good-bye to Adam, Jimmy, and Rosa. Sincerely, Sara.' "

"*Sincerely?*" Matt ran a hand through his hair. "She signed it that way?"

"She loves you, Matt," Adam said. "But she's a proud woman. If you love her, go after her. Bring her back."

"*Sincerely?*"

"She's hurt. Go after her."

How could she do such a thing? A note? A goddamn note was all she left? Damn her. "No. She's made her choice."

"No she hasn't. She's giving *you* the choice."

"She left me." He let out a hollow laugh. "The only woman I ever really wanted, and she left me."

"So go bring her back. Convince her she needs you. Tell her you love her and want to marry her."

"I won't beg."

"Who said anything about begging? Can't you just *ask?*"

The pain coursing through his body simmered, boiled, and spilled over into red-hot rage. He'd be damned if he'd ask her. She'd have to come to him and do the asking. A little begging might not be a bad idea either.

By the seventh day, Matt realized Sara was not going to contact him. He'd waited every day for her to call and make amends, his patience thinning by the second. But she hadn't. And now he was in the middle of another sleepless night. *All because of her.*

Damn that woman. He felt like giving her a piece of his mind, letting her know how miserable she'd made him. And hoping he'd made her just as miserable, which was becoming increasingly doubtful as days ticked by without a word from her.

What time was it? His fingers scanned the watch

on his wrist. 4:00 A.M. He and the early-morning
hours were becoming good friends. In the last several days, he'd spent time with each of them, tossing and turning at two, cursing at three, pacing at
four, and falling into an exhausted sleep by five.

How much longer was he going to put himself
through this kind of hell? He needed closure. Finality, one way or the other. His writing wasn't
worth shit right now, he barked at everybody, including Rosa, and he didn't even like himself.

Before he could talk himself out of it, he reached
over and picked up the phone, pressing speed dial
number one. Adam had gotten her number from
Jeff and programmed it on his phone. *Just in case,*
he'd told Matt.

The phone started ringing. It would be 7:00 A.M.
in Pittsburgh. She'd probably be awake, maybe getting ready for work.

"Hello?" It was a man's voice, thick with sleep.
What the hell? "Is this Sara Hamilton's residence?" Maybe Adam had programmed the wrong
number.

"Yeah," the man said. "I think she's in the
shower. Is there—"

Click.

Matt didn't wait to hear any more. He'd heard
enough. He threw the phone across the room, letting out a satisfied grunt when it crashed against
the wall.

Now he knew how Sara spent her nights. Now
he had his closure.

"Who was on the phone, Greg?" Sara asked,
padding barefoot into the living room.

Her brother rolled his big frame to one side of the burgundy-striped sofa and squinted a brown eye open. "Some guy," he said, letting out a yawn.

Some guy? Her heart skipped a beat. "He . . . didn't leave a name?"

"Nope." He yawned again. "Asked for you, then hung up."

Sara gnawed on her lower lip. It was 4:00 A.M. in California. Could it have been Matt, maybe calling to tell her he missed her, wanted her to come back? No, that was only very wishful thinking, something she had to stop if she were to maintain her sanity. Matt Brandon was not going to contact her. He wasn't going to call her or show up on her doorstep, no matter how many different ways she'd dreamed it. He was gone from her life. They were done.

She pulled the towel from her wet hair and started combing out the tangles. Greg's eyes were closed. "Since you have to report back to base tomorrow, I thought we'd go out tonight. Japanese, maybe?"

"Sounds great," he mumbled.

"See you at six."

"Hmmm."

Sara smiled and watched her brother drift off to sleep. Greg was a Marine, from the top of his half-inch crew cut to the soles of his laced boots. He was seven years older than her, a man committed to God, country, and family, who said what was on his mind. No pretense, no facade. No games.

She could never talk to him about Matt. Could never tell him about the heartache of loving and losing that threatened to crush her beneath its weight. He wouldn't understand, because half the time, she didn't understand it herself. Part of her was desperate to contact Matt, crawl back into his arms, no matter how temporary. But the other part, the survivor, squelched the mere thought of it.

Either way, it didn't really matter. Matt's silence told her what she needed to know. He didn't want her. Now or ever.

Nineteen

Seven months later

Matt pulled a tan and black sweater over his shirt and looked out of his hotel window. Pittsburgh in April was cold, dreary, dark, with a chiller wind that sliced through a spring jacket faster than a ground ball to first base. A slow steady rain dripped from the sky, covering the ground like a damp blanket.

He turned from the window. Some things never changed. And others . . . well, others did.

Three more days and then he could head to New York. He hadn't wanted to come here, had fought his publicist every inch of the way. But there was a lot riding on *Over the Edge*. A lot more than money. His publisher had pushed the book through, jumping every deadline, skipping over the short cuts, to get it on the streets. This was his first book since "the accident" and readers would be looking for signs that Matt Brandon still had the touch. Pittsburgh was a good launching pad. Hometown boy and all that.

So here he was, on the ninth floor of the Shera-ton, with an hour to go before his book signing, and all he could think about was *her.* She was here, in the city. So close. He cursed under his breath. It had been seven months. When was the wanting going to stop? When was he going to eat an orange or see a slice of lemon and not think about *her?* When was he going to feel alive again?

His vision was perfect. Dr. Myers had been right on target. Three months after the exam, Matt could function just as well as he had before the accident. With one exception. He no longer frequented the fashionable nightspots or trendy restaurants of his past life. Gone were the models and starlets. Funny thing was, he didn't miss them, didn't miss any of it. Not really. When Thanksgiving rolled around, instead of hopping a plane to Vegas or some other party spot, he'd stayed home and eaten Rosa's turkey with jalapeño stuffing and watched eight straight hours of football with Adam and Jimmy.

And not once did he think about *her,* not until that jerk-off commercial came on spouting the luxuries of a Caribbean cruise and zooming in on a huge buffet piled with crab claws, jumbo shrimp, filet mignon, lemons . . . Lemons! Goddamnit, lemons! Why not strawberries? Or mangos? It was a Caribbean cruise for Christ's sake; it should be something exotic. Pineapple. Coconut. Kiwi. *Why the hell did it have to be lemons?* That was it, the rest of his night was done, spent in gloomy silence, staring at the TV, cursing the jerk-off on the commercial with his too-happy voice and bleach-whitened smile.

Christmas was another bonanza of television, this one on DVD. Matt chose the *Godfather I, II, and III;* they could eat up a whole day and there weren't any commercials, no opportunity for some asshole to start gushing about love and romance. And no close-ups of lemons. But damn it to hell, if a barrel of oranges didn't come crashing down when Marlon Brando got blasted outside the neighborhood fruit stand. Fifteen, maybe twenty of those suckers rolling down the road as Brando staggered then hit the ground. Shit! Now he couldn't even watch the *Godfather* without thinking of *her.*

The week after Christmas, Amy and the boys flew in, and Matt's ten and twelve-year old nephews showed him how to celebrate New Year's Eve, pre-adolescent style. They'd blasted Lenny Kravitz on the stereo; hurled red, white, and blue streamers off the patio; tossed bunches of champagne-glass shaped confetti in the air; lit sparklers, stuffed their faces with Doritos and Cheese Puffs; and guzzled Sparkling Grape Juice from plastic cups. It was a decided difference from the live band, filet mignon, and Dom Perignon at the Ritz.

When the boys finally fizzled out around 1:00 A.M., Matt and Amy settled themselves out on the patio for a few minutes of quiet. "You were wonderful with the boys," Amy said.

Matt lifted his cup, saluted his sister. "Thank God, they're finally asleep. I'm beat."

She smiled. "Children are so incredible. Exhausting, overwhelming, nerve-racking, but absolutely incredible."

He nodded, tipped back his head and swallowed the last of his Sparkling Grape Juice. God, but this stuff was sweet. No wonder kids got cavities.

"Ever consider having any of your own?"

He was still thinking about bicuspids and sugar. "Huh?"

"Children." She rolled her eyes.

The plastic cup cracked in his hand. "I know I'm a modern guy, but I'm still old-fashioned enough to believe there should be a husband and wife before there's a child."

"I know that, silly." She tilted her head to one side, waited. "Well?"

Matt tossed the scrunched up cup on the table beside him. "Well, I'm not married, so it's not an issue."

She sighed, her gaze narrowing on him. "You know, you used to do this when we were kids. Whenever I'd ask you something you didn't want to answer, you'd played dumb, just like you're doing now."

"I don't know what you're talking about." *Leave it alone, Amy. Just leave it alone.*

"Right. And the Pope's Protestant."

"Just because Nick isn't here, doesn't mean you have to nag me instead."

"I do not nag my husband," Amy said. "I prod him . . . ever so gently."

"Nag."

"Don't change the subject." She leaned forward, braced her hands on her knees like she was getting ready for a really big secret. "What happened to all the waif-ettes? Are they too hung up on their eating disorders to have a meaningful relationship?"

"I'm done with waif-ettes." *She'd* had curves, lots of them.

"Oh?" She leaned in closer. "What does that mean?"

He shrugged. "Nothing. I just don't find them particularly attractive."

"But you used to."

"Sort of."

"Oh." She leaned back, folded her arms, crossed her right leg over her left and started kicking it back and forth. "That makes a lot of sense, Matt. You dated these toothpicks and only found them 'sort of' attractive?"

"Right. I mean, wrong. I mean, I did . . ." He closed his eyes, ran both hands over his face. "Hell, I don't know what I mean."

"Matt?"

He picked up the cracked cup, tossed it in the air, caught it. "What?"

"Are you involved with someone?"

"No." *No. No. NO.*

"Oh." She shifted in her chair. "*Were* you involved with someone?"

"It's over."

"Oh." She tapped her finger against her chin. "She wasn't one of your waif-ettes either, was she?"

"No. No, she wasn't."

That had been the end of the discussion, not that his sister wouldn't have loved to sit there until dawn, perched on the edge of her chair, dissecting every word, analyzing every movement, interpreting every silence. But he'd ended it there, walked away, and refused to let her bring it up again.

But Amy hadn't forgotten, not that woman. When he'd visited her, Nick, and the kids two days ago, she'd leaned in close and whispered that "sister's intuition" told her he was still mooning over *that* woman. Did he want to talk about it, maybe air out his feelings a little? Just a little? Matt had forced a smile and told her she had the most active imagination he'd ever seen and maybe *she* should have been the writer. And right now, he wished to hell she were the writer in the family instead of him. Then he wouldn't be standing in the middle of a hotel room, half hyperventilating because he had to do a book signing.

God, he just wanted to get this over with. Why was he so uptight? He'd done hundreds of book signings. No big deal. But never in the same city as the woman who'd jilted him the night before he would have asked her to marry him.

She'd never show at his signing. Never. He laughed, a hollow empty sound that filled the room. And if she did? Hell, he didn't even know what she looked like. And that was more pathetic than anything.

There'd been an opportunity, once a few months ago. Adam had come into his study, carrying a large manila envelope.

Matt remembered ignoring him, until he shoved the envelope under his nose.

"Jimmy gave me this."

"What is it?" He'd picked up the envelope, turned it around.

"Pictures," Adam had said. "Of you and Sara."

Then he'd turned and left. Matt remembered sitting there, in his chair, touching the envelope, tracing the lines, so slowly, like a caress. Once, he'd almost opened it. He'd even lifted the metal fastener and reached inside, brushed his fingers over the glossy prints, felt them almost pulsing under his skin. Sara . . . Sara . . . *Oh, God, Sara* . . . Then he'd yanked his hand away and tossed the envelope in the garbage. He was a fool, a goddamn, pathetic, miserable fool. But that knowledge didn't stop him from wanting to see her face, look into her eyes, even if it was only a picture. He'd tortured himself, staring at the manila envelope sticking out of the garbage can, battling between need and self-preservation, desire and logic. Just one look and her image would be ingrained in his mind forever. Eyes, nose, lips, hair. *Just one look.* Forever. Jesus, what was wrong with him? She'd left, gone home to Pittsburgh, back to the sonofabitch who'd answered the phone. That's when he'd pulled out a match and burned the damn envelope.

But there hadn't been a night he hadn't wondered what she looked like. Hadn't thought about the envelope. Hadn't tortured himself with memories of her.

He ran a hand through his dark curly hair and looked at his watch. It was time. Picking up the brown leather jacket on the bed, he headed out the door.

Sara stood in front of the bookstore, staring at the huge glossy in the window. It was Matthew Brandon, larger than life, staring down at her with those piercing, silver eyes. *Oh God, no.* He was in there, right now, just a few hundred feet away. Close . . . so close.

Three weeks ago, she'd been flipping through the morning paper, when Matt's silver gaze had jumped out at her from the front of the Arts & Life section. "Hometown Boy Returns" was the headline. She'd spent the rest of the day alternating between minibouts of hysteria and long stretches of severe depression.

Time had not lessened the pain. The wounds
were just as deep, just as raw as they'd been seven
months ago. The only consolation she had was
knowing she'd done the right thing by leaving him.
Before he had a chance to dump her. And he
would have, she had no doubt. If he'd cared about
her, really cared, he would have come after her,
demanded answers, tried to work things out.

But he'd done none of those things. She'd read
in the paper that his vision had returned, though
he'd not been spotted much in the social circuit.
In fact, reports had it that he hadn't been spotted
anywhere. A few magazines speculated as to the
possibility that months of blindness had made him
"see the light," while another headlined with
"Matthew Brandon on the Enlightened Path."
Every few months or so, Jeff dropped snippets of
information about Matt's progress, referencing it
as casual points of information.

Only once had he asked her about her level of
involvement with Matt. It was the morning after
he got back from his two-week stay with Matt. Sara
had just handed him his first cup of coffee, black,
no sugar.

"It's good to have you back," she'd said. "Jessie
and I missed you."

"Good to be back." He'd taken a sip of coffee,
smiled. "I don't think my stomach could have
taken another week of Rosa's jalapeños."

It was such an innocent statement, but the mention of Rosa linked Sara to other people in that
house, people she'd been trying to forget. She'd
forced a smile and nodded, saying nothing.

"She made this one meal, rice with pork and
chunks of tomatoes . . . and *lots* of red pepper."

"And jalapeños piled on top?"

"That's the one. Jimmy called it Firestarter."

She laughed, remembering how she'd guzzled a full glass of water after her first bite.

"Matt called it TNT."

The laugh died in her throat.

"What? What did I say?"

"Nothing." *Nothing. I'm getting used to walking around with my heart scabbed over, until somebody mentions his name and rips it open all over again.*

"Sara?"

"I'm fine."

Jeff set down his mug, rubbed his chin. "Funny, Matt says the same thing when I ask him why he looks like he's been shot in the gut every time I mention your name. Fine, fine, fine. That's all I get." He leaned forward, lowered his voice. "What happened out there, Sara? What happened between you two?"

"Nothing." She looked down at the mug of coffee perched between her hands.

"Come on, it's me you're talking to, remember?"

She shook her head. "It's too . . . difficult . . . to talk about."

"I see."

Sara met his gaze, blinked back tears. "Then you understand why I can't talk about it." She swiped a cheek with the back of her hand. "Let's just say that once again, I learned that one-sided involvements don't work."

He must've gotten the message because he never asked again. And now he was too busy playing daddy to his little girl to contemplate something as depressing as a friend's broken heart.

The wind sliced through her gray sweat outfit, jarring her back to the present, to the bookstore where her ex-lover's face was plastered against the window. She'd spent the last three weeks planning this meeting, from the oversized thermal sweats, size XXL and plain blue ball cap pulled low over her eyes and hiding most of her hair, to the folded note in her pocket feigning laryngitis. She just wanted to see him, just this once, get close to him, close enough to breathe in his scent mixed with that woodsy cologne he always wore. She could be in and out of there, mission accomplished in less than fifteen minutes with enough memories to fill her cold sleepless nights for a long time.

Sara started for the entrance, forcing herself through the double oak doors. *Keep moving,* she told herself. *Just keep moving.* She followed a group of women around a display of books. Off to the right and in full view, sat the man everyone had come to see. Handsome, smiling, self-assured, Matt shook hands with a beautiful blonde and handed her his book.

Oh God, oh God, how I've missed you.

She took her place at the end of the line. There were about thirty people in front of her, mostly women, mostly beautiful, mostly blond. Sara looked down at her sneakers and felt safe. With all of these designer bodies strutting around, he wouldn't give her a second look.

Her gaze worked its way up the line, found him. He was still as handsome as ever, his silver gaze intent, dark hair curling up around the collar, tanned skin giving him that healthy California look. But there was something about him that was different, something that had nothing to do with his renewed eyesight. She studied him. There were lines around his mouth, deep brackets carved into skin, much more severe than before. And his eyes . . . they were guarded or guarding, as though . . . as though someone had hurt him.

Ridiculous. Matt Brandon never let himself care enough to get hurt. And if he had, if he'd made that mistake, it had nothing to do with her. She was long forgotten. It was probably some new love. Maybe that's why he hadn't been in the news lately. Or maybe he'd finally fallen for Gabrielle Jontue. Loving her could make a man look like that, and then some.

She could hear his voice now. Low, deep, sweeping down the line, drawing her to him. Her palms grew sweaty. She pushed her cap lower. Reaching into her pocket, Sara pulled out the folded piece of paper.

Two more women in front of her. Her heart pounded against her rib cage, filled her ears, drowned out everything around her.

"How would you like me to sign this?"

It was him. Sara shook her head, stared into Matt's silver eyes.

He gave her a gentle smile.

She thrust the paper toward him.

He scanned it, his smile deepened. "Laryngitis, huh?" He took a copy of *Over the Edge* and scrawled a few words followed by his signature on the inside cover. "Hope you feel better soon," he said.

He started to hand the book back to her, then stopped. His face turned white under his tan. "That scent you're wearing," he said, his eyes narrowing, his words slow, cautious. "What is it?"

The perfume! How could she have forgotten about the perfume?

"What is it?" he repeated, his smile fading.

She had to get out. *Now.* Sara grabbed the book and ran, ignoring the deep voice a few paces behind, calling after her. She picked up speed, darted out of the building, zigzagging through the streets. Not until she was three blocks away, did she collapse against a brick wall, gasping for air. Even then, she kept turning around, looking for him.

Nothing. Thank God he hadn't followed her.

Her hands shook the whole twenty-minute drive home. How could she have been so stupid? She never should have gone. What had it proved? *What in God's name had it proved?* That he could still make her heart do flip-flops? That when he smiled, she felt light-headed and breathless? She shook her head. Stupid. Stupid. Stupid.

By the time she pulled into her drive, her head felt like someone had been using it as a bongo drum. Her sweats were damp, soaked in some spots from the puddles she'd blasted through on her escape route. But she was safe now. Her house was less than twenty feet away. She scrambled from the car and rushed toward the door. Once inside, she put the kettle on for a cup of chamomile tea and stripped off her sweats, opting for her faithful blue flannel bathrobe and fuzzy slippers. Two Tylenols later, Sara was snuggled in her grandmother's blue-and-yellow afghan, a cup of hot chamomile blend by her side, and a copy of *Over the Edge* in her hand.

Her fingers traced the embossed lettering on the cover. She'd helped create this book, or at least part of it. Slowly, she turned the book over and gazed at the photo on the back. Dressed in a black turtleneck and faded jeans, Matt was leaning against a stucco wall, a faint smile tugging at his lips. His arms were crossed over his chest and he was staring straight ahead, his silver eyes pensive.

This picture was different from the other jackets. It was more reserved, less inviting. Again, she thought of the look, guarded, she would call it, as though he were protecting the space between himself and the reader, lest one of them got too close, saw too much, uncovered too many secrets. The jackets of his six previous books, lying photo-side-up on the floor next to her bed were all casual, relaxed, open. She touched a finger to his mouth, traced the outline of his lips, remembering the feel of them on her skin.

Gently, she turned the book over and opened the first page. *Thank you for coming, laryngitis and all.* The next page was the dedication. One single line, that's all it was. *To everyone who believes in forever, this one's for you.* Tears trickled down her cheeks, blurred her vision. She swiped her eyes with both hands, grabbed the box of tissues beside her tea and turned the page.

At 3:30 A.M., she pulled the last tissue from the box and sniffed her way through the final sentences:

He gazed into her amber-green eyes, knowing he'd never find another love like Sara. *Marry me,* he said in a low, gruff voice, pulling her into his arms. Her smile was all the answer he needed as he lowered his lips to hers. Their love for one another would carry them through today, tomorrow . . . and forever.

Forever. Why couldn't you have loved me? Why? Sara closed the book, great sobs of anguish racking her body, tearing her soul, ripping her heart, as she gave herself up to a lifetime of lost "forevers."

Twenty

Matt shifted in his chair and pulled his cap down low. The wind whipped through Three Rivers Stadium, belting the crowd with big gusts. He pulled his jacket closer to him. Damn, but he wished he'd gotten second-row seats, number one and two. He liked those best. They were the ones he and—he pushed the thought from his head. *No,* he told himself. There was no reason to want those particular seats other than the view was better and he'd had them before. It wasn't because *she'd* been sitting beside him at the time. He just liked the seats. Period. *She* had nothing to do with it. Nothing at all.

But there was already a woman in seat two and an old man in seat one. That had been his seat. So he'd settled for row four, seat four. His gaze floated back to the man and woman. It didn't look like they were together. He was one of those die-hard Pirates' fans, outfitted in black and yellow, with a radio in one hand and a small television in the other. Probably some retired steel worker, spending his golden days following the home team.

The woman was younger, thirty-something and could've been the man's daughter, but Matt doubted it. They hadn't said two words to each other. She was all huddled up, like the cold bothered her, even though she wore jeans and a down jacket. And black mittens with yellow thumbs. She had on the same ball cap as Matt, pulled low, so he couldn't see her eyes or much else, except for her lips that were kind of pouty, no smile.

A roar from the crowd brought his attention back to the ball field. Foul ball, far left field. The rest of the inning and the next two were uneventful, five pop-outs, two grounders, three strikeouts, a double, and a single. Every now and again, he'd look at the man and woman in seat one and two. The old guy was totally engrossed in the game, radio blaring, hot dog and beer wedged between his legs. The woman just sat there, staring straight ahead. Her body might be in the seat, but her mind was definitely somewhere else.

Damnit, if she wasn't going to watch the game, she should give up her seat. To me. Maybe he should ask her if she wanted to trade; she wasn't watching the game anyway. He thought about it a few minutes, decided against it. She didn't look like she was in the mood for any kind of conversation, let alone a favor. Three beers and four innings later, the old man gathered his belonging and moved to an empty seat in row one. Matt eyed the vacant spot next to the woman. *What the hell?* Two minutes later, he slid into the seat next to her.

Might as well be polite. "Hope you don't mind—" he began, turning toward her.

She jerked her head down, like a turtle trying to get back into its shell.

"Excuse me," he began again, "I . . . hope you don't mind if I sit here."

The woman shook her head, pulled her cap down lower.

"What do you think of the game?" *Do you even know who's playing?*

She shrugged.

"Yeah, my thoughts exactly." It was a boring game, maybe that's why he'd been paying so much attention to the crowd, the woman and the old man, in particular. They had his seats, after all.

"You know you've got one of the best seats in the house." He slid his gaze back to her. "And I've got the other one."

She didn't respond, didn't even acknowledge that he'd spoken, just kept her head bent, looking at . . . what? What was wrong with her? Was she a mute, for Christ's sake? Why didn't she answer him? Was she upset? Depressed? He knew what that felt like. Maybe her boyfriend just dumped her, or her husband. He knew what getting dumped felt like, too.

He leaned forward, lowered his voice. "Are you okay?"

"Hmmhmm."

Progress. She'd made a sound. He should just let it be, leave her alone. What business was it of his if her boyfriend/husband had another girlfriend, or a boyfriend, for that matter? He should just shut his mouth and watch the game.

But God, she looked so pitiful, so absolutely pathetic, sitting there all hunched over like the life was shriveling out of her. He knew what that felt like too. "You seem . . . you seem . . . like something's bothering you."

The tears started then, a stream, slipping down her cheeks to her chin onto her coat. "Hey, I'm sorry. It's none of my business, I know. I'll shut up, okay?" *Jesus, now I've really done it.* More tears, harder. "It's about a guy, isn't it?" The words were out before he could stop them.

The woman swiped her black-and-yellow mittened fingers across her cheeks, jerked her head up and down one time.

Of course, Matt thought, *it's always about a guy. Or a woman.*

"Married?"

She shook her head, sniffed twice.

"Hmmm. Doesn't want to commit?"

Her head dipped forward so far all he could see was the back of her cap and a tiny swatch of brown hair.

"Maybe he just needs a little time to get used to the idea."

Silence. Thousands of people all around him and all he could hear was this woman's silence.

"Some guys get scared no matter how great the woman is." He should know. "They run . . . at least for a while. But if the relationship's got any substance, if it's worth it, they come back." *And the woman's waiting for him, arms wide open. Unless she's found someone else.* "And if not, well . . ." He couldn't tell her the truth, not his truth . . . *Then you feel like the biggest sucker in the world. And you bleed. And the bleeding doesn't stop; it just keeps gushing out, more, more, draining you, leaving you lifeless until you're numb from the pain of it. After a while, the hole in your soul scabs over . . . but it's always there, waiting, ready to break open and bleed all over again. And the bitch of it is, there's not a damn thing you can do about it. Not a goddamn thing.* No, he wasn't going to tell her any of that. It would be too cruel, too cold . . . too inhuman.

He opened his mouth to speak, push some balm-filled words out, but it was too late. She was already gone.

"Couldn't wait to see me again, huh?" Matt's lips twitched into a half smile.

"Hey," Jeff said, "you're leaving for sunny California in a few hours. Who knows when you'll grace this side of the continent again? Probably not until you're promoting your next bestseller." He laughed. "Besides, I have an affinity for airport food . . . something about the cardboard taste. *Mmmmm.*"

"Especially the hot dogs. Cardboard mixed with rubber."

"Right." Jeff untwisted the cap on his bottled water, took a drink. "So how's it feel to have that ugly mug plastered all over Pittsburgh?"

Matt shrugged, trying to block out the airline attendant's voice. *Flight 452 to Dallas–Fort Worth is now boarding* . . . "People probably get tired of looking at me. I know I sure as hell do."

Jeff laughed. "Not the female population. We've been sitting here less than five minutes and you've gotten the eye from just about every woman who's passed by."

"Is there something on my shirt?" Matt brushed his hands over his polo. "My face?" He rubbed his chin.

"It's your face all right, you dummy. And I guess all the rest of you. Hell if I know. I'm a guy. But my assistant still can't believe she actually talked to you on the phone this morning." Jeff rolled his eyes. "I'll be hearing about it for the next five months."

"I bet your office will be thrilled."

"Aside from me, yeah, they will be."

"I'm sure they won't *all* be doing handstands." *I can think of one person who won't want to hear my name or see my face.*

There was a long pause. "Well . . ."

"Right. Well." Matt took a sip of his water. *So what?* So what if she didn't want to hear about him? He didn't want to hear about her either. In less than two hours he'd be in the air again, away from Pittsburgh. Safe.

"How was the game yesterday?" Jeff asked.

"Boring." He thought of the woman, huddled up, hiding from something, her pain, maybe.

"She was there, you know."

Matt jerked his head up, said nothing. He knew who *she* was.

Jeff drummed his fingers on the Formica table. "Said she saw you."

"What?" Sara saw him? Yesterday? Impossible.

"Said she saw you," Jeff repeated, his voice calm, even.

"I didn't see her."

Jeff shrugged. "Said you even talked to her."

"Bullshit. The woman's a liar." He felt the blood pounding in his temples. "Is this why you wanted to see me before I left? To tell me about *her*?"

"Look, Matt, I don't know what happened between the two of you, but even an idiot can see that you're both miserable. Hell, you've both been walking around half dead since she came back here and I think it's time you talked things out. . . ."

"There's nothing to talk about."

"She's a wonderful woman."

"Great. Glad to hear it."

"She'd make a wonderful wife."

"I hear she's already had that role."

"That was low. Her ex-husband was a real bastard. Cheated on her and left her when she lost their baby."

"So I heard."

"You two are perfect for each other. Perfect." Jeff ran a hand through his hair. "Can't you just think about settling down?"

Matt clenched his jaw, said nothing.

"Make a commitment, think about loving just one woman?"

"She didn't want me." Cold truth.

"I don't believe it."

Matt shrugged. "Doesn't matter. It's over and she and I both know what caused it."

"Can't you even talk to her?"

"Listen to me, goddammit. There's nothing to talk about. Do you understand?"

"No. I really don't."

Anger pushed out his next words. "And I don't know why she'd tell you we talked," he said, his voice rising with each word. "I didn't talk to anybody except some poor, pathetic woman . . ." It hit him then . . . the hunched figure in *his* seat . . . the tears . . . the refusal to speak . . . Jesus. Sara. *Sara*. The woman in his seat had been Sara.

Sara dipped the washcloth in the pan of ice water, rung it out and placed it on her forehead. Oh God, her head was killing her. Throbbing, throbbing. It started at the ball game yesterday, a

dull ache that worked itself into a full-blown
pounding this morning, right after she told Jeff
about her encounter with Matt.

Matt. She still couldn't believe he'd been at the
stadium, sitting right beside her, talking to her . . .
like a stranger. She'd always wondered if he'd recognize her if they ever saw each other, maybe identify her, know who she was . . . somehow. But he
hadn't. He'd talked to her, said a few words. But
in the end, he'd only pitied her. She drifted off
thinking of him and how he pitied her.

A shrill ring tore through her sleep, yanking her
awake. *"Agghhhh."* She rolled to her side, pushed
the hair from her face. Her headache was better,
reduced to a faint pulsing in her temples. The ringing started again. Doorbell. Someone was at the
door. Maybe they'd go away; if she closed her eyes
again, maybe they'd just go away. It stopped, but
a few seconds later, the pounding started.

"Okay, okay," Sara yelled from the sofa. "I'm
coming." She pushed herself into a sitting position, stood up, straightened her sweatshirt and
sweatpants. "Just a minute." She ran a hand
through her hair. If it was some person selling *Red-
book* or children's encyclopedias, she was going to
scream.

She pulled the door open, preparing her "no
thank you" spiel. But the words stuck in her throat,
lodged square in the middle, blocking speech and
thought, trapping everything but the vision of Matthew Brandon standing on her doorstep.

"Sara."

She stared at him. It really was him, looking cool
and beautiful in his faded jeans and black turtleneck, like he'd just walked off the cover of *GQ.* His

silver gaze narrowed, piercing, probing, no doubt taking in her baggy blue sweats and gray sweatshirt. And fuzzy red slippers. Ugh. She shrank back a little, tried to pat her hair down. What a mess. Oh God, she didn't want him to see her like this, like some pathetic urchin, worn and tattered.

"Did I wake you?"

"I . . ." She wrapped her arms around her middle. Even a cold, remote Matt Brandon was dangerous to her defenses. "I . . . had a headache so I laid down . . ."

"I guess I should have called first." His words were stiff, forced.

"Would you like to come in?" *Say no, say you've got a prior engagement. Say anything.*

He nodded. "Sure."

Sara felt her heart pounding against her rib cage as he stepped past her and entered the living room. He stood there, next to the Peace Lilly, drinking in the tiny room: the overstuffed couch and faded rocker, the ceramic pots stuffed with lavender, the windowsill filled with African violets, the canvas splattered with ten different shades of blue.

"A little smaller than what you're used to," she said, trying to find something safe to say, anything to break the awkward silence.

His gaze swung back to the windowsill and the six African violets perched on the edge. Two purple, two white, two pink. "It's you, Sara." Had his voice softened, just a little? "Totally you."

"It's home."

"Right. Home." He cleared his throat, jammed his hands in his pockets. "So, how are things?"

"Fine. I'm keeping busy." Since she'd come

back from California, she'd signed up for classes in yoga, tai chi, feng shui, Asian cooking. Anything, *anything* to keep her mind off Matt Brandon. She'd even joined a book club discussion group that met once every two weeks, but she'd dropped out when they selected Matt's book for discussion.

"I'm pretty busy too," he said. "Book tours, speaking engagements, plotting my next book." His gaze settled on her.

"Great. You must be very excited." *Damn you, Matthew Brandon, why'd you come? Why?*

"*Over the Edge* could be as big as *Dead Moon Rising.* I've got some in the car, let me go grab one for you and sign it."

Sara raised a hand to stop him. "That's okay," she said. "I've already got one." Her voice faded out as she remembered the scene at his book signing. At least he didn't recognize her, thank God.

"Oh? Where is it? I'll sign that one."

You already did. "Hmm. I don't know where I put it." She scratched her head, shot a sideways glance at the rocker. Half of *Over the Edge* lay exposed, right in the middle of the seat, the other half was covered with the yellow-and-blue afghan.

Matt followed her gaze. "And . . . there it is," he said, walking over and snatching it from its spot.

"Hmm. How about that." She twisted her fingers behind her back, watching as he flipped the pages open. Any second now, and he'd know.

He looked up, confused. "Sara?"

"Yes?" *Play dumb, until the last possible second, play dumb.*

"*Thank you for coming, laryngitis and all.* The woman with laryngitis, the one who ran away, that was you?"

She nodded.

"You didn't really have laryngitis at all, did you?" His silver gaze was on her.

"No."

"Why? Why'd you pretend? And why'd you run away?"

"I guess I just didn't want to face you. Not then, not there." *Not here, either.* "I know it was a stupid thing to do, but it was easier than putting either of us in an awkward situation." She tried to laugh, but it fell flat. "Can you imagine us meeting for the first time since . . . since California?" She shook her head, feeling suddenly light-headed. "It would not have been a good scene. And imagine the gossip. No. I saved us both a lot of grief by just pretending."

"Is that what you do when you want to avoid something, Sara? Pretend?"

She ignored his question. Her reasons for doing things were none of his business.

Matt took a step toward her, stopped a few feet away. "Sara, aren't you going to answer me?"

"No." She looked away. "Can I offer you something to drink? Lemonade? Tea? Coffee?"

"You can offer me an answer for starters."

Her right temple was starting to throb. "Well, then, I'm really glad you stopped by, especially with your busy schedule . . ." *And now it's time for you to go.*

"I didn't know that was you at the game yesterday."

Her gaze swung back to his. "Jeff told you, didn't he? That's what this is all about, isn't it?"

"He said you were upset." He reached out,

touched her shoulder. She flinched. "Why, Sara? Why would you be upset?"

Maybe because you broke my heart. "I don't know. I just didn't expect to see you again."

"Oh, I get it. Your morals finally caught up with you, huh?" The left side of his jaw twitched. "You couldn't face me. That's it, isn't it?"

"My morals? *My* morals?" Both temples were pounding now. "That's a joke, right? Well, excuse me if I don't laugh."

"You're the one who left me," he said, bitterness coating every word out of his mouth.

"Semantics, that's all it is." She balled her hands into fists, nails digging into skin. "You would've dumped me as soon as you regained your vision."

"Oh really?" He took a step closer. "And how do you know that?"

"I know. Can't we just stop this? What difference does it make now?"

"Is that why you ran home and hopped into bed with another guy?"

"What?!"

"I know, Sara." His lips flattened into a straight line. "I called you about a week after you left. Seven A.M., Pittsburgh time. Some guy answered, said you were in the shower."

"Oh my God." She covered her face with her hands. "It was you. *Oh my God.*"

"Yeah. Oh my God. So don't play the wounded victim. *You* left me. *You* broke the trust." His voice cracked. "You. Not me."

She lifted her head, peeked through a tangle of hair. "I . . . I haven't been with any man," she said, her voice shaky.

"Sara—"

"It was Greg."

"For Christ's sake, I don't want to know the bastard's name."

"Greg," she repeated. "My brother."

"What?" Matt pushed the hair out of her eyes, stared at her. "What did you say?"

"My brother was staying with me. He's the one who answered the phone."

"Jesus." He ran both hands over his face. "You mean all this time . . . I thought . . ."

"I was never with another man."

"So tell me why you left."

"I had to," she said. A tear trickled down her cheek. "After our last night together, I knew I had to leave." Her voice wavered. "Because if I didn't go then, I never would." Another tear fell. "I'd stay as long as you'd have me, desperate and hoping, until there was nothing left and I was sucked up dry." She hesitated a second, then pushed on, past months of grief and anguish. "Please understand, Matt. I had to go." It was a whisper, a plea.

"Why?" The brackets around his mouth deepened. "Why couldn't you have just waited until morning and talked to me about it? Do you know the first thing I thought about when I woke up?" He plowed a hand through his hair. "I was going to apologize for acting like such a jerk. And then I was going to tell you I loved you, even though I was probably the last one to figure it out."

More tears stung her eyes. *Oh God, what have I done?*

"There's more," he said. "After I spilled my heart out to you, told you all these wonderful things, I was going to ask you to be my wife." There was pain in his eyes, real, deep, visceral. "But you were gone."

Sara buried her face in her hands.

"Look at me, Sara."

Her head inched up.

He reached out, touched her cheek. "You're so beautiful," he murmured, trailing his fingers down her face. "So damned beautiful."

"No." She let out a sharp laugh, backing away from his touch. "I'm just me. Ordinary. *Always* ordinary." She sniffed. "Nothing like what you're used to. You would've tired of me. You know that."

"You *are* beautiful. But you were beautiful even when I couldn't see you. Do you know why?" He took her hand, brought it to his lips. "Because you *care* about people. And you make them want to care about themselves, want to do better, *be* better. Live by a code of honor and decency. I'd never tire of that."

He pulled her to him. "You made *me* want to be better, Sara," he whispered in her ear. "And I will always love you for that."

She froze. *And I will always love you for that.*

"Did you hear that, Dr. Hamilton?" he asked, letting out a long sigh. "I just told you in a roundabout way that I loved you." He planted a small kiss near her ear, sending shivers through her whole body. "Now, I'm telling you in a very direct way that I'm making a *commitment* to you." He pulled her closer, closer, until their bodies were pressed against one another. "And I want one from you."

She trembled against him. "I love you, Matt. I've loved you for so very long."

"Then be my wife," he said, cupping her chin with his fingers. "Love me. Forever."

Forever. She smiled, leaned forward and placed a soft kiss on his lips. "Forever," she whispered, "I will love you, Matthew Brandon, forever."

Much, much later, Sara lay snuggled in Matt's arms, listening to his slow steady breathing. Her fingers rested on his shoulder, skin to skin. He was here. In her bed. In her life. It was so much better than a dream.

"Hello, beautiful." His voice was soft and warm.

Beautiful. When he called her that, when he touched her or looked at her with those silver eyes, she felt beautiful.

"Hi," she murmured, turning her head to look at his face. His eyes were closed but he was smiling.

"You wore me out. I'm dead," he said, sliding his hand down to her hip.

"You're just out of shape." She rolled over, her bare breasts rubbing against his chest. "Nothing a little practice won't cure."

He laughed. "You know, Jack Steele had this same problem."

Sara reached out and smoothed back his rumpled hair. "I read all about it. In detail," she added.

"So you know the cure," he said.

Her gaze flew to his. He was watching her, a teasing glint in his eyes. "Six times a day? Really, Matt," she tsk-tsked him. The way he was looking at her sent shivers down her spine.

"Okay. I'll settle for three," he said, pulling her on top of him.

She laughed. "I guess I should be thankful to Jack. After all, if it weren't for him, you wouldn't be here."

"Good old Jack," Matt said, smiling at her as his hands worked down her back, toward her buttocks.

"What's going to happen to him now? He's in love. He's getting married. His MO's blown to pieces." Sara planted little kisses on his chest, her fingers circling his nipples.

"Don't you worry about Jack," he said, stroking her legs. "He's still investigating. But now he's got a partner."

"Ah, a partner," she murmured, rolling her tongue around a copper nipple. "That could be *interesting.*"

She felt his body jump in response.

"Very interesting." Her tongue trailed down the flat planes of his stomach, sucking, licking.

"He'll have more sex," he groaned. Her tongue darted inside his navel. "Better sex," he rasped.

She lifted her head and met his hot silvery gaze. His breathing was quick and shallow, as though he'd just finished a race. Too bad, he wasn't anywhere close to the finish line. Sara ran her tongue over her upper lip and smiled, a slow smile telling him she was just getting started.

"Well, you're going to need a research assistant," she said, her voice husky, low. "And I think I'd be the perfect candidate."

His gaze burned every inch of her body, sending tingling sensations pouring through her like fire. "Yes," he said. "You're the *perfect* candidate." His lips turned down. "But . . . did I mention . . . this was a long-term assignment?"

"Oh?" she asked, lowering her head. Her hair brushed over his stomach.

He sucked in his breath. "It could take . . . a . . . lifetime," he finished with a groan.

"I'm counting on it," she murmured, moving lower. "I'm counting on forever."

ABOUT THE AUTHOR

I started writing my first romance novel when my children were babies. I would read fairy tales to them during the day and work on my own version of "happily ever after" when I tucked them into bed. As is so often the case, life got in the way, and I ended up tucking that first novel into an old 286 computer for seven years, until one day I was searching for computer games for the kids and found it, all 120 pages of unfinished business! From that moment on, I knew I wanted to tell the rest of that story and then another and another. And so I am thrilled to be publishing my second novel, Paradise Found. I am equally thrilled to be the mother of three and stepmother of two (yes, that equals five!) extremely unique, energetic children, ages 11 to 18. Our house is always a little crazy, never quite clean, full of raucous laughter and good food. It's full of animals, too, a black lab and a goldfish. (The gerbils, unfortunately, didn't make it for this book.) When I find a few quiet moments, I read, garden, experiment with my own interpretation of art, walk my dog, or plot my next scene. And sometimes I even get to spend a little time with my very patient, very understanding husband, who keeps me on course and is without a doubt my biggest fan.

I would love to hear from readers c/o Zebra Books.